I0585495

BACKSLIDE 2

KEITH THOMAS WALKER

KEITHWALKERBOOKS, INC

KEITHWALKERBOOKS

Publishing Company
KeithWalkerBooks, Inc.
P.O. Box 690
Allen, TX 75013

For information write
KeithWalkerBooks, Inc.
P.O. Box 690
Allen, TX 75013

ISBN-13 DIGIT: 978-0-9850500-2-3
ISBN-10 DIGIT: 0985050020
Library of Congress Control Number: 2017917788
Manufactured in the United States of America

Second Edition

Visit us at www.keiththomaswalker.com

CONTENTS

MORE BOOKS BY KEITH THOMAS WALKER

Blurred Lines: The Monster
Blurred Lines: Cop Killer
Blurred Lines: Copycat Killer
Blurred Lines: Mister Me Too

Asha and Boom Part 1
Asha and Boom Part 2
Asha and Boom Part 3

Backslide
Backslide 2

The Realest Ever
The Realest Christmas Ever

Prom Night at Finley High
Fast Girls at Finley High
Bullies at Finley High

Jackson Memorial
Jackson Memorial 2

Brick House
Brick House 2
Brick House 3

Threesome
Threesome 2

Take One of Mine

Take one of Mine Part 2

Fixin' Tyrone
How to Kill Your Husband
A Good Dude
Riding the Corporate Ladder
The Finley Sisters' Oath of Romance
Blow by Blow
Jewell and the Dapper Dan
Harlot
Plan C (And More KWB Shorts)
Dripping Chocolate
Sleeping With the Strangler
Life After
Blood for Isaiah
One on One
Election Day
Evan's Heart
Poor Righteous Poet
Might be Bi Part One
Harder
Primal Part One
Hotline Fling

Visit www.keiththomaswalker.com for information about these and upcoming titles from KeithWalkerBooks

PART ONE
CAPS AND GOWNS

CHAPTER
1

Tell me
Your secrets
Your worries
Your fears
Enlighten me
Your joys and your sorrows
Have you ever been frightened?
Who hurt you?
Please tell me his name
Trust me
With your heart
And I'll do the same
Enrich me
Your soul is sweet nectar
I suckle
Your history
Your joy and your pain and your tears
I'm listening

"HAROLD SCOTT?" KOLE Stone asked.

A sliver of dread tiptoed down Dana's spine as she nodded. She felt like she was divulging too much information, though it seemed unlikely Kole would attempt to exact revenge for something that happened nearly thirty years ago – in Chicago no less. As far as she knew, Kole didn't have any connections in the Windy City and had never traveled there. Plus, Harold was in his late-thirties when the incident occurred. There was a chance he had died by now.

But still, given all she knew about her man and had seen firsthand, Dana couldn't say with complete certainty that Kole wouldn't find it necessary to defend her honor. She was hesitant as she looked up at him and nodded. Her head rested on his massive chest as they cuddled on a king-size bed in his home. The moon shone brightly through the large windows on the west side of the room. Outside the temperature was a sweltering 92 degrees, despite the fact that the sun had relinquished its hold on the skies above Overbrook Meadows hours ago. Inside, Kole had his thermostat set at a pleasant seventy-two.

"But that was so long ago," Dana said. She closed her eyes again and allowed her memories of the Scott family to flood her consciousness. Some memories were best left forgotten, but Kole was curious about the time she'd spent in foster care. Dana couldn't provide an honest answer to his inquiries without telling him about the family that left her the most traumatized.

"How old were you?" Kole asked. His eyes were open the last time Dana checked. He stared at the ceiling fan spinning quietly above them, though Dana was sure his mind's eye was elsewhere.

"I was thirteen. That was my fourth foster home. The first one was with the Brewers," she said, attempting to steer the conversation to more tepid waters. "I was the only foster child there. I was with them for four years, until Mrs. Brewer ended up getting pregnant. They'd been trying for ten years before I got there. They had finally accepted that it was impossible; God wasn't going to bless them with a child. But lo and behold, she got pregnant when she was 42. They kept me around for a few more months, just to make sure it was going to stick, and then they sent me back.

"I guess that's the good thing about taking on a foster child, instead of doing a full adoption. If we don't work out, you can send us right back, like a pair of shoes that didn't fit right."

Rather than comment on the cruelty of the system, as Dana hoped, Kole took a deep breath and asked, "What happened to that guy, Harold? He went to jail for what he did to you?"

Again Dana felt an uncomfortable twinge of trepidation as her upper body rose and fell with his inhalations. Kole lie topless, wearing nothing but his boxers. Rather than a blanket, Dana's body was draped over his. The slow rise and fall of his torso made her feel as if she was resting on a massive beast.

"No," she said. "He never got arrested. They just moved me out. They had other foster children in the home, and they all stayed." This outcome still bothered Dana three decades later, though she rarely shared the story. All told, she couldn't think of more than five people she had told. She hadn't mentioned it at all since she migrated to Texas.

"How the hell does that work?" Kole wondered.

Dana sighed. Behind her closed lids, her eyes filled with tears. She prayed none of them would spill on the wolf's chest.

"We had an argument before it happened," she revealed. "I wasn't doing good in school, and Mr. Scott put me on punishment. I didn't like it, so we argued. I think they were on the verge of putting me out anyway. I never liked that family. I was young, but I knew some things. Some of the foster parents, they would take on kids because the city paid them. Sometimes neither the husband or the wife worked. They got a check every month. The more foster kids they had, the more money they got. I felt like the Scotts were doing that. But I was thirteen, so what the hell did I know?

"When I went to school the next day, I told my teacher what happened. She called the police and CPS, and they did this big investigation. I got moved out of the house right away, so I don't know much about that part, but I know Harold never got charged. He said I made up the story because I was upset with him over my punishment. There wasn't any physical evidence, and none of the other kids reported anything, so they took his word over mine."

"And he was free to go on raping little kids?"

Dana reached to rub Kole's shoulder, which had grown tense during the conversation.

"He didn't rape me," she said. "I told you it never went that far."

"But he touched you."

"Not really. He tried to. I stopped him."

"You said he reached under your blanket. You said he touched you."

"And I said I stopped him."

"You said you were asleep, and you woke up to him touching you. How you know what he did while you were sleep?"

Dana cursed herself for revealing so much. This pillow talk had taken a turn for the worse.

"I know he never penetrated me," she said definitively. "I know that for sure."

"Why are you taking up for him?" Kole wanted to know. He spoke softly, but his voice grumbled like an idling 18-wheeler, especially with her head pressed against his chest.

"I'm not," she said. "I just don't want you getting upset about something that happened a long time ago. I appreciate that you care so much, but it's over now. That's in my past. I moved on."

Kole considered that for a moment. Dana hoped he'd let the topic die, but he asked, "Do you ever think about the other kids? The ones that were still there when you left? The ones that came later? The little girls."

Dana's throat caught, and a tear did spill then. She didn't want to draw attention to it by wiping it, but there was no doubt Kole felt the moisture in her breaths. "I did think about them," she confirmed. "I still do. I feel bad for not being able to help them."

"I know it's not your fault. I didn't say that."

"I was only thirteen. I did everything I was supposed to do. I told the right people. I gave my statement. I swore that everything I told them was true."

"I know. I'm not saying you didn't." Kole wrapped a strong arm around her and squeezed comfortingly. "I know you did all you could. It's that pervert I'm worried about."

"You need to let it go," Dana suggested. "Like I have. I lived with those other kids. Two of those girls were younger than me. I had nightmares after I left that house. I still wonder what happened to Emily and Cheryl." She sniffled. "But if I can move on with my life, you can let this story die. I'm sorry I ever told you."

"Don't say that," he said, stroking her arm. "I'm glad you told me. I need to know about your past. So, you never knew your parents?"

She shook her head. "No."

"You don't know nothing about them? Never tried to look them up when you got older?"

"I know my mom was in prison when she had me. Before that she was living on the streets. Prolly a prostitute or addict – or both. She had eighteen years to find me when she got paroled. I used to hope she would show up and take me away from some of the stuff I was dealing with. But she never did. I guess I got bitter as time went by. By the time I graduated high school, I was glad she never came."

"I feel you," Kole said. "But if you ever change your mind, I'll help you look for her."

"I don't think I want that. If I have a change of heart, I'll let you know."

Dana lie quietly, listening to his heartbeats. After a while she said, "What about you, Mr. Mystery Man?"

He chuckled at that. "What you mean?"

"You've never been very open about your past."

"That's not true. I told you a lot."

Dana couldn't argue that point. While it was true their relationship was shrouded with mystery in the beginning, in the past year Kole had been forthcoming with virtually any information Dana requested. Getting him to open up about his *feelings* remained a challenge, but when it came to facts about his life, Kole no longer felt the need to keep secrets.

Dana knew he had a mother and four sisters who lived in Texarkana. She had never been there, and she wondered if the city was as *country* as Kole made it sound.

"Tell me about your step-father," she said. "You said he was the reason you left your family and came to Overbrook Meadows."

Kole didn't speak for a few seconds. She thought the memory might be too uncomfortable, even after all these years, but he finally responded gruffly. "Ain't much to say about Tyrone, 'cept I couldn't stand him back then, and I can't stand him now. He's the reason me and my mama don't get along. Don't think I'll ever forgive her for choosing him over me."

Dana looked up at him. Even with the scant lighting, she could see that he was still staring up at the ceiling. She wanted to ask a follow-up question, but she knew Kole would let the story unravel at his own pace, if he chose to continue.

"I was ten when he started coming around," he recalled. "Before that, my life was perfect – or at least that's the way I remember it. Mama never worked. She had five kids; me being the youngest one. My pops, he was a hardworking man. Brought home the bacon. Took care of the family. Everything changed when his shirt got caught in some machinery at the plant. Sucked him in and broke nearly every one of his bones before spitting him out."

Dana gasped silently, but Kole's voice didn't change as he spoke.

"They give us a hundred thousand," he continued. "Today, I think we would've got a million for something like that. We prolly could've got more back then, but my Mama hadn't never seen that kind of money. She took the first check they offered her, and it was a wrap. We buried my pops, paid off the house and lived off the settlement money until it started to run dry. I was seven when my dad died. My mom kept her legs closed until I was nine. That's when she started going out again; staying out late, 'cause she didn't wanna have these men up in the house. But in a little city like that, word gets around.

"My first fights was with kids at school calling my mama a ho. I wouldn't let nobody speak negative about my mama. I defended her through thick and then – till Tyrone showed up. I didn't like him from the beginning. Rubbed me the wrong way from the moment I met him. He had this look about him; the way he dressed, the way he smiled; like he had everything figured out, and everyone around him was just pawns on his chess board.

"Tyrone was a womanizer, which I probably could've overlooked. But he took it upon himself to start raising me, like he was my father, and I wasn't never cool with that, especially when he started putting his hands on me."

Dana had never heard this portion of the story. She wanted to know if Kole's expression revealed emotions his voice did not, but she remained deathly still. She felt like any movement on her part might break the spell, and the way he was opening up to her would come to an end.

"He didn't beat the girls," Kole went on. "I don't know if my mama told him not to, or if it was something in Tyrone that told him it wasn't right. But my sisters got a pass, for pretty much whatever they did. He'd lecture them, and sometimes they'd cry just from that. But with me, Tyrone told me the bible said if you spare the rod, you spoil the child. I didn't even know what a *rod* was until he found one and started beating the shit out of me with it."

Dana sighed. Kole continued speaking.

"I wasn't a bad kid. At least not the kind that would deserve that type of punishment. But when it came to Tyrone, the more defiant I got, the more he tried to whoop it out of me. I think

I was twelve when I finally stood up to him. Had to. Mama wasn't doing nothing to help. Tyrone beat my ass, and I got right back on my feet. Blood was dripping off my face, but I looked him dead in the eyes and told him if he ever hit me again, we would go at it. I told him I didn't care if I lost. We could have it out every day from then on till one of us got killed.

"That's when Mama finally intervened, but it wasn't like I expected. She told me I had to go stay with my Uncle Benny. She packed my bags herself. I ain't gon' lie; I hated her for a long time. It wasn't until I got older that I found out what lengths a woman will go through to keep a roof over her head and provide a father for her children. I don't hate her no more, but that don't mean I forgive her for choosing Tyrone over me. I don't think I can ever forgive her for that."

Dana's eyes welled again. She knew Kole didn't intend for her to despise a woman she'd never met, but she couldn't help hating his mother at that moment. She felt like Kole was making excuses for her. Dana was a single mother herself. She raised her son for seventeen years with no help from any man.

Then again, Dana went to college and had a well-paying job. And she only had one child, whereas Kole's mother had five.

Even still, if any of her boyfriends had ever abused her child, she'd kill him herself. It would never reach the point where Tariq had to defend himself from a monster in his own home.

"I liked staying with my uncle," Kole went on. "Uncle Benny was a hard worker. He worked at the same plant where my father died. But he hustled on the side too. Every city, no matter how small, has a population of crackheads. People said my Uncle Benny was wrong for serving them, but I saw it as supply and demand, even when I was a kid. Those fiends wouldn't go to rehab if my uncle stopped selling, so why shouldn't he make the money? Somebody was gonna profit off their addiction.

"Anyway, about a year after I moved in with Benny, he got the job offer of a lifetime. Overbrook Meadows was building another rendering plant, and they wanted him to be a supervisor.

We loaded up everything we had in the back of his truck, sold his house with the furniture still in it, and hightailed it up outta Texarkana as fast as we could.

"At the time, I vowed to never return, but I could never cut my family completely out of my life. Tyrone died five years ago. I went to the funeral to offer my condolences and make amends with my mama. Later that night, I went back to the cemetery to piss on that motherfucker's grave. I took a bottle of whiskey with me, so I'd have plenty piss. I think I stayed out there till damn near sunrise, drinking and pissing. I paid for Tyrone's headstone. I drenched that motherfucker with piss."

Dana's eyes widened, though she wasn't too shocked by this revelation. This story paled in comparison to some of the things she'd seen Kole do with her own eyes, like choke the life out of a gorilla-size gangster named Brass.

"Unfortunately for my uncle," Kole said, "things didn't pan out like he thought they would when we got to Overbrook Meadows. He got laid off from his job after six months and couldn't find anything else that paid as good. He had to fall back on hustling to pay the bills and take care of me. One thing about Uncle Benny was he always kept it real with me. He didn't like slanging, and I didn't like him doing it, but it is what it is. Overbrook Meadows wasn't no different than Texarkana, when it came to dope.

"But my uncle always promised he would leave them rocks alone when he got a good-paying job. And he did it too. It took a few years, but he got another supervisor job at the Miller brewery; the one off 35. But just when things were finally looking up for us, he ended up getting snuffed. Some punk shot him in the back one night after he got off work. Took his wallet and took off. Wasn't no need for that. Benny would've gave it to him, if he would've asked. That's when I learned life's a bitch, and she don't take no prisoners. Benny had his faults, bumped his head a few times, but in the end, he was trying to do right. Ain't no telling where he'd be today, if he had a chance to live his life. Hell, ain't no telling where *I* would be..."

Dana sucked air between her teeth. She didn't know what to say about the tragedies that plagued Kole's childhood. *I'm sorry* seemed too inadequate. Rather than speak, she continued to caress his torso. His house was completely quiet. It was brand new, built from the ground up. But at that moment, not even a creak from the home settling disturbed the silence. The void of sound was broken by Kole's deep voice when he spoke again.

"I was sixteen when my uncle died. That was around the time I started having trouble with the gangs at school, and me and Moon realized we'd have a better chance of defending ourselves if we stuck together. It started out with just us two, and, well, you know the rest."

Dana did know how that story ended. Kole and Moon accumulated a squad of likeminded individuals. As their crew grew larger, they created structure, discipline and directives, and The Organization was born.

The interesting thing was, Dana couldn't say she wished none of these bad things had happened, because if not for Tyrone, Kole may have never come to Overbrook Meadows. If not for his uncle's death, Benny may have kept him out of trouble, and there would be no Organization. Kole never would've come to her doorstep last summer and offered to help with a problem Dana was having with MMG (the Murder Meadows Gang). The butterfly effect had never been so poignant.

"Sorry for all the gloom and doom," Kole said, picking up on her inner conflict.

"No, it's alright," she said, looking up at him. "If life was always sunshine and rainbows, we wouldn't appreciate it."

"You right about that," Kole agreed.

"Thank you for telling me about your parents and your uncle," she said. "I know you trust me." Her voice was barely above a whisper. "You trust me with your heart and with your memories, the good and the bad, just like I trust you."

Kole didn't speak, but his eyes responded to her. His dark orbs were intense and reassuring.

Hoping for a more lighthearted conversation, Dana said, "Can you believe Tariq's graduating tomorrow?"

The room was as dark as her man's skin, but she sensed a smile spread across Kole's face. She felt a slight variation in his body temperature.

"It's a big day," he confirmed. "I'm proud of that boy."

His sentiments warmed Dana's heart, even though Kole had never taken on a full-fledged "father figure" role for her son. Tariq was a senior in high school when they started dating; way past the stage of needing nurturing, as far as the teen was concerned.

But while he may not have looked up to Kole in a fatherly light, Tariq certainly valued him as a role model. The irony of this wasn't lost on Dana. She knew her man had a past that included everything from drug dealing to coldblooded murder. But Kole's past was exactly that: *His past*. He was now recognized as a man who set goals for himself and accomplished them. He was strong-minded and compassionate. Kole was loyal to his family, friends and his woman. He was a nurturer and a provider. These were all traits Tariq recognized and appreciated as much as Dana did.

"I'm surprised Brendon's gonna be walking the stage with him," Kole commented.

"I am too," Dana said, though she hated to feel that way. "I don't think he would've made it, if it wasn't for you."

"*Me*? How you figure that?"

"You know you scared that boy straight."

Kole chuckled. The sound of his amusement, with Dana's ear pressed to his chest, lightened her heart.

He said, "You think so, huh?"

"Yes, you know you did. I'll never forget the look in his eyes when you snatched those beads off his neck. I've never seen anyone cower like that," she said with a laugh. "He thought you were about to open a can of whoop-ass. I swear to God, I thought he was gonna pee on hisself."

Kole laughed too. "I guess I can take a little credit for turning him around."

"You're coming to the graduation, right?"

"Of course. Why would you even ask?"

"I don't know," she said, looking up at him. "Maybe you had more pressing matters to attend to."

"More pressing than watching Tariq get his diploma?" he asked, stroking her arm again. "No way."

Dana expected this response, but it still made her heart flutter. She rolled to her stomach and stood on her arms, one on either side of his torso. She crawled forward until she straddled him fully, and they were face to face. She lowered her head and kissed him softly. Kole's hands moved to her sides, and he returned the affection.

As the kiss deepened, his touch set off small fires that grew steadily as they descended from her ribcage and converged in her lower belly. She slipped her tongue inside his mouth. Kole grunted quietly before licking and sucking it. His hands moved to her back, and he drew her closer, until her breasts rested on his chest, and she could feel the desire between his legs.

Inhaling slowly, she sat up and stared down at him. The bulge of his manhood was intimidating. She watched his eyes as she squeezed and then stroked it through his boxers. Kole's lips glistened from their kisses. His mouth was closed. His jaws flexed in the darkness.

Dana took a deep breath as she caressed him. In the past year, they had made love countless times, but the size of his erection never failed to give her butterflies. In the beginning, her ecstasy was laced with an underlying fear that it would hurt when he stroked her into submission. There was still some of that fear now, but her anxiety was mostly caused by anticipation. Her clitoris began to swell when she pulled his boxers down, exposing him fully.

Her mouth watered when she wrapped both hands around his piece. She once considered that an odd reaction, but she no longer questioned or resisted her natural impulses. She and Kole were in a committed, monogamous relationship. He didn't balk about getting a checkup early on, so they could eliminate condoms from their lovemaking.

There was no hesitation as she scooted down the bed until she was face to face with his manhood. She closed her eyes and slowly took him into her mouth. Kole's legs stiffened beneath her, and she heard him release a pent-up breath.

Dana did not consider herself a master of fellatio, especially when working with something as large as Kole's tool. But she'd made a conscious effort to improve this facet of their foreplay. So far, her efforts had paid of splendidly. She didn't have to take him all the way in – couldn't if she wanted to – because Kole's most sensitive region was under the fat head. She titillated this area with her tongue and her lips as she bobbed her head up and down. Rather than swallow her saliva, she let the moisture seep past her mouth. She used it as a lubricant while she stroked his shaft with her fist, always making sure her hand followed her mouth all the way to the top.

Kole liked it sloppy.

And though he'd never admitted it, Dana knew he liked it loud. The sound of her slurps and sucks made his toes curl. Dana felt them, because she squatted on them on purpose. His toes told her more about how well she was doing than the grunts he emitted when he neared his climax.

Kole also liked it when she tried to deep throat him, and her gag reflex kicked in. He liked the sound of her muted cough and the feel of her tonsils gripping his meat.

He reached for her head, but not to stop her. Not yet, anyway. His fingers slipped into her hair and remained there. Dana opened her eyes and watched him watch her. She deep-throated him again until her eyes glistened with tears. She felt his toes clench again a moment before a squirt of pre-cum coated the back of her throat. Kole stopped her then. He sat up and used both hands to push her face out of his lap.

Dana continued to stroke him with her hand. She knew Kole cared about her, and he had trouble discussing why he didn't like to finish in her mouth. The closest she ever got to an answer was, "I can't do you like that," which led her to believe he considered the act *beneath* her. Maybe, in his world, that was something only a whore would allow. In the year they'd been together, he only came in her mouth twice. Both times she had to swat his hands away and literally fight for his cum.

Tonight she tried a different approach. While holding his dick like a microphone, she licked the tip and squeezed, bringing more of his pre-cum up the shaft. She rubbed the head across her mouth, coating her lips as if his essence was lipstick. She licked it off and then licked him, maintaining eye contact the whole time. She knew he was close, because his eyes grew darker, and the pulsating in her fist grew more intense.

She asked him, "Do you love me, Kole?"

His eyes narrowed, as if he couldn't figure out what that had to do with anything that was happening at the moment.

"You know I do," he breathed.

That was true. Dana knew it because he showed her in so many ways on so many days. He didn't say it often – not at all in the beginning. But in the past six months, she could get him to acknowledge his feelings for her if she asked. He might not ever voice those words without being prompted, but Dana was okay with that. Actions speak louder than words.

"Tell me you love me," she whispered against his dick.

He continued to frown, but his erection did not ebb. He asked her, "Why?"

She grinned. "Because a girl needs to hear it every now and then."

She wouldn't have been surprised if he replied, "*I told you last month.*" But he didn't.

His eyes softened, and he said, "I love you."

She smiled. She didn't give a damn if she had to force it out of him. Every time he said it, she felt like the luckiest woman in the world. She told him, "If you love me, cum in my mouth."

He frowned again. Before he could question the correlation, she said, "That doesn't make me a freak. And even if it does, I'm only a freak for you; in your bedroom."

He shook his head. "But you ain't gotta do that."

"I want to," she said seriously. "And I know you want to."

"Nah, I'm—"

"I don't want my man cumming in some other bitch's mouth, 'cause he don't wanna do it to his girl. Everything you need is right here," she said, and sucked him down again.

His toes curled beneath her. He said, "I would never cheat on you."

Dana came up for air long enough to tell him, "Then cum in my mouth, Kole. Please. I need my protein shake."

Her dirty talk made his eyes widen as much as her tongue did. He gradually reclined on the mattress, but not all the way. He propped himself on his forearms, so he wouldn't miss any of the show. The thrill of him giving in to her needs, coupled with him saying he loved her, gave Dana's tongue and jaws renewed strength. She sucked him like they were teenagers. It didn't take long before Kole reached again, but she narrowed her eyes, and his paws returned to the bed and gripped the sheets instead.

She watched the rise and fall of his chest increase speed while losing stability. His stomach tightened as his eruption rolled downhill. The explosion made Dana's eyes bulge. The first squirt went all the way to the back of her throat. The pulsating in her fist became even stronger, each one bringing another burst of the protein shake she sought. She had to swallow twice to avoid spilling any of it. Kole watched her with a sense of awe and gratitude. She continued sucking when he was spent. Kole gradually lie back fully, his eyes slipping closed, his chest rising and falling, as if he'd been working out.

Dana's smile was ear-to-ear when she finally backed off. Her elation was only rivaled by her longing for him. For now, Kole was still as hard as a rock, and she had a tsunami in her panties. She quickly stripped them off and crawled on top of him, until he could feel the heat of her wet center on his manhood. Kole opened his eyes and watched her.

"Damn," he muttered. "I get pussy too?"

Dana grinned and sucked air between her teeth as she lowered herself and guided him in slowly. When he was fully submerged, and her walls caressed him just right, Kole closed his eyes and did something he'd never done before.

He told her, "I fucking love you."

Dana didn't know which one of her emotions he tapped into with that unprompted declaration, but she couldn't ride him for more than a minute before a mind-splitting climax buckled her like she got struck by lightning.

Her voice quavered. *"Oh shit..."*

Kole chuckled when she collapsed on his chest. "Hmph. Lightweight."

He gave her a few moments to recover before he rolled her onto her back and mounted in the missionary position. Dana squealed when he plunged in balls-deep.

"Let me show you how to do this thang," he muttered.

"Show me," Dana breathed between gasps. *"Shit! Baby, show me!"*

CHAPTER 2

Sharp as a tack
So handsome
Endearing
Courageous and thoughtful
My child
Though you're clearly
A man
I think back to when I held you dearly
In my arms
And you looked up to me
And I clearly
Saw greatness in your dark, brown eyes
Even as you smiled and sucked your pacifier
On this day
As you step across that stage
Your future's as bright as I've always prayed
And my eyes shed freely
These are tears of joy!
Though a man now
You'll always be my baby boy

ON FRIDAY AFTERNOON, Dana and Kole went to the Wilkerson Greines Center to celebrate the end of a major chapter in Tariq's life. Once there, Dana hooked up with Courtney, one of her good friends from work. With just the three of them, Dana felt outmatched by the hordes of family members that showed up to support some of the other students. She considered what Kole said about finding her mother one day. Maybe she had a whole slew of family members she'd actually like, despite how she felt about her birth-giver.

She doubted if any of them would've travelled all the way from Chicago to support a graduate they didn't even know. But still, Dana wanted the best for her child, including a racket of cheers when he walked across the stage to accept his diploma (even though the principal kindly instructed everyone to hold their applause until the last student's name was called).

The ceremony was beautiful, from start to finish. Finley High's band was one of the top three in the district, and they were on point that day. The only downside was when the choir tried to match the band's perfection with a song one of the students wrote.

As they sang, Kole leaned over to his woman and told her, "They should've went with '*I Believe I Can Fly*.' But it sounds like they would've jacked that up too."

Dana laughed and relayed his comment to Courtney, who sat on her other side.

Dana's heart began to kick when Tariq's row of students made their procession to the stage. In the bigger scheme of things, his high school diploma would pale in comparison to the other goals he'd reach in his lifetime. But it was the springboard for everything else.

My baby made it!

Dana had tears in her eyes when they finally called Tariq's name. She screamed her head off and was happy to hear others in the audience cheering for her pride and joy. She tracked the sound and was delighted to see Brendon's family going crazy for her son.

She took a gazillion pictures and then fell into the arms of her boyfriend. Kole hugged her tightly, as if he was Tariq's father.

Dana wished she had met him ten years ago, so he could've at least worn the *step*-father hat.

CHAPTER
3

WITH OVER TWO thousand guests in attendance, it was a hassle finding Tariq after the students were dismissed. Dana played cameraman for the next thirty minutes, taking pictures of Tariq and everyone who stopped by to give him a hug. Dana thought her son had never looked so handsome. She felt the same way about Brendon when the best friends finally linked up.

"Look at you!" she told him, admiring his shirt and tie. "First time I've ever seen you in anything but a tee-shirt."

"I tried to wear one!" Brendon joked, or at least she hoped it was a joke. "But the principal said they wouldn't let me walk if I did."

"Well, that was a good call," Dana told him. "Where are you and your family headed after this?"

"I'm not sure. Y'all going out to eat?" Brendon asked.

"We're planning to," Dana said. "Tariq wants to go to Buffalo Wild Wings, of all places..." She gave her son a look for his questionable restaurant selection.

"Don't look at me like that," Tariq said, grinning. "You know hot wings is my favorite food!"

"But it's your *graduation*, baby. We can take you anywhere you like. I can't believe you're passing up Red Lobster. You love that place."

"I ain't trying to break you," Tariq said. "You need to save your money for when I start bumming off you when I get to college."

"Don't worry about that," Dana said, her eyes gleaming. "You can eat wherever you want. It's your big day!"

"For real," Kole said. "You can pick another restaurant, if you want. It's my treat."

"I appreciate it, but I'm good with hot wings," Tariq stated.

"Me too," Brendon chipped in. "Can we go with y'all?"

"How many you got with you?" Dana asked.

"It's about ten of us. We'll pay for our own food."

"No, I got it," Kole insisted, much to the delight of Brendon, who's eyes lit up.

"For real?"

"Yeah," Kole told him. "Let us know when y'all ready to take off."

"Shit – I mean, excuse me! We ready now!"

"Let's get a move on," Kole told him. "It's gonna be hell getting out of here. We wanna make it to the restaurant before a lot of other families start showing up."

"Ain't nobody picking *Buffalo Wild Wings* for their graduation dinner," Dana muttered.

But she was wrong about that.

When they arrived at the restaurant, her group had to wait twenty minutes for their table. Sure enough, they spotted two of Tariq's classmates with their families as the hostess led them to their seats.

Tariq couldn't resist throwing in an *I told you so*. "Mmm hmm. Guess I'm not the only one who knows this place is the bomb!"

"I'll be glad when you're gone to college," Dana said good-naturedly.

The graduation dinner was lively and sentimental. Even Brendon's seldom-seen mother showed up and looked surprisingly presentable. Dana couldn't tell if she was still strung out on crack.

Either way, she was glad the woman pulled it together long enough to celebrate her son's accomplishment.

Brendon's aunt Victoria hadn't seen Kole since he went to her apartment last summer and put her in her place in regard to the mischief Brendon was getting into. Victoria didn't appear to harbor any ill will. Dana guessed that was because Kole was picking up the ticket for the whole get-together.

While they dined, the boys discussed their plans for the future. Tariq got accepted to Florida A&M, while Brendon planned to attend Overbrook Meadows Community College in the fall.

"What made you pick that school?" Victoria asked Tariq. "What they got over there?"

"I'm majoring in Animal Science," he informed her.

That only deepened her puzzlement.

"I wanna be a vet," he said, "at a zoo."

That brought a round of oohs and ahhs from Brendon's family.

"You wanna help deliver those baby elephants?" one of Victoria's children asked.

"Yeah," Tariq confirmed, "and care for any of the animals that get sick; giraffes, penguins, lions and snakes too."

"That's cool!" Brendon's aunt said.

But his mother frowned. "Uh-uhn. I can't be messing around with no snakes. You should let them *die*."

Everyone laughed at that.

Not to be outdone, Brendon said, "I'm thinking about transferring to that school when I get a couple of years of community college under my belt."

Dana was pretty sure she kept her expression neutral, even though that was the *last* thing she wanted to happen. She didn't like the idea of Tariq going all the way to Florida, but the bright side was it got him away from his knuckleheaded best friend. But what were the odds of Brendon making it that far anyway? Dana felt guilty for having such little faith in him, until his own aunt voiced the same opinion.

"Boy, you know you ain't going to no damn *Florida*! Yo ass barely got through high school!"

Everyone laughed, but Dana could tell Brendon was offended.

"Oh, I can't get through two years at community college?"

"You know you can't," Victoria said. "Especially since you won't have nobody making you go, like you did in high school. If you sign up for a bunch of classes, you ain't gon' be doing nothing but wasting money. They don't give you your money back when you drop out."

"You said I wasn't gon' be able to keep a job," Brendon told her. "I been at the Italian Inn for six months now. What you got to say about that?"

"You right," Victoria conceded. "You have kept that job. I don't know how, but–"

"It's 'cause I'm a good worker," Brendon interjected. "They love me there."

"I heard you be stealing those waitresses' tips," his aunt announced.

Brendon couldn't force a smile anymore. He scowled and asked her, "Man, why you can't never say nothing nice? How y'all expect a nigga to do something with his life, when I ain't got nobody who believe in me?"

Everyone's eyes grew large, and an uncomfortable silence settled upon the table. Dana was surprised Kole was the first to speak.

"I gotta agree with Brendon on this one," he told Victoria. "And that's saying something, 'cause I don't think I've ever agreed with him on *anything*." His humor brought a few chuckles and eased tensions considerably. "Today's a day to be proud of these boys," he continued. "These *young men*," he said, correcting himself. "I had my doubts that Brendon would make it out of high

31

school, but he did. I didn't know he had a job, but if he's managed to keep it for six months, that says something too.

"Truthfully, Brendon can do anything he sets his mind to. I know it, because I seen it plenty of times, and I did it myself. But even if you don't got nobody in your corner," he said, addressing Brendon directly, "that don't mean you should give up and find somebody to blame. If I was you, I would try even harder – not just for myself, but to prove everybody wrong."

Brendon nodded, and his expression softened. "I appreciate that, Kole."

"Yeah, and I'm sorry," Victoria said to her nephew. "You can do anything you set your mind to."

Brendon rolled his eyes at her for stealing Kole's motivational speech, but then he smiled. "Thanks, Auntie. I'ma be somebody. Watch. I'll show you."

"Show me, then," Victoria said. "'Cause I'm damn sho' gon' be watching!" She grinned and looked around for their waiter. "They serve alcohol here?"

CHAPTER 4

DANA AND KOLE didn't travel to the graduation together, so it was just her and Tariq on the way home from the restaurant. Even this late in the game, she wasn't done attempting to steer him to a closer school.

"I cried when you walked across that stage," she told him. "I think I'ma cry even more when you pack up your bags and head to Florida."

"You'll be alright, Mama." Tariq was still beaming, clutching the four greeting cards he received during dinner. All of them contained money. Victoria had the least to contribute. There was only a twenty-dollar bill in her envelope. Kole outdid everyone with ten, crisp one hundred-dollar bills.

"I was looking at Texas Lutheran's curriculum the other day," Dana said. "You know they offer that Animal Science degree too."

"You want me to go to *Texas Lutheran*?"

"You don't have to say it like that. That's a good school."

"It's a *little* school," Tariq said. "And it's too close. It's only twenty minutes away from the house."

"What's wrong with staying close?"

"It'll be like high school all over again. I can come home every day, let you wake me up in the morning."

"No, there won't be none of that," Dana assured him. "You have to wake your own butt up."

Tariq shook his head. "It's too close," he reiterated.

"What about Texas Southern?" Dana asked. "Or Abilene Christian? You got accepted to both of those schools too."

"Florida offered me a full ride."

"Abilene did too."

"So what you're saying is, you want me to go somewhere close."

"It's not, I mean, what's wrong with that?"

"Why, Mama? You don't trust me?"

Dana looked over at his caramel-colored complexion. Her little man wasn't so little anymore. Tariq had been taller than her since his freshman year of high school. He now had a struggling moustache and a decent tuft of hair on his chin.

"I trust you," she said. "It's just, that school is pretty close to the beach."

"Not really, but what does the beach have to do with anything?"

"That whole spring break crowd," Dana said with a cringe. "You'll be around all those dope heads when they get to partying."

"There's dope heads everywhere, Mama. I been around them the whole time I been in high school."

"But I knew where you were every night. Once you get to Florida..."

Tariq waited, but she didn't finish the sentence. "So, you don't trust me," he said again.

"I do," Dana promised. "It's those *other* people I don't trust. You – you're not just my only son. You're the only family I got."

"I know," he said, his eyes softening. "I'm gonna be alright. Do you want me to call you every night, to let you know I'm safe in my dorm?"

She grinned. "No, Tariq. I'm not asking for all of that."

"You sure? We can face time, so you'll know I'm tucked in with my blankie."

"Alright, smart-ass."

He laughed, and then asked, "What about Kole? I didn't think you'd miss me too much with Kole around."

"Having Kole in my life doesn't change how I feel about you," she informed him.

"Are y'all gonna shack up when I leave?" Tariq wondered. "You spend the night there almost every day."

Dana was surprised by the question. She only spent the night with Kole a few times a week. Tariq had an active social life, so she didn't think he minded.

"Does that bother you?" she asked.

"Naw. I'm just saying, y'all might as well live together. Then you won't miss me so much."

"Oh, so you wanna hand me off to your friend," she said with a grin, "like the ugly chick at the party who won't stop following you."

Tariq laughed.

"Kole and I both have our own homes. I don't think either of us is ready to give one up right now."

"If y'all get married, one of you will have to sell your house," Tariq deduced.

"Who said anything about marriage?"

"Really? You don't wanna get married?"

"I don't know," she said with a shrug. "Maybe one day."

"*One day*? Mama, you dang near *fifty*. What are you waiting for?"

"*Fifty*? Boy I'm *forty-one*!"

"You're not getting any younger. What's wrong? Kole's not the one? I thought you loved him."

Dana wasn't sure how their talk about college had led to this. "Kole and I are fine," she said, eager to get him off her case. "What we have is perfect, just the way it is. We don't need a ring to define our relationship."

Tariq watched her for a moment and then shook his head. "Is that *you* talking right now, or is it Kole?"

Until that moment, Dana was sure that was the way *she* felt. She didn't like how Tariq made her question herself.

"What about you and Sabrina?" she asked, blatantly rerouting the conversation. "She got accepted to UTA, right?"

Tariq nodded. "Yep. She'll be in Arlington in the fall."

"How does she feel about you going to Florida?"

"'Bout the same as you. She asked if I wanted to get married before I left."

"*What*?" Dana almost stomped the brakes in the middle of the freeway. "She's just trying to lock you down. I hope you told her no!"

"I did," Tariq said, laughing. "You should see the look on your face right now."

"You're only eighteen! What the hell makes her think you wanna get married this young? That girl done lost her damn mind!"

"Chill, Mama. I already know what's up. She didn't mean no harm. She's just scared. I told her I wouldn't even *think* about marriage until after college."

"Hmph," Dana said, brooding. "Good."

"I guess marriage ain't in either of our futures," Tariq commented, returning his attention to the money in his lap.

Dana was glad to hear that – on his side, but a part of her was disappointed by the comment. She knew Tariq didn't mean any harm, so she let it go and told him, "I'm proud of you. You're already making good, adult decisions."

He grinned and said, "Thanks, Ma. But trust me, I know how hard it is for single moms. Everything I've accomplished is because of you."

"No, baby. You did it all yourself."

"It's okay to take a little credit," he told her.

Dana giggled. "Okay. Just a little."

"I love you, Mama."

"I love you more, baby. To the moon and back."

CHAPTER
5

ON SATURDAY, DANA was midway through her shift at Jackson Memorial when she received a text message from Kole. Her work as a radiology tech had been stressful that evening. Kole's text put a smile on her face. He didn't say much; it was just the fact that he was thinking about her:

Hey, babe

She texted the same back to him: Hey, babe

After a moment, her phone vibrated again, which made her more giddy. He replied: You off tomorrow?

She told him, Yes

He typed, Moon invited us to a graduation party. Wanna go?

Moon was Kole's best friend of nearly thirty years. The men had always been as thick as thieves. Moon was Kole's right-hand man when Kole ran a dangerous underworld group called The Organization. When Kole stepped down two years ago, Moon took over as the head honcho. He was still operating in that capacity, but Dana loved him. More than anything, she was glad Kole had relinquished the reins.

In regard to the graduation party, she told him, Of course. What time?

Kole said, It starts at 5

Dana typed, I'll be ready. Can't wait!

She was grinning when she backed out of the message and returned her phone to her purse. When she swiveled her chair back to the front of the department, she noticed her coworker Courtney watching her.

"What's up, girl? Who you talking to, got you smiling like that? Better be Kole."

"Look at you, all in my business," Dana said with a giggle. "Yeah, that was Kole."

"Y'all got plans for tonight?" Courtney wanted to know.

Dana didn't get off until 10:30, but she was off tomorrow, so a late date-night wasn't out of the question.

"No," she said. "He invited me to a graduation party tomorrow."

"Who graduated?"

"I don't know," Dana said. "I didn't even ask."

"You just happy to go out with him," Courtney guessed.

Dana nodded. No point in denying what was written all over her face.

"I'm glad I finally got a chance to meet your *mystery man* yesterday," Courtney commented. "I was starting to think there was something wrong with him, like some of the other folks up here."

That was news to Dana. "Really? People talk about my boyfriend?"

"You know people talk about *everything*," Courtney replied. "Don't act like you new to this. How long you been working at this hospital?"

"A long time," Dana acknowledged. "But I didn't know people were talking about me."

"What you expect?" Courtney asked. "Folks know you got a boyfriend, but you never post pics of him on Facebook. I don't think there's any pics of you and him together. Even when y'all go out, you'll post something like, '*Date night*,' but it will only be a picture of your plates."

"You stalking my Facebook page," Dana asked, but she was smiling, so her friend didn't take offense.

"We're friends on Facebook," Courtney commented. "In real life too. I don't have to stalk your page to see the stuff you post. It pops up on my timeline."

"And because I don't post any pics of Kole, people think he doesn't exist, like I'm making him up or something?"

"Either that or he's married," Courtney informed her. "That's the story most people are going with."

"Most people like who? People in this department?"

"I love you, but I'm not gon' start naming names," Courtney said. "I'm just saying I've heard people talk about it. A couple even asked me about it. I told them they should ask you, if they're so interested."

"Good," Dana said, frowning now. "They need to mind their own business."

"Yeah, that's one way to look at it," Courtney replied.

Dana looked at her sideways. "Don't tell me you're one of the ones who was thinking he wasn't real..."

"No," Courtney said with a grin. "I was one of the ones who was thinking he's married."

"Wow. I guess I should thank you for being honest."

"Since we're talking about it," Courtney said, rolling her chair closer, "why don't you ever post any pics of Kole? I know he's the one who doesn't want you to."

"Oh yeah? How you know that?"

"Girl, please," Courtney said with a smack of her lips. "Any woman who has a man as fine as Kole would be showing his ass off every chance she got. Don't play."

Dana chuckled. "Yeah, it's him," she admitted. "Kole doesn't do social media."

"It's one thing for him to not be on social media himself," Courtney countered. "But not wanting his pictures on there at all, that's a little different. That's usually one of those, *I don't want my wife to see me*, type of moves..."

"He's not married," Dana assured her.

"You know that for a fact?" Courtney asked, narrowing her eyes.

Dana nodded. "Of course, girl. You think I'm crazy? I'm at Kole's house damn near every night. Either that, or he's at my place. If he has a wife, they haven't seen each other in over a year. But Kole's never been married."

"So there's still a little mystery to him," Courtney noted, "if he doesn't want his picture on Facebook."

When it came to mystery, Dana couldn't say her friend was wrong. She encountered plenty of confusing and curious moments when she and Kole started dating last summer. That was a few months after their first attempt at romance, which ended with him dumping her unceremoniously for no good reason (or so it had seemed). Dana was grateful Kole finally sat her down and explained himself fully, exposing more about his past than she wanted to know at the time.

She now understood the complexities of her man more than any woman ever had. But from the outside looking in, she understood why Courtney had doubts. Unfortunately, Dana couldn't fill her friend in on any of the things she was concerned about. The fact was, Kole was a dangerous man with equally dangerous enemies. Dana could put her own life in jeopardy if one of them found Kole via her Facebook page. Even though Kole had retired from The Organization, there was blood on his hands that would never wash off.

"I don't think Kole's the first person in the world to avoid taking pictures," Dana told her coworker. "If that makes him mysterious, I guess it is what it is. I know what I got, and I don't care what people think about it."

"That's cool," Courtney said. "Like I said, I seen him with my own eyes, and I'm happy for you. Y'all make a great couple. I can tell by the way y'all interact that you love each other. He's a good man. And *Lawd have mercy*, he's fine as hell. You a lucky girl."

"Thanks," Dana said, smiling again.

"How long before y'all get married?" Courtney wondered.

"Who said anything about marriage?"

"You been with him for over a year," her friend noted. "Don't tell me you haven't thought about it."

Dana shook her head. "I don't think that's gonna happen for us."

"That's what *you* want, or is it him?"

Dana was struck by a sense of déjà vu. Didn't she just have this same conversation with Tariq?

"We haven't talked about it, but I don't think Kole's the marrying type."

"If you haven't talked about it, what are you basing that on?"

"Well, he's 42 and he's never been married. No kids, either."

"And the plot thickens," Courtney commented.

"Girl, I'm through talking to you," Dana said, turning her chair back towards her desk. "No matter what I say, you try to make a story out of it."

"Hey, at least I'm on your side," Courtney told her. "I'd rather ask and hear it from you than speculate on my own."

Dana didn't respond to that, but she appreciated her friend's candor.

CHAPTER 6

ON SUNDAY, KOLE showed up at 5 pm to pick Dana up for what she learned would be a barbecue at Moon's place. Kole had a key to her home. He stepped into her bedroom wearing dark jeans with a dark tee. The shirt wasn't form-fitting, but it was nearly impossible to conceal Kole's physique, no matter what he wore. He never hit the gym, but he had a workout regimen he'd maintained since high school. His exercises included running, sit-ups, pull-ups and at least five hundred pushups a day.

The way his chest and shoulder muscles bulged under his shirt made Dana think every infomercial she'd seen for a new fitness machine was a sham. She got lost in Kole's dark skin and darker eyes as she looked him up and down. Her boyfriend wore a thin moustache and goatee with enough stubble on his cheeks to qualify as a burgeoning beard.

"You look nice," he said as he approached her. Kole's voice was deep; easily overpowering the music emanating from her cellphone.

Dana wore a flirty sundress that had spaghetti straps and a cinched waistline. The dress ran out of material midway down her thighs. The brown highlights in her hair matched her sandals. Dana's skin was nearly as dark as her man's. Her breasts weren't very large, but her thighs and ass made up for it, as was evident when Kole immediately gripped her backside when they hugged. The feel of his strong hands sent a flash of muted lightening from her stomach down between her legs.

If they were attending an event they hadn't already RSVP'd for, Dana would've backed towards the bed and asked if they really needed to be on time. As it was, they were already a few minutes late to Moon's get-together.

"How are we supposed to be there by five, if you don't get here till five?" Dana wondered. She spoke over Kole's shoulder as he hunkered down to embrace her. Her eyes slipped closed. She relished their closeness. She smiled as she inhaled his cologne. The underlying scent of his manliness was equally pleasing.

"Nobody shows up to a barbecue on time," he said as he backed away.

Dana's body craved him the moment they were no longer touching, like an infant that was not ready to be placed in the crib.

"Your friend loves to barbecue," she commented.

"You know Moon would never pass up a chance to show off his grills," Kole agreed.

Dana had experienced Moon's culinary skills a few times. And yes, Kole did mean *grills* – plural. Moon was one of few cooks Dana had met who lit up two grills and a smoker and tended to all three effortlessly. If not for his involvement with The Organization, Dana thought he could open a restaurant, like his wife Carla. But when it came to Moon, his criminal activities came first. Everything else was a hobby.

"Good," Dana told her boyfriend. "'Cause I'm hungry. Does he want us to bring anything? Ice, beer?"

"Nope," Kole said. "Just a graduation present for his niece."

"I hope you didn't go all out, like you did with Tariq," Dana said. "I wish you would've told me you were giving him that kind of money."

"Why," Kole asked with a smirk. "What would you have done about it?"

Dana realized she had no recourse. "I would've gave him something different," she said. "Your card put my little check to shame."

Kole laughed. It was a hearty chortle that made laugh lines appear in the corner of his eyes. Growing up, humor had been a rare emotion for him. He experienced it a lot more frequently since he started dating Dana. She was happy to be the one to provide that for him.

"How much did you give him?" he asked her.

"Five hundred."

"Shit, I wish I got that kind of money when I graduated. My mama and them wasn't even coming to mine, so I didn't bother going either."

Dana's heart sank. The things Kole had experienced never ceased to amaze her. As she peeled back the layers of his life, she hoped he'd reveal positive memories. But for the most part, he did not.

"I did get a gift, though," Kole recalled. "Me and a few partners went to the gambling shack to celebrate. We got four bottles of rum from the bootleg guy. We stayed in that place all night, getting drunk, trying to holler at them grown women.

"Most of us lost the little money we brought with us, but Moon was feeling them dice that night. He went on a run and ended up winning three hundred dollars. Everybody was telling him to let it ride, but he scooped it up off the floor and handed it to me. I asked him, 'What you giving me this for?' He told me, 'That's yo graduation present.'"

Overall, Kole's story was dark. But like him, it had tender moments. Dana's eyes watered as she listened to him.

"You ready?" Kole asked, as if he didn't notice her emotional state.

"Yeah." Dana turned away from him and wiped her eyes. "Let me grab my purse."

CHAPTER
7

MOON DIDN'T LIKE to refer to his home as a *mansion*, but that was the word Dana would use to describe the sprawling eight-bedroom complex. Made mostly of brick, the compound stretched a whole city block, with nearly an acre of St Augustine grass in the front yard and several more acres in the back.

The first time she visited, Dana had to ask her boyfriend how this home vibed with Moon's supposed low-key profile and his lack of taxable income.

Kole had grinned and told her, "Me and Moon have one of the best lawyers in the business. By *best*, I mean crooked as hell. He set us up with money laundering operations. Moon took it a step further and got a sweet inheritance from a long, lost aunt. The inheritance just happened to be enough to pay for this house."

"Moon had a rich aunt?" Dana asked.

"Hell no. This particular aunt never even existed outside of paper."

"What kind of lawyer can do that?" Dana had wondered.

"Like I said; the best in the business."

Moon's driveway was almost large enough to be declared a parking lot, which was necessary for his niece's graduation party. Kole pulled in at 6 pm and parked amongst nearly a dozen vehicles that had already arrived. He and Dana were greeted by Moon's lovely wife Carla when they entered the home. The foyer was breathtaking, rivaling some of the megachurches Dana had visited. The hostess was just as beautiful.

"Kole! *Look at you!*" Carla gushed, throwing her arms around him.

"Hey, Carla," he said and hugged her tightly. "You're looking as lovely as ever."

Carla backed away beaming. She was a delightful woman with rosy cheeks and wide hips. Despite her husband's ill-gotten gains, Carla was never one to sit and home and play happy-housewife. She was the owner of a restaurant named after herself. Among other specialties, they served the best meatloaf Dana had ever tasted.

"I see Dana's still sticking around," Carla said and took the woman's hands. She pulled her close for a hug and a kiss on the cheek. "I knew it was something special about this one," Carla said. "Kole never had a serious girlfriend," she told Dana. "Or *any* girlfriend, for that matter. Least not one I've ever met. How'd you do it?" she wondered.

Dana blushed and shrugged coyly. "I don't know, Miss Carla. I ask myself that same question."

"Now, don't you go thinking you're so lucky to be with him," Carla said, offering Kole a playful frown. "I can see that *he's* the lucky one to have you in his life. So," she said, staring into Dana's eyes again, "any wedding bells in your future?"

"Whoa, what are you doing?" Kole asked, stepping forward. "Everybody's trying to have a good time here. What are you talking about?"

The smile on his face made Dana giggle.

"Boy, us having a good time ain't got nothing to do with what I asked this woman," Carla told him. "If you wanna *keep* having a good time, you better do right by her. I know you can see she's a keeper."

"Yeah, and I'm definitely gon' keep her away from you!" Kole teased. He wrapped a possessive arm around Dana's waist and pulled her away. "Where my man at?" he asked, leading her down the hallway. "Nice seeing you, as always," he called back to Carla.

"Mmm hmm," she said, her lips set in a pout. "Nice seeing you too, Kole. Dana, you need to come find me, when him and Moon get full of that liquor. I got a few tips that'll get that jackass to jump the broom!"

"*Jesus*," Kole muttered when they were further away. "Why is everybody so worried about what we got going on?"

"That's like, the third person that's asked about us getting married, in the past two days," Dana commented.

"What?" Kole was surprised to hear that. "What'd you tell them?"

"What do you think I told them?"

He studied her features, glad to see she was smiling. "I hope you told them to mind they damn business."

"You want me to say that to Tariq?"

His eyes widened. "Tariq asked about us?"

She nodded. "He wanted to know what our plans are, after he leaves for college."

Kole shook his head. "Backstabber. And I just gave that lil' nigga a thousand dollars."

Dana elbowed him in the ribs. "Don't be calling my baby a *lil' nigga* – or a *backstabber*. Maybe the people asking aren't the *only ones* curious about what's going on with us."

"Who else wants to know?" Kole wondered.

Rather than respond, she batted her eyes.

Kole's mouth fell open. "Hey, wha, what are you doing? Everybody's trying to have a good time here. Why you tripping?"

Dana rolled her eyes and muttered something under her breath.

"What was that?" Kole asked.

"I said Carla's right: *You're a jackass!*"

"But you love me, though."

Dana didn't reply, but her smile said it all.

48

"*Love is in the air*," a deep voice boomed a moment before Kole's best friend rounded the corner.

Moon was a large man; more stout than fat, but his gut had been getting away from him for the past few years. He had a bald head and strong arms that pulled his comrade in for a bro hug. Dana watched the men with a twinkle in her eye. Very few people could put a smile on her boyfriend's face like Moon did.

"Glad you could make it," the host said when they backed away. He turned to Dana and took her hand. "It's always good to see you, Dana. You having any trouble keeping my boy in line?"

Before she could respond, Kole said, "Ain't nobody keeping me in line, and you know it. I does what I wants to."

Dana's jaw dropped, and Moon's eyebrows rose. She had a great rebuttal for that, but Moon winked at her before turning to his friend.

"Oh, is that right?" he asked Kole. "So I guess you been staying out all night, hitting up the bucky-nekkid whenever you feel like it. Coming home drunk and smelling like stripper oil..."

"Oh, hell no he hasn't!" Dana interjected.

"Yo, that's 'cause I don't want to," Kole said with a chuckle. "That's *my* choice."

"Yeah, you choosing not to get your love boat anchored!" Moon joked.

"More like *torpedoed*," Dana threatened. "Start coming home at all hours of the night if you want to..."

Moon laughed at that. His amusement rumbled through the entire first floor.

"Look at you," Kole said, "always wanna stir up some mess."

When Moon got his chuckles under control, he said, "I'm just getting you back for how you used to do me and Carla."

"I ain't never did nothing like that," Kole protested.

"Oh no? What about when you drove her to the strip club and had her drag me up outta there?"

49

Kole grinned at the memory. "That was a long-ass time ago. Y'all had just got married."

"But you did it," Moon insisted.

"She made me!" Kole argued. "You know how persistent your wife can be. Plus you was wrong for leaving her home alone on her birthday."

Dana's eyes widened. "*Moon!*" she said, slapping his arm.

The big man burst into laughter again. "I was gonna go home," he told Dana. "Time just got away from me. I'm giving him a hard time, but your man did the right thing." He faced Kole again. "Might've saved my marriage. You know Carla still gets onto me about that night."

"Good," Kole stated.

Moon looked Dana's way again and said, "You know, it's little things like that that makes Kole a good man. He a little rough around the edges, but he knows what it takes to keep a woman happy."

"He does," Dana agreed. The smile that lit her face when she looked her boyfriend in the eyes was so palpable, even Moon's heart thumped sweetly.

He gripped his friend's shoulder and said, "That's love right there. I don't know what you're doing to keep her smiling like that, but whatever it is, you better keep it up."

In a rare display of public affection, Kole looked Dana in the eyes as he responded to his friend. "I will. Putting a smile on her face is damn near the only thing that matters to me these days..."

CHAPTER 8

WHEN IT CAME to parties, Moon was known to throw one helluva shindig. By ten o'clock all the guests had arrived, and the celebration was in full swing. Most of the guests were tipsy, courtesy of an endless flow of beer and hard liquor. The woman of the hour, eighteen-year-old Destiny Yates, couldn't have been more pleased, especially when it was time to lavish her with graduation gifts. In lieu of bringing any food or drinks to the party, everyone knew to provide something special for the graduate, and boy did they show out!

Dana lost count of how many cards Destiny opened. All of them were filled with cash, which the graduate stuffed into an empty Crown Royal bag. As full as the bag was when she was done, it didn't compare to the gift her favorite uncle got her. Moon led everyone to the driveway, where a fiery orange Dodge Charger had appeared, seemingly out of thin air. A huge, red bow sat atop the hood. Destiny squealed like a much younger girl when Moon handed her the keys. As anxious as she was to hop inside, she took a moment to show her gratitude; hugging Moon tightly and showering him with kisses.

By midnight, Moon closed the lid on his barbeque pits, and the party started to wind down – for the youngsters. The adults remained full of cheer. Dana suspected this would turn into an all-nighter. She was glad she hadn't drunk too much, but she couldn't say the same about the food she'd consumed. Moon's ribs were so tender, she could literally shake the meat off the bones. She felt like she'd eaten enough meat and beans and potato salad to last the rest of the year.

She reclined on one of the patio chairs and watched her man across the yard. Kole had his back to her, but she could tell by his gestures that he was laughing. He was surrounded by half a dozen men who were all members of The Organization. Despite their party attire and the smiles on their faces, Dana knew they were extremely dangerous. She felt completely safe as she reclined in the chair and rested a hand on her swollen belly.

She didn't realize she had dozed off until her eyes flashed open, and she sat up with a start. She looked around in confusion, thinking she couldn't have heard what she thought she heard. But as the fog cleared from her mind, her eyes confirmed the worst possible scenario: People were running, falling and ducking, knocking over tables, chairs and drinks. Women were screaming, children too.

And then she heard it again – eight to ten quick shots – in rapid succession.

PAP!PAP!PAP!
PAP!
PAP!PAP! - PAP!PAP!PAP!

Dana's eyes widened to the size of doorknobs. The blood in her veins turned ice cold, restricting circulation and rendering her completely frozen. She couldn't breathe. Her terrified eyes scanned the yard, in search of the man she cared about the most. Kole was not standing where she'd seen him last. None of the men were. Some had hunkered down behind Moon's hulking pecan trees. Others were running, both towards the gunfire and away from it.

Dana tried to sit up just as a hard object slammed into her from the left side. She and the chair fell hard to the pavement. There was scarcely time to react to the pain or the shock before she felt hot breath on the side of her neck. The breath smelled of liquor, but the orders it barked sounded completely sober.

"**Stay down! Don't move!**"

As horrified as she was, Dana's blood ran hot again when she realized it was Kole. While others sought to ensure their own safety, he had thrown caution to the wind and ran to protect her. He shielded her with his massive body. Because of him, Dana didn't utter one scream, or even a gasp. Tears filled her eyes as she gritted her teeth. She tried to reach up and hold him, so Kole wouldn't rise to his feet and endanger himself further.

But as her fractured consciousness quickly mended itself, she realized that whatever had happened was done, and neither she nor Kole was the target. Beyond the chaos of the partygoers, she heard tires peeling as the shooter made his escape. She heard voices – angry, distressed voices – demanding someone open one of the gates. She heard soulful wails from women.

"*Oh my God! Noooo! Lord, please, noooo!*"

"*He's hit! Yo, he's hit!*"

"*Get up, dog!*"

"*Who the fuck was it?!*"

"*Yo, he's hit! My nigga bleeding!*"

"*They shot that girl!*"

"*Get up, dog!*"

"*What the fuck, cuz?! Who the fuck was it?!*"

"*Somebody open this goddamn gate!*"

"*Moooon! Nooooo! Moooon!*"

At that moment, Kole rose to his feet. Dana looked up at him with tears in her eyes. He stared down at her quizzically. He looked around slowly, more dumbfounded than shocked. He looked down at Dana again and took a deep breath before stiffly walking away from her. She rolled to her side and watched him. Tears flowed down her cheeks when Kole took off, sprinting now. And then he turned a corner and was out of sight.

CHAPTER 9

BY THE TIME Dana made it to the gate that separated the backyard from the front, the ghastly deed was completed. Murder and mayhem had been achieved, while an old Isley Brothers song played unimpeded from a stereo in the backyard.

If I go ooooon my way without you
Whooooaa... Where would I go?

Dana saw blood splattered on Moon's extensive driveway, blood on some of the cars that had come to celebrate an adolescent's accomplishments. People were screaming, women mostly, but not exclusively.

Angry men ordered guests to "*Move yo damn car!*" while other angry men hopped in vehicles that were not blocked and pursued the shooter.

Between the legs of distraught partygoers rushing to and fro, Dana saw three bodies on the pavement. The first was a man in his mid-twenties. He looked to be deceased, though the four people attending to him swore he was still alive. The second was a young girl, possibly a former classmate of the graduate. She wore a tight, short skirt, which had ridden all the way up to her panties. Dana was provided a glimpse of her wound before a crowd of men closed in on her. She'd been shot in the thigh. Tears skated from her bloodshot eyes.

The girl repeatedly screamed, "*I'm dying! They killed me!*" but Dana didn't believe that was the case.

While it appeared a bullet had severed a major artery, at least one of the men kneeling beside her knew the basics of first aid. He implored her to, "*Calm down. Shut the fuck up!*" as he yanked his belt from his waistline. He looped it around the injured girl's leg, higher than her bullet wound, and cinched it so tightly Dana couldn't help but wince.

The third victim was obviously the intended target. The man of the house had taken three shots to the torso. All of his wounds were leaking blood profusely. His wife was on her knees beside him, screaming bloody murder. She wore her husband's blood on her hands and on her dress. Kole sat flat on his ass, cradling his best friend's upper body in his lap. Around them, stunned and powerless men from The Organization paced and cursed and knelt to render aid and then stood again when they saw there was no use. Moon's eyes were open and transfixed on the other side.

In the midst of the chaos, sat Kole, stoically; as if everything around him was on fast-forward, while he was on pause. He held his friend, staring straight ahead but watching nothing. People were yelling at him, some pleading. Dana couldn't tell if he heard them. She couldn't tell if he was in shock or if he was quietly contemplating his friend's death and the impact it would have on the community.

Dana had never seen him like that. Tears streamed down her cheeks. She tried to approach him, but like everyone else, there seemed to be an invisible wall separating Kole, Carla and Moon from the rest of the guests. Dana's legs went numb, and she dropped to her knees ten feet away. The pungent smell of gun smoke filled her nostrils.

Kole looked up at her. The couple locked eyes, and Dana saw misery and tears in his. Beyond that, she saw hell. She saw fire and destruction, the likes of which Overbrook Meadows had never known.

As he watched her, Kole reached absently and wiped the tears from his eyes. When he lowered his hand, Dana saw that he had smeared his friend's blood across his face. Her body shuddered when she realized it looked like war paint.

Atlantis
Is back to you
I'll aaaalllllways
Come back to you

PART TWO
FLATLINE

CHAPTER 10

THE WAITING ROOM in Jackson Memorial's ER was not large enough for the number of people who showed up after the shooting. Most of the men were from The Organization. Wearing masks of anguish, denial and devastation, they occupied nearly every chair, bench and walkway. They gathered outside and smoked and swore vengeance. They bombarded the clerk at the information desk, demanding an update on Moon and the other two victims.

The overwhelmed hospital staff called security, who in turned called the Overbrook Meadows police for backup. But even with ten uniformed men on the scene, Moon's men were not deterred. One officer asked them to disperse and was met with stiff resistance.

"Why we gotta go? You ain't told nobody else they have to leave!"

"We got a right to be here!" another chipped in. "Y'all got our people back there. We need to know what the hell's going on!"

"The doctors are doing their best to help everyone," the policeman assured them. "But you people out here–"

"*You people*? The hell you mean?"

"Racist-ass cracker!" a brooding demon named Lawrence exclaimed.

Another officer stepped forward and stood shoulder to shoulder with the first. "This has nothing to do with race! This is about you creating a scene – all of you! You're in here pacing, yelling, cursing. Do you see any of the other visitors acting like that?"

The few visitors there who were not associated with Moon's shooting lowered their gaze, rather than take credit for their good behavior.

"Man, this some bullshit!" another thug commented. "Y'all want me to leave, you gon' have to arrest me! Take my black ass to jail!"

"Me too! Gone put the cuffs on me!"

"Gon' have to take all of us!"

The cop debated whether to reach for his radio or back down. He chose the latter. "You can stay if you want," he conceded. "But you're gonna have to give these people at the desk a break. We don't need you going up there asking for an update every five minutes. And all of you can't be walking around, blocking the entrances. Plus there's no smoking at this hospital. All of your friends outside have to take that across the street."

Dana watched the back-and-forth from a seat she was fortunate to snag when she and Kole first arrived. She expected more aggression from Moon's men, but a henchman she knew by the name of Byrd stepped forward.

"We'll follow your rules," he told the cop. "But it ain't no more chairs, so you can't blame us for walking around."

Flustered, the cop told him, "Just – just stay out of the doorways and away from the information desk. If you want an update, only *one of you* needs to go up there."

Byrd was a tall man with dark skin and short hair. The blood stains on his shirt and pants were mostly dry. He nodded and rejoined his group.

Dana couldn't get her grief under control as she sat anxiously, cradling her cellphone in her lap. She knew Moon personally, but it was Kole's anguish that cut the deepest. In the

almost two years she'd known him, she'd never seen him cry.
Given his harder-than-stone exterior, she didn't think that was an
emotion he was capable of. He didn't cry much at the scene of the
shooting or during the drive to the hospital, which made the few
tears he did shed much more distressing. The fact that she could
do absolutely nothing to alleviate his pain made Dana feel helpless
– just as helpless as she felt sitting in the waiting room, while
Kole, Carla and a few others were allowed in the exam rooms.

Watching the men from The Organization introduced a
sense of dread to Dana's grief. They were already talking about
retaliation, though, as far as she could tell, no one had the slightest
idea who might be responsible for the shooting. The thought of
Kole getting involved with whatever revenge plot they cooked up
chilled Dana to the core, but she knew it was inevitable.

Outside of Carla, no one in the hospital loved Moon more
than Kole did. Kole's love might even outshine Carla's, because
he'd known Moon much longer. The best friends had experienced
countless dark days together as they clawed their way out of the
trenches and handcrafted The Organization brick by brick.

Dana waited until she stopped crying before she called her
son. She wanted to step outside for the conversation, but she
knew her seat would be taken the moment she vacated it. There
were already half a dozen women standing in the waiting area.
None of the men were on their gentlemanly behavior that night.

Tariq didn't sound worried when he answered the phone,
so Dana knew he hadn't heard the news yet.

"Hello? Mama?"

"Yeah."

The miserable quality of her voice immediately put him on
edge.

"What's wrong? Where are you?"

"At the hospital," she revealed. "There was a shooting at
Moon's house."

"What? Who – are you okay?"

"Yeah. I'm fine. But some people got hurt. It's—" She sighed and couldn't stop her tears from falling again. Her voice quavered when she told him, "Moon – *he's dead*. I think he's dead. Some more people got shot."

Tariq had only met Moon once, but he knew what he meant to Kole. The boy was also familiar with The Organization.

"Is, is Kole alright?" he asked.

Dana shook her head and told him, "No. He – he's not doing well. He, he was right there when it happened. I've never seen him like this. Everybody, it's, it's crazy here. People are going crazy."

"What hospital you at?"

Dana could tell her son was up and on the move.

"Do you need me to come?" Tariq asked.

Even if it wasn't well past 1 am, Dana wouldn't dream of her only child being in the midst of the bloodlust that was fermenting in the waiting room.

"No," she told him. "I'm fine."

"When are you coming home?" The concern in his voice broke Dana's heart.

"I'm not sure. Probably not tonight. Kole – I need to be here for him."

"Do you, maybe you shouldn't be there, Mama. I don't want anything to happen to you."

His worry was palpable. Dana wished she could be there for him. But, even though she hated to accept it, Tariq was not a child anymore. She hoped he wouldn't think she was putting Kole ahead of him.

"I'm sorry, baby. I can't come home right now. I need to be here for Kole."

"But Mama, what if it's some people trying to hurt him? I don't want you to get hurt, just because you're with him."

Tariq was aware of most of the atrocious things Kole had done in the past as well as the bad deeds he'd accomplished since he and Dana started dating. Despite it all, he never suggested his mother steer clear of her ominous boyfriend. In fact, Tariq had always considered Kole's loving arms the safest place for his mother.

"Kole wasn't the target," Dana said, though she had no way of knowing if that was true. "He's hurting right now, and I can't leave him. I'm sorry. I'll be home as soon as I can."

Despite his misgivings, Tariq had no choice but to yield.

"Alright, Mama. Please let me know when you leave the hospital."

"I will, baby."

He sighed and said, "Tell Kole I'm sorry about his friend."

"Okay. I'll talk to you later."

CHAPTER
11

KOLE DIDN'T EMERGE from the ER until 3 am. None of the dozens of men from The Organization had left yet. A handful of them rushed to him, seeking favorable news and guidance. Dana rose to her feet as well, but she stood on the outskirts of the crowd, rather than fight for his attention.

The look in Kole's eyes was the most solemn she'd ever seen. His expression was deadpan. Dana thought he was still in shock. He didn't speak much, but judging by his demeanor and body language, she knew no miracle had transpired within the past few hours. Moon was gone. Dana had to wait until they were alone to get an update on the other two victims.

After speaking to the men, Kole scanned the crowd until he spotted his woman. The gaze he fixed upon her was chilling. The clothes he wore to the graduation party were dark, but she could make out the dried blood. Thankfully he'd washed his hands and cleaned the blood from his face since the last time she saw him.

He approached her slowly. When they were close enough to speak without raising his voice, he said, "You ready?"

Dana nodded. She stared into his eyes, hoping for a glimpse of his state of mind. But Kole's emotions were shuttered. He reached into his pocket and produced his car keys. He handed them to her, which was another move he'd never made. Kole once joked that he'd rather ride in the back of a police car than in the passenger seat with a woman at the wheel.

There were no jokes tonight.

Dana took the keys and followed him to the emergency room exit. She looked back before they stepped outside and saw all of the men from The Organization watching them. These men were as tough as they come, but that didn't stop tears from welling in their angry eyes.

Dana knew they were watching Kole. She felt the weight of the world settling on her man's shoulders. She didn't have to ask what they expected of him. The grim reality was a cross she too had to bear. Her stomach churned, and she nearly vomited as she turned and caught up with her boyfriend.

CHAPTER
12

CONVERSATION DURING THE ride home was almost nonexistent. Kole answered a few basic questions, but Dana could tell his mind was elsewhere, and he'd rather not speak at all.

He told her, "There was nothing they could do for Moon. He was dead at the scene. They tried CPR on the way to the hospital, but they pronounced him as soon as they got there."

"I'm sorry," Dana said. She kept her eyes on the road, because every time she looked over at him, Kole's blank stare frightened her. He looked like he might pull out a pistol and take his own life at any moment. *"I'm so sorry, Kole."*

Tears streamed from her eyes, but Kole's cheeks were dry. He didn't respond.

"How's Carla?" Dana breathed. She didn't realize how asinine her question was until he ignored it.

"The other people," she said, "are they okay? That girl...?"

Kole shook his head but said, "She gon' be alright. They got her to the hospital in time."

"What about your friend?" Dana dared to ask, "the other guy that got shot?"

Kole took a deep breath and blew it slowly from his nostrils. Dana didn't think he'd answer, but he finally told her,

"Got shot in the back. He alive, but they say he got hit in the spine." He sneered.

Dana chanced a glance in his direction and wished she hadn't. Kole's eyebrows were bunched together. She hadn't seen that look in his eyes since he choked a rival gang member to death with his bare hands. Dana was fortunate to be there to save that man's life, but she doubted if *anyone* could buffer Kole's vengeance once he found out who shot up Moon's party – and why.

"He might not make it to the morning," Kole continued. "He on a breathing machine. Ain't looking good. If he do make it, he ain't gon' walk no more."

Dana's heart squeezed like a vice. She felt he'd ignore her next question, but if it was possible to know who she should pray for, she had to ask.

"What's his name?"

Kole surprised her by replying right away. "Jimmy. Jimmy Jackson. We call him Slim Jim."

Dana sucked in a shuddering breath and nodded. "What are you gonna do?"

She wasn't surprised when Kole shut down again. He didn't say another word for the rest of the drive home.

CHAPTER 13

KOLE WOULD NOT take a seat when they arrived at his place.

He stormed down the hallways, his fists balled, his features set in an expression Dana could describe as nothing less than *murderous*. She didn't attempt to follow him. She went to the master bedroom, knowing his warpath had to end there at some point. He was filthy and needed a change of clothes. He was exhausted and needed to sleep.

But for the next hour, his pacing did not pass her doorway. Dana sat on the edge of the bed in complete silence. When she could no longer hear his footsteps or his deranged muttering, she left the room; her stomach a huge jumble of nerves. She found Kole in the den, breathing roughly, tears spilling from his eyes. The sight of his distress put her in the same condition. She cautiously approached and knelt before him. But he stood abruptly and stepped past her, nearly knocking her over in the process.

"*Kole!*" Dana cried after him.

He did not respond.

Dana stared at his hulkish back and shoulder muscles until he rounded the corner and was out of sight.

CHAPTER 14

SHE HAD RETURNED to the bedroom when she heard his voice. She didn't realize she'd cried herself to sleep, but Kole's alarm clock revealed it was 7 am, three hours later than the last time she checked. Forcing her weary, puffy eyes open was not a simple task. She slipped from the bed and followed her man's voice to the front room. When she was close, she hesitated in the hallway and listened to him speak.

"Them motherfuckers *got* to know something." Kole's voice grumbled like a werewolf. "You been over there?" he asked. "Maybe showing up in person will jog their memory. Him too. All them niggas! I ain't leaving no stone uncovered. I don't give a damn if they run to *Vietnam*. I'ma be right there waiting on they ass!"

Dana's heart rattled in her throat as she stepped into the room. Laying eyes on Kole kicked her apprehension up another notch. It didn't appear he had slept at all. He had dark bags under his eyes. His hair was unkempt. His lips were dry, his teeth bared. Even worse were his bloodshot eyes and the caked blood on his clothes and sneakers.

Dana knew, without any doubt, that Kole would make good on his promise to pop up out of a rice paddy, if Moon's killers fled to Vietnam. She couldn't shake the thought that he'd be consumed by his own destructive fires this time. Maybe everyone around him would burn.

He looked up at her and snarled. Dana didn't want to believe she was the target of his annoyance, but all of their interactions in the past six hours said otherwise.

"I'm on my way," he said into the phone and ended the call.

He rose to his feet and walked past Dana, as if she wasn't standing there. For the first time ever, she found the scent that wafted from him unpleasant. It was a soft, coppery odor mixed with his musk and anxiety. She stepped on pins and needles as she followed him to the bedroom.

Kole finally shed his bloody clothing but headed for the closet, rather than the bathroom. He emerged a minute later with fresh jeans and a new tee shirt. Dana had never known him to be indifferent about his hygiene. Her eyes were filled with concern as she took a seat on the corner of the bed. Kole sat on an ottoman and bent to tie his sneakers.

"Kole, please talk to me," she said.

He looked up at her briefly before returning his attention to his shoelaces. When he was done, he returned to the closet and reappeared a second later with his gun and holster. He positioned the holster on the small of his back and concealed his weapon there.

Dana thought he'd leave without saying two words to the woman he loved, but Kole did have something to say.

Before he left the room, he looked her in the eyes and said, "I think you should go home."

He turned and marched down the hallway. A few moments later, Dana heard him exit the house through the kitchen. She followed him to the garage but not in time to see him back out. The garage door slowly made its descent as she stood in the doorway.

She closed the kitchen door. As she returned to the front room, she took slow, deep breaths to avoid hyperventilating. So distracted by Kole's appearance, she didn't notice the big-screen television was on. She saw that he'd been watching the news. She was not surprised by the top story of the day. As upset as she already was, Dana had room for more disgust when she saw Overbrook Meadows' new police commissioner on the screen.

An ardent Trump supporter, Joseph "Mad Dog" Humphries likened himself to Sheriff Joe Arpaio of Arizona. Not many liberals were happy about him bringing his "hard-nosed brand of justice" to Overbrook Meadows, but politically, the city tended to lean towards conservatives, and Humphries handily defeated his opponent.

Dana took a seat on the sofa and rubbed a tense spot on her temple as she listened to the new commissioner offer his take on last night's tragedy:

"We have to take our city back!" Mad Dog declared. "These *street gangs*," he spat, with clear contempt, "they've been terrorizing the good people of Overbrook Meadows for too long! It's gotten to the point where joggers don't feel safe. Our elderly citizens are afraid to step out the door to check their mailbox. We've all seen them; rolling down the street, blasting that offensive music, standing on the street corners with their pants down and their underwear showing.

"Last night, a sweet, innocent young lady wanted to celebrate her high school graduation. Her family threw her a big party. But even *that's* not a safe event anymore. Three people were shot; one killed. One may never walk again. And for what? Bragging rights? Just so some..." He had to catch himself to stop from cursing on the local news. "Just so some *hoodlum* can say he's bad; he's a tough guy now?

"Well, I'll tell you what, if you're so tough, why don't you do us a favor and come down to the station and turn yourself in?! 'Cause that's where you're gonna end up – either that or lawfully put down by one of my officers. Why don't you save us the trouble of shooting you, you coward, 'cause you damn sure ain't worth the bullets!"

Mad Dog took a moment to calm himself before saying, "I wanna tell the *good* people of this community not to fret. Dark times are upon us, but with God on our side, and the highly trained officers on our police force, the devil will not win! *You hoodlums and thugs will not win!*" The commissioner was so animated, a few drops of spittle flew from his mouth. His face was reddening by the second.

"To all the predators listening: Expect some changes out there," he said, pointing at the camera now. "Expect your comfy, little lifestyle to get a lot tougher in the days to come. All of you gun-toting losers who'd rather rob and kill instead of getting a job, *like a real man*, know this: Your days are numbered. Every move you make, we're gonna be right on your ass, until every last one of you is behind bars where you belong!"

Even the news anchor was momentarily at a loss for words when the interview ended, and the producer cut back to the studio.

"Well, um, you heard him," the reporter stated. "All of the thugs in Overbrook Meadows, you've been warned."

Dana turned off the television and sank rather than recline on the sofa. Never did she imagine the tough talk of an asshole cop would have her rooting for the bad guys. But her boyfriend was a bad guy, and he was out on those mean streets right now. Kole probably wasn't doing any of the dirt that would put him on the new commissioner's radar. But if he planned to avenge Moon, it wouldn't take long before Mad Dog sicced his deputies on him.

Dana's mind was so fried, she felt like she was going crazy. She wondered if it wouldn't be a good idea to take Kole's advice and simply leave – and never come back.

CHAPTER
15

For the one who was there
When it all began
For the laughs
And the tears
For the countless sins
Hell-bound and loving it
Never tried to pretend
We were saints and not goons
Good times came to an end
When they snuffed out your candle
Time ceased to exist
For you and for me
Man, I can't take this shit
Your memory will never fade
Legend status on a billion
Everybody tilt your bottle
Spill some liquor for a real one

KOLE WORE HIS sorrow like a heavy load as he made his way to The Moonlight on the south side of town. The early morning sun was bright and beautiful, but it couldn't overpower the darkness that engulfed him and paved the way on the gritty streets. He felt sick in every fiber of his being. His ailing heart sucked in fresh blood and turned it to poison. The infected blood fueled his desire for vengeance. He drove slowly, staring straight ahead, with little regard to anything going on in his peripheral. It was a wonder he didn't run over a pedestrian before he made it to Moon's club twenty minutes later.

The Moonlight was one of few bright spots on that side of town. The area was a cesspool of gang activity, drug trafficking and all the ills that came along with it. Moon's club catered to this crowd, but the nonviolent initiative he established when he purchased the building over a decade ago had never been challenged.

Moon maintained discipline at his nightspot with an overwhelming show of security on Friday and Saturday nights, but everyone knew it was his ties to The Organization that people truly feared. A fight at the club might warrant no more than a stern warning, but if someone was foolish enough to pull out a pistol, going to jail would be the safest place for them. They'd still have to make amends with Moon when they got out.

Kole had a set of keys that gained him entry into the club. Normally a bear-size brute named Hootie would've accosted him in the doorway, but Hootie was not there that day. With his employer murdered the night before, the security guard may not have known if he was still employed.

While he waited for his comrade, Kole strolled casually through the club. Last summer, a carload of thugs fire-bombed the place in retaliation to evil deeds performed by Kole and The Organization. True to his word, Moon repaired and renovated the property in less than three months. The Moonlight was now bigger and more beautiful, with nary a scent of gasoline or smoke. The dance floor was spacious and pristine. The bar was stocked with the latest and classic spirits. Staring at the liquor, Kole was tempted to take a seat and drink his sorrows away.

But there was much to do.

He returned to the main entrance when he heard the doors push open. He made it in time to see Byrd step into the foyer. A top lieutenant in The Organization, Byrd was Moon's righthand man and second in command. He and Moon didn't make as formidable a duo as Kole and Moon had, but he was a force to be reckoned with.

It didn't appear Byrd had gotten much sleep either, but he looked fresher than Kole. He stared at his former boss for a few seconds, taking in Kole's eyes and demeanor, before he reached and gripped his hand. The men came together for a bro-hug that lasted longer than usual. When they separated, Kole headed to the bar and planted himself on one of the stools. Byrd followed him and did the same.

"What's the word?" Kole asked, facing him

Byrd shook his head. He was a tall, dark man in his late twenties. Back when Kole was the leader of the group, he appreciated Byrd's bloodlust and his seemingly nonexistent conscious. He once kidnapped a woman who happened to be the baby-mama of one of their rivals. She was pregnant at the time. Byrd didn't hurt her too badly before their rival backed down from his aggressive behavior. But he certainly hurt her.

"Ain't no word," he told Kole with a sigh. "I been on the phone all night. Don't nobody know nothing."

Kole shook his head. He bared his teeth and replied, "That's bullshit. Don't nobody make a move like that without somebody knowing about it."

"You right," Byrd agreed. "But whoever knows about it ain't talking – not right now at least."

"What about you?" Kole asked him. "You been with my nigga damn near every day. You don't know about any beef Moon had?"

Byrd continued to shake his head. "Everything been straight, just the usual high-capping every now and then."

"The usual? Nah, man. Ain't nothing *usual* right now. I need to know everything. Who been bucking up lately?"

"One of our boys got into it with a couple of them MMG cats a few weeks ago," Byrd informed him. "But we handled it. Me and Moon rolled up on them personally, and they apologized."

Kole was surprised to hear that. The Organization had an unsavory history with MMG, also known as the *Murder Meadows Gang*. That was the crew responsible for setting Moon's club on fire last year. After Kole had a one-on-one fight with their leader and emerged victorious, both cliques agreed on a truce.

"What was it about?" Kole wanted to know.

"Turf," Byrd said. "Same as always. They tried to move in on some of our territory, and you know we wasn't having it. But like I said, me and Moon talked to 'em and got it squared away. Wasn't no hard feelings."

"Is Brass still the top dog over there?"

Byrd nodded. "Yeah. Him and Ice," he said, referring to Brass' younger brother.

"I think we need to pay them a visit," Kole commented.

Byrd nodded. "I don't think it's nothing there, but I guess it won't hurt."

"Who else?" Kole asked.

"Ain't been no beef," Byrd assured him. "If somebody had it out for Moon, you know I'd tell you. Don't matter how farfetched it was. I wanna know who did this just as bad as you. It don't make no damn sense. And the way they did it – came right to his house and got him in front of his family, his wife – that's some disrespectful shit. I swear before God I'ma wet everybody who had anything to do with it."

Kole didn't doubt his friend's resolve. "Have you talked to Carla?" he asked.

The question caused Byrd to lose nearly all of his bravado. He lowered his gaze and shook his head. "Naw. I was gonna call her this morning, but..." He trailed off, rather than explain why he didn't. He looked up and asked Kole, "What about you?"

"Not since we was in the hospital. I'll probably check up on her today. Kinda hard to look her in the eyes," he revealed. "Feel like she might blame me for what happened."

"You? Naw. Why would she blame you? You been out the game for a while. Whatever problems Moon had, you far removed from it."

"But me and Moon been friends since high school," Kole said. The full scope of what he'd lost hit him suddenly, like a bowling ball to the gut. Kole grimaced, but didn't break down again. "Maybe she feels like I could've said something to get him to retire when I did."

"She might think that," Byrd acknowledged. "But you and me know that ain't true. You talked to him about retiring plenty of times. He stayed in The Organization because he liked what he was doing. He loved it. If anything, Carla will blame *me* for what happened. I was supposed to be there for him. I'm the one that's always supposed to have his back."

Byrd couldn't stop from tearing up. Kole did not take his show of emotions as a sign of weakness.

"You wasn't working last night," he offered. "Nobody expected you to be on your guard at a party."

"But I'm *always* supposed to have his back," Byrd insisted. "I should've been right beside him. I didn't even see what kind of car they took off in. Nobody did."

"That just means we gotta work even harder to get to the bottom of this," Kole told him. "I'ma need you to keep your head straight. For all we know, they coming for *all of us*." He waited a few beats and asked, "You good?"

Byrd wiped his eyes and nodded. "Yeah, man. I'm good."

CHAPTER 16

MMG DIDN'T HAVE an official headquarters, but Kole knew the top leaders hung out at a hole-in-the-wall club on the south side, not far from The Moonlight. The last time Kole visited the locale, it was to save Dana and Tariq, after they were targeted for execution by the gang. The ordeal started over a misunderstanding and ended with Kole flatlining Brass with a rear-naked choke. If not for Dana's CPR skills and her determination that no one die that night, MMG and The Organization might still be at war. As it was, they ended their conflict and vowed to live in peace.

Despite the truce, Kole felt a sense of doom as he pulled into the parking lot. He looked over at Byrd and asked, "How you wanna play this?"

Not surprisingly, Byrd deferred the decision back to him. "It's whatever. Tell me what you want me to do."

Kole surveyed the building and noticed a couple of soldiers standing near the entrance. The men were already eyeing them warily.

"We can both go in," Kole offered. "But they'll have us closed off."

"And outnumbered," Byrd pointed out.

"We definitely outnumbered," Kole agreed. "But I don't think they'll do anything stupid in broad daylight. I'ma go talk to those dudes," he said, his eyes on the men who were watching them. "I'll see if I can get Brass to come out. If I go in, and I don't come out in five minutes, you take off and gather the troops. If I'm still not answering my phone by the time y'all get back, go ahead and light this place up."

"I think we need to gather the troops *first*," Byrd countered. "Why you wanna risk it?"

"'Cause I don't think they want that kind of drama," Kole guessed. "They know what's gon' happen if they kill me."

Byrd didn't look like he agreed with that assessment, but he didn't have anything better to offer, so he nodded.

"Move to the driver's side when I get out," Kole said as he opened his door. "I got a strap in the glove compartment. If any of them approach the car once I'm inside, that prolly mean they wanna take you out before you can call for help. So you might as well get to busting."

Byrd wasn't a coward, but it was clear he liked the plan even less now. Kole was liable to get them both killed. But he kept his mouth closed as Kole exited the vehicle. Byrd stepped out on his side and moved to the driver's seat. He popped the glove compartment open and confirmed there was a pistol inside. He removed it and placed it on his lap.

The men loitering in front of Brass' club were in their early thirties. Neither of them was a novice. After watching Kole exit the car and Byrd switch places with him, they expected trouble and were prepared for it. One reached into his pocket and kept his hand there. The other removed a firearm from his waistband and held it at his side. Kole appeared to be unarmed, but they couldn't say the same for Byrd. They knew Kole wouldn't have time to gun them both down, so they guessed he was a diversion.

Though he had stepped down from his leadership role in The Organization, Kole ran the group for twenty-five years, so he wasn't surprised to see recognition in the men's eyes. He took in their disposition, their weapons and their state of unease before coming to a stop fifteen feet away.

"I ain't armed," he lied.

"What the hell you want?" one of the men asked. He had big lips and big teeth.

Kole recognized him as one of the gang members who was at the club the night he and Brass had their big showdown. As he recalled, Gator Mouth had reached for a weapon, while soldiers from The Organization secured the scene. The move got him lumped up, with a gash under his afro. The afro had grown back into place, and Kole couldn't see the wound now.

"Wanna talk to Brass," Kole stated.

Gator Mouth looked from Kole to the car idling in the parking lot. Was this an assassination attempt? If so, Kole had to be a fool, if he thought Brass would thoughtlessly step into an ambush.

"Man, you better get the fuck outta here," the second man said. He had short hair and fair skin. Both of his arms were fully covered with MMG tats.

"I ain't leaving till I talk to him," Kole replied.

Despite having no visible weapon, his size and boldness was more formidable than both of Brass' guard dogs. Gator mouth stared him down for a few seconds before checking on Byrd again.

He said, "Tell that nigga to get out the car."

Kole shook his head. "That ain't happening. I know it's a bunch of y'all in this club. Why you scared of lil' old me?"

"Ain't nobody scared of you," Gator Mouth quipped. "You a fool for bringing yo ass around here. You know we ain't got no love for y'all."

"Why don't you go get Brass," Kole suggested, "before something stupid happens? Don't you think Brass wants to make this call?"

Gator Mouth looked to his tatted friend. "Man, let me go tell 'em what's up. You okay with watching him?"

The tatted man was the one with his weapon exposed. "If something pops off, I got this one. I don't know about the one in the car, though."

"This the one that's important," Gator Mouth told him. "If you feel like they trying to do something, make sure you kill this nigga." He nodded towards Kole.

Kole shrugged and kept his mouth closed.

Gator Mouth disappeared inside the club, while his friend tried his best not to look shook as he held Kole hostage. Thankfully the tense scene only lasted thirty seconds. The first goon reappeared with several people following behind. One of them was the notorious Ice.

The last time Kole saw this man was the same night he choked his brother to death. Ice had tried to intervene, and soldiers from The Organization delivered a swift beat-down. Undaunted, Ice had managed to crawl to Brass when Kole finally released him. Realizing he was dead, Ice's heart-wrenching screams haunted Kole to this day.

You got him! You won!
Why you didn't let him go?!
Why you didn't let him go?!

Ice only had one scar on his face that bore testament to the horrors of that night. The scar was above his right eye. Kole noticed it as Ice stepped forward, into the sunlight, but Gator Mouth reached and pulled him back.

"Watch out, he got a shooter in that car."

Ice checked where the man pointed and took a step back into the doorway. Byrd would have to move the car closer to get a shot at him from that position.

Ice returned his attention to Kole. A deep sneer marred his otherwise handsome face.

"You got some nerve, coming 'round here. The hell you want, Kole?"

"I don't want no trouble," Kole assured him. "Just wanna talk to Brass."

"Anything you got to say to my brother, you can say to me."

Kole shook his head. This back-and-forth was reminiscent of their last encounter. "You really wanna do this?" he asked.

Ice continued to sneer at him, as did his followers. "I know you ain't talking shit," he said. "You only got one dude over there. What's to stop us from splitting yo wig right now?"

Everyone in his crew was armed, most of them openly. Kole knew he didn't stand a chance, but he couldn't stop from pushing things to the limit. For Moon, he would go much further than that.

He took a step forward and said, "I'm standing right here."

Ice pushed past his crew and met him head on. But another figure appeared in the darkened doorway. This one was as big as a gorilla, with a thick neck and big, strong arms. He reached and grabbed his brother's shoulder, drawing him back into the foyer.

Brass stepped to Kole, and the two men stared at each other for what felt like an eternity. Kole hadn't seen him since their epic brawl. Although Kole got the best of him, Brass had put up a helluva fight and gained respect from The Organization. Kole didn't fault him for pulling a knife during their altercation. He hoped Brass didn't hold a grudge after having his air supply cut off for so long, his heart gave out.

Finally the MMG leader asked, "What you doing over here?" His voice was deep and gravelly. Compared to Ice, Brass was the ugly duckling in his family. But his street fame had propelled him to legendary status, where looks no longer mattered.

Before Kole could respond, Brass said, "I heard about what happened to Moon. You know we ain't have nothing to do with that."

Kole watched him carefully. "I don't know that unless I hear it from your mouth. I heard there was an issue with some of your boys a few weeks ago. Moon had to ride by and tell them to move around."

"That's old news," Brass countered. "If we had a problem with it, we would've done something way before now. But it wasn't no problem. My peeps told me what happened, and I got on them for being out of bounds. They didn't like the way Moon came at 'em, but they wasn't mad enough to do nothing stupid – not without telling me first."

"You sure about that?"

"Ay, you need to watch your mouth," Brass stated, his eyes narrowing. "I done already told you, you ain't running nothing. You got lucky the last time you came over here. Don't think I won't whoop yo ass right now, if you keep talking shit. You better stay in your lane..."

Kole almost took a swing at him. It pained him to let a man disrespect him openly, but he swallowed his pride and remained still, for Moon's sake.

"Now, as far as your question," Brass went on, "ain't nobody in my crew gon' take out an OG without telling me. Ain't no freelancing over here. Everything that happens goes through me."

Kole wasn't the best lie-detector, but he believed the man was telling the truth. If MMG was responsible for Moon's death, they could've admitted it at that moment and did the same to Kole. Byrd may have managed to escape, but with their leader and former leader murdered, The Organization's infrastructure would be severely damaged, possibly irreparably.

"I'ma get to the bottom of this," Kole said. "When I do, anybody who had anything to do with it – anybody who even *knew about it* before it went down – I'm going after them with everything I got."

"I know you ain't threatening us," Ice spat.

Both of the leaders ignored him.

"If I hear something, I'll let you know," Brass said. "Till then, you need to get from around here, Kole. Don't nobody over here fuck with you."

Kole took the OG's advice – not because he was concerned about his safety, but because he'd exhausted this lead.

When he got back in his car, Byrd asked him, "What they say?"

Kole told him, "They don't know nothing."

"You believe 'em?" Byrd asked as he got the car moving.

Kole nodded slowly.

"What's next?" Byrd asked.

"Bideker Street."

"You plan on chasing down every OG in the city?"

Kole nodded. "One of them bound to know something."

"What happens if we run into the one who did it?" Byrd wondered. "Don't you think they'll try to take you out?"

"If they do, you'll know who killed Moon. Gather the troops and let 'em have it."

If Byrd had reservations about Kole offering himself as the sacrificial lamb, he didn't mention it. He slowly rolled out of the parking lot and made a left, headed to Bideker Street.

CHAPTER 17

POPCORN, THE LEADER of the Bideker Boys, didn't know anything about Moon's murder. Kole also struck out with OG Kody from Polywood and OG Damon from Truman Street. It took the better part of the day to track down eight more gang leaders. They all had the same response: *We don't know nothing. If we hear anything, we'll let you know.*

Aside from that, Kole noticed an increased police presence on the streets that had everyone concerned.

OG Kush from Berry Hill told him, "These laws damn near got everything shut down. They rolling through like this 'cause of Moon?"

"That's what I hear," Kole told him.

"Shiiit, they'll prolly catch whoever done it before you get your hands on 'em," Kush predicted.

"Don't matter. I'll still get 'em," Kole said coldly. "No matter where they go."

The sun had set when Kole and Byrd headed back to The Moonlight. His phone sounded off in his pocket, and he saw it was Dana calling. He was surprised she hadn't tried to contact him sooner.

He answered, "What's up?"

"Just wondering where you were," she said, her tone guarded. "Is everything alright?"

"Yeah," Kole said with a sigh. "On my way to The Moonlight."

"Have – did you find out anything?" she wondered.

"Nope. Nobody knows anything. But the streets will start talking, sooner or later."

"Are you coming home?" she asked.

Kole wasn't surprised she was still there. She wouldn't abandon him in his time of need, just as he wouldn't abandon her.

"You didn't work today?"

"No, I'm off. I couldn't have worked, even if I wanted to – not after what happened last night. I went to check on Tariq. We had lunch. I took care of a few things at home and came back, waiting on you."

"Thanks for coming back. I wanna see you, but I don't know what time I'll be home."

"It's okay," she told him. "I'll be here. Please be careful."

Kole couldn't promise to do that, so he didn't bother lying. "I'll see you in a little bit."

CHAPTER 18

BACK AT MOON'S club, the sense of nostalgia was stronger than it had been earlier that day. Everything reminded Kole of his best friend. He expected Moon to walk up to him at any moment and say, "Man you should've been here last night! We had bitches lined up from wall to wall! Even the ugly niggas was winning!"

Instead, the darkness inside the nightclub resembled the bottom of a grave. Kole stepped behind the bar and grabbed a bottle of Crown Royal. He popped the top and took a swig straight from the bottle. He passed it to Byrd when he sat across from him. Byrd took a drink and passed it back to him. Kole barely grimaced as he turned it up again.

"You know you gotta step up," he said after his second drink. "It's time for you to run things now."

Byrd nodded slightly. He had ambitions to lead The Organization one day, but he never imagined the passing of the torch would come like this. He took another drink and sighed.

"What that mean?" Kole asked him, reaching for the bottle.

Byrd looked up at him. He was constantly taken aback by how menacing Kole appeared, even when he wasn't trying to. "I'm ready," he said.

Kole continued to stare at him with those piercing eyes. "You sure?"

Byrd nodded. "I'm sure. But do you think this is the best time? The guys, they're all out of sorts right now. They wanna find whoever did that to Moon, before anything else. They look up to you. I think you should take over for a while, until we get to the bottom of this. After that, I'll be ready to run things."

Kole's heart skipped a beat as he turned the bottle up again. He knew it would come to this, didn't he? The Organization was in his blood. He retired, but he couldn't completely sever his relationship with the group, not while his heart was beating. He had avoided rejoining their ranks for his peace of mind and lately because it was the right thing to do for Dana and Tariq. In any other circumstance, he would've offered to be an advisor at best. But for Moon, all options were on the table.

He nodded. "Alright. I'll take over, till we find the killer. But once that's taken care of, you gon' be on your own. That lifestyle, it ain't for me no more."

"I understand," Byrd said. "I don't wanna draw you back into it no more than you wanna be in it. But you know how to get to the bottom of things better than anybody else. You the best, when it comes to that."

Kole couldn't dispute that. And as the liquor coursed through his system, he decided he didn't want to dispute it. Byrd was an excellent enforcer, but he didn't have lava flowing through his veins like Kole did. He didn't have demons in his chest that were begging to be set free.

"We'll get 'em," Kole said and took another pull from the Crown.

"No doubt," Byrd agreed, rubbing his hands together. "Ay, pour some of that out for Moon."

That was a ritual Kole would've preferred to do outside (or not at all, considering someone had to die for the honor). But for his best friend, he could care less who'd have to clean up the spill.

BACKSLIDE 2

He tilted the bottle of Crown until the remaining contents spilled onto the floor. The liquor splashed on his shoes like blood.

He could barely hold it together when he said, "For Moon."

"For Moon," Byrd repeated. His eyes were wet as well.

CHAPTER 19

If I could have a moment of your time
To hold you close
Your chest to mine
Our heartbeats would intertwine
Your smile would captivate my mind
Your breath sends tingles down my spine
Your lips
Your tongue
Taste sweet like wine
I'd surely die if I could dine
On your love
And your words
And your touch
Sweet divine
Babe, I'm begging
For just a moment of your time

DANA MET KOLE in the kitchen when he staggered in at 10 pm. She didn't think he could look much worse than he did when he left this morning, but she could smell the alcohol on his person – not just his breath – and his inebriated, zombie-like movements made her heart shudder. He still wore the stench from the day before. The whites of his eyes were nearly all crimson. It was a wonder he had made it home safely. Dana wouldn't be surprised if she checked the garage and saw a fresh dent on his bumper or fender.

She pushed her grief and panic aside and hurried to support him. She took his keys from his hand and placed them on the counter. Kole watched her quizzically for a moment, as if wondering how she gained entrance to his home. And then he sighed and shuffled towards the living room. Dana stood before him, walking backwards, ready to catch him if he fell, though she'd probably be pinned beneath him till sunrise if that happened. It was unlikely she'd be able to free herself from his dead weight.

Kole lurched with both arms out, supporting himself on the hallway walls. He made it to the front room without tumbling. Dana hoped he was heading for the couch – a bed would've been even better – but he staggered to the bar instead. She was horrified to see him reach for a bottle of whiskey. The cap didn't give him as much trouble as she hoped it would. He twisted it off and turned the bottle up like it was water. Dana brought a hand to her face and covered her mouth, blocking a whimper from escaping her lips.

Since they'd been together, she'd never forced Kole to do anything, didn't think she could if she tried, but she couldn't stand idly by while he drank himself into a coma. She walked around the bar and took his hand. He was agreeable when she tried to lead him away, but he grunted his disapproval when she reached for the bottle in his other hand.

"Please, Kole. Leave it there," she implored him.

He frowned at her. Dana was undeterred. She reached again. He held his arm away from her, but his movements were sluggish. She easily stepped past him and snatched the bottle. She placed it on the bar and wrapped her arm around his waist, turning him away from it. Kole's nostrils flared as he sighed in defeat. Dana took him to the couch, and he plopped down heavily.

She knelt before him and undid the laces on his shoes. She noticed one of his sneakers was sticky with what she assumed was more alcohol. After removing his shoes and socks, she fought back tears as she rubbed his feet. Kole moaned his appreciation.

She asked him, "Do you want me to give you a massage?" and he nodded.

"Here," she said, rising to her feet. "Sit here."

She helped position him on the floor and sat on the sofa behind him, her legs straddling his torso. She pulled his tee-shirt up. He raised his arms to facilitate the removal. Kole's shoulder and back muscles were awe-inspiring. His dark skin was flawless. Dana kneaded his neck and trapezius muscles. Kole held his hands to his sides and casually rubbed her bare feet.

She asked him, "Did you find out anything?"

He shook his head. His voice wasn't as slurred as she thought it would be when he spoke. "Nobody knows nothing. But we'll find them."

"You think it was more than one person?"

"I know it wasn't somebody he invited to his house," Kole stated. "There wasn't a fight or argument or nothing. Somebody came there with the goal of taking him out. I don't think they could've accomplished that working alone. At the very least, there was a getaway driver."

"How do you plan on figuring it out?" Dana wondered. His muscles were taut beneath her fingers. "Baby, please relax," she told him.

"I don't know how I'll figure it out," Kole acknowledged. "But I will. Somebody will talk, sooner or later. I got a lot of people asking questions."

"People like who? The Organization?"

Kole didn't respond to that.

"Are you going back to them?" Dana pressed.

They didn't start out on the right foot, when it came to honesty. But as their relationship deepened, Kole found that keeping secrets from her always did more harm than good in the long run.

He said, "I have to, for now. They need me to get to the bottom of this. I don't know if the killers have some sort of agenda. Maybe they want to take them all out."

"But wouldn't that put you at risk, if you go back?"

"There's always risks," Kole stated. "Everybody takes risks. Even you; every time you get behind the wheel of a car."

"You know what I'm talking about."

"What am I supposed to do, roll over and take it?"

"There's a lot of people in The Organization. They can take care of this. They don't need you."

"I'm not gonna sit on my hands and do nothing."

Dana could hear the agitation in his voice and feel it in his muscles.

"Moon was my brother," he said. "If you don't do nothing when someone messes with your family, then you ain't nothing."

Dana knew Moon wasn't his real brother. But after all they'd been through, she understood why he'd refer to him as such.

"I ain't sitting this one out," Kole said. "If you got a problem with it..."

Dana's heart froze. She held her breath, but he never finished the sentence. She didn't know if she should feel relieved that he didn't say what was on his mind or anxious because of the ultimatum he almost gave her. She continued to massage him, and gradually the tension subsided.

"Do you plan on running The Organization, or just helping them?" she asked.

"I'll be in charge. But only until I find out what's going on," Kole assured her. "Then I'll back out again, and things will be like it was."

But you said we couldn't be together, if you were part of The Organization. You said your involvement could cause trouble for me and Tariq, and you never wanted to put us in harm's way.

Does this mean you're going to leave me again, like last time? Am I supposed to sit idly by, with our future up in the air, until you decide to leave the gang for good this time? Do you expect me to wait for you?

Are you worth it?

These questions went unasked and unanswered.

After a while, Dana noticed his head start to slump forward. She asked him, "Do you wanna go to bed?"

He nodded. He tried to make it to his feet but seemed unable to do so. Dana moved to help him. When she got him up, he draped an arm over her shoulders and leaned heavily onto her as they made their way down the hallway. Dana didn't have the strength to fully support him, but she did her best. Gradually they made it to the bedroom. Rather than fall onto the bed, Kole headed for the bathroom.

Dana stood watch over him, while he leaned over the toilet with one hand flat against the wall. He fumbled with his zipper with his other hand, so she unfastened it for him. She backed away while he relieved himself and then sprang into action when he turned towards the tub rather than the door.

"What are you doing?"

"Gotta take a shower," he muttered.

Dana was grateful he finally gave some thought to that, but, "Baby, I don't think you should right now. You're gonna fall and hurt yourself. Here, at least let me help you…"

He was already topless, and she had taken his shoes and socks off in the living room. That was half the battle. She pulled his pants and boxers down his legs and knelt to get them the rest of the way off. Kole held the shower curtain rod while he lifted his feet, one at a time. Dana prayed it would hold.

Before she rose to her feet, Kole took hold of his manhood and thumped the top of her head with it. Dana looked up at him frowning. He grinned. She shook her head, not sure what to make of that or the fact that his erection was growing steadily.

"You should get in the shower with me," Kole suggested, "in case I fall."

Dana's frown intensified. She wondered if he was as inebriated as he seemed. But seeing a smile on his face, even it if was a perverted one, was a better alternative to the mood he'd been in for the past 24 hours. She ignored his dick slap and reached past him to turn on the water. Kole stepped into the tub before she had time to check the temperature. She quickly stripped down to her birthday suit and joined him.

Kole didn't speak during their shower. With his back to her, he leaned forward, with his palm against the tiles. The warm water flowed over his head and down his body. Dana lathered up a bath sponge and scrubbed his back and armpits. She washed his neck, arms and knelt to clean his legs. She tried to maintain focus on the task at hand, but it was hard not to marvel at his nude physique. His back fanned out like a deck of cards. His waist was slim, his legs proportionately muscular. His ass was pleasingly round and tight.

Despite the mountain of delectable man flesh standing before her, intimacy was not on her mind. But when she reached around to wash his chest and stomach, Kole placed a hand over hers and guided it down further. Dana encountered his stiff piece, which had grown considerably since they got in the shower. She was glad he didn't turn to see her confused expression. Nothing she had ever read indicated sexual release was helpful with the grieving process. She assumed it was the alcohol driving his passion.

Whatever the case, Dana was a caregiver by profession and by nature. She cleaned him with the sponge and then dropped it and used the soap as a lubricant. She stroked him slowly. He responded with deep, guttural moans of pleasure. The muscles in his ass flexed as he pumped his hips, effectively fucking her hand.

When the remaining soap was rinsed away, the friction she provided became less desirable. Kole turned and looked her in the eyes. His presence in the shower was all encompassing. Dana's breath caught in her throat. Her clitoris swelled when he placed a hand on her shoulder and pushed down, guiding her to her knees.

This was *not* a day Dana wanted to get her hair wet.

This was not what Kole should want the day after holding his dead friend in his arms.

The conflicting emotions made her heart thunder. She felt guilty for the oasis rippling between her legs as she took him into her mouth. She felt self-conscious when she looked up and saw he was watching her with low, inebriated eyes. She didn't have to work her neck. Kole grabbed the back of her head and stroked her mouth, much like he had done to her hand. No one had adjusted the water, but it was much hotter now. The stream sprayed over his shoulders, down his swollen pecs and abs. It drizzled in her face, mingling with the saliva dripping from her mouth.

Despite the spontaneity and peculiar timing of the event, it was clear Kole cared for her and took her wellbeing into consideration. When he slammed in too hard, and she winced, his strokes became softer. When she pulled away from the death grip he had on her hair, he loosened his fingers. She felt his pre-cum building seconds before she tasted it. She closed her eyes, thinking he'd finish in her mouth, but he pulled out abruptly. She opened her eyes and saw him reaching for her hand.

He helped her to her feet, and together they stepped out of the tub. Dana didn't have time to turn the water off before he turned her towards the doorway. Her eyes were wide as she yielded to his directions. He guided her forward, until her thighs encountered the bed. He pushed her upper body flat against the mattress. He spread her legs and gazed at her wet center for a moment before stepping closer. He rubbed his pulsating head against her opening and then slammed in hard – all the way in on the first thrust.

Dana couldn't stop a surprised and pained yelp from escaping her. Subconsciously she tried to crawl away from him. Kole grabbed her hips and yanked her back. He accentuated the move with another hard thrust, making their skin clap like thunder. Dana's moans mingled with screams as he settled into a rhythm that was always hard, sometimes slow, but always *hard*. Her body eagerly responded to him; producing more lubrication. Her walls gripped him tightly. Her clitoris pulsated, loving the constant stimulation.

Kole's strong hands moved to her ass. He gripped her cheeks so hard she expected to find bruises in the morning. He still hadn't spoken. His moans of pleasure were more like growls. Dana felt a bolt of lightning streak down her spine when she came. She gripped the sheets and buried her face in the mattress, screaming as loudly as she wanted to.

Her sporadic convulsions pushed Kole to the limit seconds later. He grabbed her hips again and yanked her towards him with each of his final strokes. She thought she'd black out when he slammed in so hard and stayed in for so long, she could feel him in her chest.

Beyond the freight train sound of blood rushing past her ears, she thought she heard a wolf howl. Her legs trembled so badly, she didn't think she'd be able to make it to the bathroom to turn off the shower.

CHAPTER 20

"WE RAN UP in there ready to make an example out of her."

An hour after their lovemaking – or fucking, depending on your point of view – Dana lie on her side with Kole behind her spooning. He had an arm draped protectively over her. She loved the feel of their closeness. She loved that despite appearing completely drunk earlier that night, he was coherent now, and he wanted to talk. This was probably not the type of pillow talk a traditional couple would appreciate, but nothing had ever been normal with Kole.

The incident he was describing happened when he and Moon were twenty-four and twenty-five respectively. Dana wasn't sure why he chose this particular story to share with her, but she was attentive and intrigued. Any time Kole wanted to talk about his past, she was all ears.

"It wasn't what she stole from us," he went on, "it was the principle of the matter. See this chick – her name was Alisha – she'd been one of the best customers for that crew. She was a ho. She was a thief. A liar, a conniver. She would do whatever it took to get that rock. She wasn't bad looking, either. If she would've settled down a little bit and got with a good dude, someone who loved her, they could've turned her life around.

"But Alisha, she was what you'd call a *crack monster*. She would burn whatever bridge was in front of her for that dope. Steal from her mama, it didn't matter. The homies we had working that block had to skin her up a few times over debts she couldn't pay. But as soon as she got the money, she'd come right back. She was loyal. That's why it tripped us out so much, what she did..."

Dana didn't interject the obvious question, because Kole was a great storyteller, and he liked to go at his own pace. He checked on her attentiveness from time to time, because it was getting late, and she had her back to him.

"You woke?" he asked.

"Yes, baby. I'm listening."

"Oh, okay," he said. "So Alisha was having a real bad week when she decided to go stupid on us. I heard she was staying with one of her aunts, and she got kicked out. She had a boyfriend that was trying to help her get right. But he saw it wasn't no use, and he took off. Alisha had been borrowing from my crew again. She was expecting some kind of crazy-people check from the government, but that fell through.

"She went and donated plasma the day she burned us. They gave her thirty dollars. She went to my crew hoping they'd cut her a deal, but she already owed them fifty. They took what she had and threatened to kill her if she didn't come up with the other twenty.

"I don't know if you know anything about donating plasma," Kole said, "but that's a long, annoying experience. They put this needle in your arm; damn thing's as big as a golf tee. You gotta lay there with your arm out straight, pumping your fist. Sometimes you in there for two hours. After Alisha went through that and got her money took, she said, '*Fuck it*,' you know? She was gon' get high that day *some way, somehow*, come hell or high water.

"She had scored from my crew so much, she knew where they stashed their rocks. It was under a trash can, not far from

98

where they posted up. Alisha called 9-1-1 and said there was some gang members out there with guns. The laws showed up four cars deep. Some of my guys took off. Some just put they hands up and got arrested. When the smoke cleared, Alisha ran up and grabbed the sack out from under the trash. Her dumb-ass didn't even care that a bunch of people saw her do it. She wanted to get high so bad, common sense didn't matter."

Kole wasn't being very descriptive, but Dana could see the scene playing out in her head. When he didn't speak for a few seconds, she said, "I'm awake. Finish the story."

"Just checking," Kole said and stroked her arm. "The boys wanted to handle it," he went on. "But this was a big deal, so me and Moon decided to take care of it personally. Letting it slide was not an option. We caught up with Alisha that same night; found her in a motel about five miles from where she stole the dope. We ran up in there, pistol gripping, ready to beat her ass or maybe worse. But what we saw shook me to the core, Moon too. If I live a hundred years, I'll never forget it."

"What'd you see?" Dana asked, going against her own rule to be patient.

"She had two kids in there," Kole said, "couldn't have been no more than two or three. They was old enough to know they Mama wasn't doing right. They was twins, still in dirty-ass diapers. Alisha was in there smoking up a storm, right in front of them. Whole room smelled like crack. Had them babies crawling on that dirty motel floor, crying, begging they mama to feed them. She had enough crack to trade for a thousand dollars' worth of groceries, but she didn't have one slice of bread in there."

Dana's eyes filled with tears. She didn't say anything, out of fear that he wouldn't finish the story if he knew how it affected her. Her vivid imagination was a curse now. Kole didn't say if the babies were boys or girls, but she could see both of their ashen faces in her mind's eye. She took a deep breath and let it out slowly, hoping he wouldn't notice her body shudder.

"Shit made me so mad, I wanted to break her neck," Kole said. "But Moon stopped me. He said them kids done seen enough, and we wasn't finna add to they misery. I remember he said it just like that. They didn't need no more *misery* in they life. Moon could've been a philosopher, if he was born in a different time. He knew how to use words and really *think*, on another level."

"So, what happened?" Dana wondered.

"Moon surprised the hell out of me," Kole said. "He took the kids outta there and got 'em settled in the car. Then he went back and got what was left of our dope from Alisha. He told her she had till tomorrow morning to do the last of her smoking and hoeing, and he was gonna come pick her up and take her to rehab. He said she wasn't getting her kids back from him till she completed a program.

"When we got back in the car, I told him he was a fool. Ain't no way in hell Alisha was gon' get herself together overnight. And what the hell did he plan to do with them kids till then? Moon said, 'Don't worry about all that. Let's just get 'em cleaned up and fed, and we'll deal with the rest later.' I told him *he* could deal with it later, but he needed to drop my black ass off *first*. I didn't want nothing to do with them snot-nosed bastards."

Dana frowned at his callousness.

Kole chuckled. "I was an asshole back then," he said. "I can admit it. Anyway, just like I predicted, Alisha was gone by morning. Nobody knew where she was. In the meantime, Moon had taken them twins home and got his girlfriend to help look after 'em. He went looking for Alisha every day, for a good month. I went by his place one day, and this nigga was chilling in the living room with them twins and his girlfriend. They was watching kid movies, eating popcorn and shit. I pulled him outside and asked, 'What the hell is going on? Why you still got them goddamn babies?' You know what Moon told me?"

Dana had no idea.

"He said after he got 'em cleaned up that first night and gave 'em something to eat, they went right to sleep, and he had never seen anything so beautiful. If it was anybody but Moon, I woulda slapped the shit out of him. He said he got attached to 'em, and he couldn't turn 'em over to the police. He held out hope that he could help Alisha get herself together, and she'd raise 'em right.

"It took another month for us to finally track her down. And as you prolly guessed, she said she wasn't going to no damn rehab. Moon got so mad, he lumped her up pretty good. He told her he'd been taking care of the twins for two months, and they was good kids. They didn't deserve to be raised by no damn crackhead, and she didn't deserve to have them.

"The next day he made the decision I told him to make on day one. He called CPS and said he had two kids that had been abandoned by their mother. I wasn't there when they came and got 'em, but his girlfriend told me Moon got real emotional. He hugged them babies like they was his, and then he took off by himself when his girlfriend asked if he wanted to talk about it."

Dana had tears in her eyes as she listened to the story. It was hard to imagine the Moon she knew doing any of that, especially at such a young age.

"That's a side of Moon people didn't know about," Kole said, as if reading her mind. "Yeah, he did his dirt, me and him, but my nigga had a heart of gold. He didn't deserve to go out like that, at his own home, in front of his family. I'ma..."

He sighed. Dana heard his throat contract as he swallowed down his grief. She sensed he was crying but did not roll over to look into his eyes. She knew he wasn't comfortable with these emotions and didn't want to disrespect him.

"I'ma *destroy* everybody who had anything to do with it," he stated. "I'm sorry if – I don't know what that means for us."

Dana didn't either. She loved this man with all her heart, but Kole had his mind set on committing murder in the first degree. Possibly multiple murders. She understood why he felt the need to avenge his brother. But in doing so, he'd put their relationship in jeopardy. He could get sent to prison or murdered himself. Did he not care enough about her to take a different course of action? He wasn't blind with rage at the moment. The decisions he was making were bold and calculated.

Kole stopped speaking, and after a while she heard him snoring lightly. Dana closed her eyes but once again found sleep elusive.

PART THREE
HITTERS

CHAPTER 21

Shall insults flow forth wild and free?
And then we'll fight, or should I squeeze
Off six quick shots. Frankly I need
Your blood, woman. I want you to bleed!
Please tell me, did he meet your needs?
His manhood, did it make you cream?
His soft lips, did they speak of me
Or kiss your private places? Dream
Of darkness, deadly shadows. Dream
Of fury, keen and focused. Streams
Of terror that bombard your dreams

THE NEXT MORNING, Kole got a call at 7:30 am. He rolled out of bed nude and tracked his ringtone to the bathroom, where he'd left his pants last night. He didn't make it before his phone stopped ringing. He removed his cell from the pocket, but no one answered when he returned the call. It wasn't a number he recognized.

Back in the bedroom, Dana lifted her head from her pillow and watched as he approached the bed. She'd seen him naked plenty of times, but *damn*. Morning wood had him looking delectable. Her nipples hardened at the sight of his semi-erect piece. She started to say something, but Kole's phone rang again. This time he answered right away.

"Who's this?"

"Kole?" The caller was male. His voice was scratchy, without much bass.

Kole frowned and asked again, "Who's this?"

"Lewis," the caller said.

That narrowed it down to three people Kole knew. Based on the scratchy voice, he felt comfortable guessing, "The crackhead?"

"Yeah," Lewis confirmed, taking no offense to the title. "I got some news for you; about Moon."

Kole's eyes widened. From across the room, Dana felt his heartrate increase.

"What you got?" he asked. His frown was gone now, his eyes dark and serious.

"Some hitters moved into a motel over here the day before yesterday," Lewis informed him. "They took off the night Moon got shot. Ain't seen 'em since."

The statements didn't provide a lot of information, but the tip was huge. *Hitters* was another term for *hitmen*. While it was possible their arrival and departure had nothing to do with Moon, Kole found the timing suspicious – if the snitch's information was credible.

"How you know they was hitters?" he asked him.

"'Cause I know one of those dudes," Lewis said. "I know how he get down."

"What's his name?" Kole asked.

"It's, um... Wait, hold up. Maino said y'all was offering some kind of reward for whoever could point you to them niggas."

Maino was a member of The Organization. Kole was glad his soldiers had put the word out, but he was frustrated with Lewis' stalling tactic. The possibility of being so close to the name of one of Moon's shooters made the hairs stand on every inch of his body.

"Yeah, I got you," Kole assured him. "What's the name?"

"Man, I ain't saying you ain't gon' pay me," Lewis countered. "I'm just saying, I'd feel a lot better about giving them dudes up if I had the money *first*. I gotta make some moves; get from around here after I give you this info. I don't want them niggas coming for me next."

Kole sneered. Dana sat up, her heart squeezing uncomfortably.

"Where you at?" Kole growled into the phone.

"The Sunset," Lewis said, referring to one of the more seedy motels on the south side. "Room 14."

"Listen," Kole said, "if I come all the way over there, and you ain't got nothing for me, you know I'ma stomp the dog shit out of you, don't you?"

Dana's eyes bulged. She was aware of Kole's violent tendencies, but it had been a while since she'd seen it firsthand. The fact that he was staring right at her made the threat even more disconcerting.

"I got something for you," the dopefiend insisted. "I wouldn't have called you if I didn't. I wouldn't mess around like that."

"Alright," Kole said. He turned away from the bed and pulled one of his dresser drawers open. "I'll be there in fifteen minutes."

He snatched a pair of boxers from the drawer and quickly put them on.

Dana had a good idea what was going on, but she asked him, "What's happening?

Kole didn't respond. He was on his phone again. He stepped into the closet as he dialed a number. Byrd sounded like he didn't get much sleep.

"What's up?"

"I need you to meet me at the Sunset," Kole told him. "Crackhead Lewis say he got some info for us; say a couple of hitters moved in there the day before Moon got shot. They bounced right after."

"Word?" Byrd didn't sound drowsy at all now.

"How long it'll take you to get there?"

"Shit, ten minutes."

"I'll be right behind you."

Kole disconnected and dressed in black Dickies with a black tee. He stuffed a snub-nose revolver in his hidden holster. Back in the bedroom, he sat on an ottoman and put his socks and shoes on.

"Kole, are you gonna talk to me?" Dana sat on the side of the bed now. She didn't pull the sheet up to conceal her nudity.

He looked over at her, marveling at how beautiful she was. How innocent. He finished lacing his sneakers and looked her in the eyes. He asked her, "Would you ever testify against me?"

Dana's eyes widened. Her heart kicked even harder. She shook her head. "No, Kole. You know I wouldn't."

He asked her, "Do you know what plausible deniability is?"

Dana did, and she was surprised he asked her that. He never had a problem talking about his evil deeds before.

"Kole, you can tell me," she assured him. "I would never tell the police anything about you."

He nodded. "I'm gonna talk to a guy who might know something," he said, rising to his feet.

"And, and then what?"

"If it pans out, I'll deal with it."

Kole headed for the doorway. He looked back and watched her for a second. Dana thought he had more to say. Whatever it was, he thought better of it and left the house without another word.

CHAPTER
22

HE EXITED THE freeway on Berry. He didn't make it ten blocks into the south side before a black and white swooped in behind him and hit the lights. Kole grimaced as he pulled over. Everything on his person and vehicle was legit, but a black man could never be *too legit* in the eyes of the law.

Two officers exited the cruiser and approached his car on either side. Kole rolled down both windows before they had to request it.

"Where you headed?" the cop on the driver's side asked. He leaned down and peered into the car, standing a safe five feet away.

The policeman on the right violated Kole's privacy just as thoroughly. Both men had their hand on the butt of their service weapon.

"What crime did I commit?" Kole asked the one who had spoken to him. He kept both hands on the steering wheel. Other than his head, his body was completely stiff.

"I asked where you was headed?" the policeman replied.

"I'm minding my business," Kole stated, not wanting to antagonize him, but he was also unwilling to accept this type of harassment. "What'd you stop me for? What crime did I commit?"

The policeman ignored him. "You got any drugs or weapons on you?"

Kole looked at the second cop. Both men were white. He didn't want to assume this stop had anything to do with racism, but there was no denying some white men relished the authority a gun and badge gave them over minorities.

"Yeah, I got a pistol," Kole revealed, because he was legally required to do so.

His comment didn't cause the stop to go from zero to 100, but it certainly intensified things.

"Keep your hands on the wheel," the first cop said. "Don't move."

"*Don't move a muscle*," his partner reiterated.

They ordered him out of the car, gave him a thorough pat-down and momentarily confiscated his weapon.

One of them asked, "What you need a holster like this for?"

Kole replied with the same question he'd been asking for the past few minutes, "What'd you pull me over for?"

After running his license and determining Kole had no warrants, his vehicle registration was up-to-date, and he was not a felon in possession of a firearm, they returned everything and allowed him to continue on his way.

"What'd you pull me over for?" Kole asked angrily before getting back inside his car.

"You're in a high-crime area," the cop informed him. "Just a routine stop."

"You just gon' violate my rights, 'cause I'm in a bad neighborhood?"

"You got a problem with it, take it up with the commish."

Kole wanted to press the issue, but he knew it wouldn't get him anywhere, and he had business to attend to.

He spotted Byrd's car in the parking lot when he got to the Sunset Motel. Kole hadn't been there in a while. The place was as rundown as he remembered it. The risk of rape, robbery and assault was ever-present there, especially after nightfall. The only clientele who found those risks acceptable were dealers, hookers, johns and fiends who couldn't afford a better place to engage in their illegalities. Byrd exited his vehicle and met up with Kole as he stepped out of his car.

"What took you so long?" Byrd wanted to know.

"Damn laws hemmed me up," Kole told him.

"For what? You straight?"

"Yeah, I'm good. They didn't have no reason to stop me," Kole told him. "Guess it got something to do with that crackdown they doing."

Byrd nodded. "Yeah, they serious about that. Homies having a hard time doing anything. I told everybody to lay low for the rest of the week."

"Good idea."

"But how's that gon' affect us finding Moon's killers?"

"It ain't," Kole stated. "We can shut everything down *except* that."

In Room 14, Kole was grateful to find Lewis sober. The dopefiend was fair-skinned and handsome, despite his rough lifestyle and the havoc crack was wreaking on him internally. Kole closed the door once he and Byrd were inside. He sneered at Lewis' deplorable living conditions. The room was a replica of the motel Moon had saved Alisha's twins from.

"What you got for me?" Kole asked, his arms folded over his torso.

"One of them named Nero," Lewis said. With his next fix so close he could taste it, the information flowed like water. "They from Dallas. They had a room two doors down, was in a gray Sonata. It wasn't a rental, but I think it had some dummy plates. The dude that was with him, I don't know his name. They checked-in Friday afternoon and was gone most of the day. They came back Friday night, and then one of them took off again. I don't know where he spent the night.

"On Saturday, they was going in and out all day. They came back late that night, got whatever they had in the room and took off. They was gone for good that time. Wasn't but a couple hours later I heard Moon got killed. I can't prove them niggas had something to do with it, but I'm pretty sure they did."

Kole looked Byrd's way. They both found the information valuable.

"You said you know for sure they hitters..." Kole said to Lewis.

"I don't know nothing about the second one, but I know Nero," Lewis replied. "He came down and killed Rodney Shaw a couple years ago. People say Rodney was finna snitch on somebody. Nero got some more bodies under his belt in Dallas. He prolly killed more people here. He a hitter. I'm positive."

Kole asked Byrd, "You know 'em?"

Byrd shook his head.

"You say they from Dallas?" Kole asked Lewis.

The crackhead nodded. "Nero is. Like I say, I don't know the dude he had with him, but I know he ain't from around here."

"How I find Nero?" Kole wanted to know.

The snitch shook his head, hoping this wouldn't detract from his payment. "I don't know. I ain't been to Dallas in a hot minute."

"Tell me what they look like," Kole said. "Tell me everything you remember about them; they car, what time they left. Everything."

Lewis didn't have much more information than he'd already provided, but he talked for another five minutes. Before they left, Kole instructed Byrd to give him a few hundred dollars.

On the way back to their cars, Kole told Byrd, "Ride with me." Once they were inside his vehicle, he asked him, "What you think?"

"Sounds promising," Byrd said, scratching his chin. "We know it was a hit, and it wasn't nobody who got invited to the party. Some out-of-towners are probably the only ones dumb enough to take Moon out. If some hitters showed up like that and split right after, I'm pretty sure they was here for Moon. I ain't heard of nobody else getting killed in the past two days."

Kole nodded, staring straight ahead.

"The question is why," Byrd stated. "Who ordered the hit and *why*?"

"Once we find Nero, he might not be able to tell us why," Kole deduced. "But he can tell us who paid him."

"You think he'll roll that easy?"

"I didn't say nothing about easy. Hell, I hope it *ain't* easy."

Byrd grinned. "Okay. How we gon' find Nero?"

"I know some cats in Dallas who might know him," Kole said. "They pretty deep; into a lot of stuff. They helped us out last year when we was looking for Brass. You remember the ones who followed him from the funeral, kept eyes on him until he went to his club?"

"You talking about Legend and Timber?"

"Yeah, that's them. The only problem is I don't know how to get in touch with them. They were Moon's connects."

Byrd thought for a moment. "Moon got a lot of connects, and they all in his phone. I think he got they names coded."

Kole agreed that was the best place to start the search. "You don't have his phone, do you?"

Byrd shook his head. "I'm pretty sure Carla got it."

Kole sighed inwardly. He loved Carla to death, but meeting with the grieving widow was not something he looked forward to. He hadn't spoken to her since the shooting.

"*Damn*," he grumbled. "You coming with me. I don't think I can deal with her by myself."

Byrd nodded. "For sure. Let go."

CHAPTER 23

MOON'S HOME LOOKED a lot different in the morning sun. But Kole didn't think he'd ever stop seeing his best friend's blood splattered on the driveway. He couldn't bring himself to drive or park over the spot where he cradled Moon in his arms as he took his last breath. Kole could tell Byrd felt the same way. Neither of them spoke as he pulled to a stop and they exited his Infinity.

Carla answered the door after a notably long wait. Kole was about to try the doorbell again when she pulled it open. She wore a nightgown and the look of a woman who had nothing left to live for. She hadn't put on makeup or touched her hair, probably since Moon died. Her nose was red from wiping and blowing it. The puffy bags under her eyes told a tale of woe that broke Kole's heart.

But upon seeing him, her expression changed. Kole wasn't surprised to see loathing in her watery eyes. She looked over at Byrd with the same resentment, and then focused her venom on the one she'd known the longest.

"What you want, Kole?"

Of course she blamed them for Moon's death. Her anger was misguided, but it wasn't uncommon in their line of work.

"I'm sorry for what happened," he told her. "You know I loved Moon like my flesh and blood. I'm just as hurt as you are."

"Oh really?" Carla snapped. "So you know what it feels like to find out your dead husband's been fucking some other bitch?"

Kole's eyes widened. "What?"

"Don't act like you don't know what I'm talking about! Don't tell me you didn't know about *Brenda*!"

Brenda was Moon's girlfriend of over five years. Kole often found it odd that his friend could maintain a side-chick for so long, while going home to his loving wife every night. But who was he to judge? What Moon chose to do in the privacy of his bedroom(s) was his business.

Carla took his lack of response as an admission. "*You knew*!" she shrieked. "You let him play me for a fool, all these years! *You knew*!"

"Hey, calm down," Kole said, looking around at her neighbors' houses. She didn't live in the type of neighborhood that would tolerate this sort of rachetness.

"*Don't tell me to calm down*!"

"Look, let us come in at least," he said, stepping forward.

Carla didn't immediately move out of the way, but Kole's statement was not a request. He continued forward, until she had no choice but to back into the foyer.

"*Why, Kole*?" she bellowed, crying now. "*Why would you let him do that to me*?"

"What do you know about Brenda?" Kole asked when they were all inside. He looked back to make sure Byrd closed the door.

"*Everybody's* talking," Carla informed him. "You'd be surprised what kind of dirt will get uncovered when somebody dies. Everybody's looking at me like, 'You didn't know?' I keep telling these bitches, '*Hell naw, I didn't know*! You think I'd stay with him if I knew he had another woman?' They're all telling me, 'He been with her for *so long*, I thought you was cool with it.' *Why, Kole*? Why do y'all no good bastards do that shit? Why'd you let him do it?"

"Listen, Carla, I'm sorry. But I didn't come over here to talk about that."

"Of course you didn't, Kole! 'Cause you're a goddamn liar, just like Moon! I bet you're cheating on Dana, too! Why don't you leave that girl right now, so she can go on with her life? You know you ain't no good! Ain't none of you sorry bastards worth a damn!"

Her face crumpled as she broke down. Kole was compelled to pull her close and wrap his arms around her. She resisted at first, but he was strong, and at the moment, she was very weak. She sobbed into his chest.

"*Why, Kole? Why you let him do that to me? I loved him! Why would he do that to me?*"

"Listen," Kole said. "I know you're upset. This is a very hard thing to find out after somebody dies. But just because Moon did that stupid shit doesn't mean he didn't love you. He's still the same man he was before he died."

"*No, he's not!*" she bawled.

"Yes, he is, Carla. And you know it. It's just like that time I ate at your restaurant and told you how good your cornbread was. You told me you ran out of real butter and had to use that fake shit. I still liked that cornbread just the same."

She looked up at him, frowning. "It's not like that at all, Kole."

"I know it's not," he conceded. "But I made you stop crying." He grinned sheepishly.

She shook her head and then pushed away from him. "I hate you."

"No, you don't. 'Cause I'm the same Kole, just like he's the same Moon. If he had a weakness for that girl, Brenda, that was his *only* flaw. Either way, he loved the shit out of you, came home to you every night. Why you worried about some random broad calling him her boyfriend?"

"'Cause he *embarrassed* me, Kole! He made me look like a fool!"

"He made you look like a fool? Really? Well, tell me where Brenda's restaurant is. Where her ten-bedroom house at? What's in her bank account, a couple thousand?"

"We only have eight bedrooms," Carla corrected him.

"And that bitch can barely afford her *one*," Kole said. "So who's really looking like a fool?"

Most of what he said about Brenda's account and living conditions was not true. But Kole didn't expect Carla to do the research. Even if she did, she wouldn't do it before he and Byrd took off.

"But you knew about her?" she asked, softening now.

"I don't see how the answer to that question will bring you any peace," Kole stated. "If you wanna hate me for not keeping Moon alive, do that. But don't hate me for not living his life for him. I told him you was a good woman. I told him you was the only woman he needed. And that's where I left it. A man can't do no more than that."

Carla didn't like it, but she seemed to accept that. "Are you cheating on Dana too?" she asked.

Kole shook his head. "No. I'm not."

"Yeah, right. I'm pretty sure when you end up dead, we'll get the truth."

"Damn. That's some cold-blooded shit to say."

"I didn't mean it," she said. "But I'll tell you one thing, if that bitch Brenda shows up at the funeral–"

"You not gon' cause a scene at Moon's funeral," Kole warned her. "You wanna whoop her ass, I'll take you over there right now. But you not gon' do no shit like that at my brother's funeral. You ain't disrespecting Moon like that."

The change in his demeanor made her back down.

"Well, what the hell you come here for anyway?" she asked.

"I need Moon's cellphone."

"Which one?"

"All of them. I got a lead on his killers. I need one of his contacts to help track them down."

She stared at him for a moment, narrowing her eyes, before turning and leaving them in the foyer. She returned a minute later with two cellphones. "Here."

Kole took them. "Thanks."

"You think it had anything to do with them white boys?" Carla asked.

Kole frowned. "What white boys?"

"Some guys came to the restaurant about a month ago," she told him. "Moon was there by hisself. I was making dinner for him, when I heard him arguing with somebody. When I went to check on him, he had already kicked them out. I asked what it was about. He said it was nothing, just some punks talking noise."

Kole looked back at Byrd. He shook his head and shrugged.

"I never heard anything about that," Kole said to Carla. "What'd they look like?"

"I didn't get a good look at 'em. I just saw they was white and all tatted-up. Looked like trash to me."

Kole gave that some thought. "I'm pretty sure Moon would've told me or Byrd about it if it was serious."

Carla nodded. Before he left, she said, "Whoever it is, promise you'll make them suffer, for what they did to Moon."

In her eyes, Kole saw the same fires that consumed his soul.

"You know I will," he replied, and he and Byrd exited the house.

When they got outside, Kole told him, "Thanks for having my back when she was going off on me."

"I had your back," Byrd said.

"Yeah, *waaaay* the hell back there."

117

CHAPTER 24

I done did time with my homey
Flip a brick from a dime with my homey
4 am filling clips
Hop in the ride and dip
Windows spitting fire with my homey
Night shift in the dope house with my homey
Flush it down when the law come for my homey
The missus calling
You know I got your back
Take that broad to the motel, big homey
Repping Overbrook Meadows for my homey
'Bout to wet up the D-Town for my homey
Get off my case
Woman, stay in your place
Don't tell me not to get down for my homey

AFTER LEAVING CARLA'S house, Byrd tried to find Legend or Timber's number on Moon's cellphones.

He shook his head in frustration. "All the contacts are coded," he told Kole, "just like you said."

"He never told you his system?" Kole wondered, "with the two of you working so close to each other."

"No, it never came up," Byrd stated.

"He told me something about it a while back," Kole said. "Shouldn't be too hard to figure out, if we start with the people we know and work our way backwards. We can go to The Moonlight, so we'll have time to sit and think about it."

Byrd said, "Bet."

"What do you think about what Carla said about those white boys?"

"I'm pretty sure Moon would've told me, if it was something serious," Byrd said. "Could've been some panhandlers, for all we know."

Kole nodded. "Yeah. Maybe."

CHAPTER 25

THE MEN FOUND The Moonlight dark and gloomy. As he strolled through the desolate building, Kole began to wish they had chosen a different location.

"You remember when Moon had that issue when Webbie and Lil Boosie came up here?" Byrd asked.

Kole grinned at the memory. The rappers had received a warm welcome, for the most part. But a local gang harassed them on stage, demanding they settle a longstanding drug debt.

"Moon ran up on that stage like Suge Knight," Byrd recalled, "told everybody who had a problem with the artists to meet him out back."

"He had fifty goons waiting for 'em when they got there," Kole said. "Them fools was shook. Thought Moon was finna massacre 'em."

"He didn't, though," Byrd recounted.

"That's what made Moon special," Kole said, realizing how much he hated to speak of his friend in the past tense. "He could've handled it one way, but he took the time to hear them boys out. Turned out their grievance was real."

Byrd chuckled. "I ain't never gon' forget the look on Webbie's face after the show, when Moon told him and Boosie they had to pay their debt before they could get back on their tour bus. Boosie had plenty of security, but they wasn't ready for that."

"Moon was always fair," Kole noted. "He knew those rappers would never perform at his club again if he pulled that move. He took that loss, because it was the right thing to do. I was telling my woman last night how they don't make 'em like that anymore."

"No doubt," Byrd agreed. "The whole game's gonna be a little more shady with him gone."

The men took a seat at the bar. Kole got to work on Moon's main cellphone, while Byrd took a gander at the other one. In Moon's phone, Kole found his number saved as "*PV.*" Byrd's number was saved as "*YW.*"

Next to him, Byrd found his phone similarly coded. "It's got something to do with the alphabet," he announced.

Kole told him, "No shit, Sherlock."

"Oh, okay. I guess you close to figuring it out then."

"I'm closer than you."

"Bet a bill on it."

Kole told him, "Bet."

He went around the bar and found a pen and notepad. He returned to his stool and did an image search for the alphabet on his cellphone.

"Oh, we using pens and paper?" Byrd commented.

"Only a fool wouldn't use the tools at his disposal," Kole told him.

"Hmph."

Lemon was another member of The Organization whose phone number Kole had memorized. He searched the number on Moon's phone and found the contact saved as "*OM.*"

He frowned at the three names and initials he'd jotted down. It didn't make sense. Kole tried one more number he knew by heart. Brenda was saved on Moon's phone as "*YZ.*" With that, Kole cracked the code.

"You got it yet," he asked Byrd.

Byrd shook his head. "Everybody's got two letters, but they don't match up with the alphabet – not numerically, anyway."

"Yeah, they do," Kole informed him. "He did it backwards, with the first and last letters of the name."

Byrd stared at him in confusion.

"The first and last letters of my name are *K* and *E*," Kole explained. "But instead of saving me as *K-E*, he counted backwards in the alphabet. K is the 11th letter, but if you go backwards, the 11th letter is *P*. E is the 5th letter, but if you go backwards, it's *V*. So instead of saving me as *KE*, I'm saved as *PV*."

Byrd shook his head. "I still don't get it."

"That's 'cause you dumber than a box of rocks," Kole joked. "Anyway, we looking for Timber's number. T is the..." He counted the letters on his phone. "It's the 20th letter. But when you count backwards, it's *G*." He jotted that down. "R is the... 18th letter. But when you count backwards, it's... *I*. So Timber's number should be saved as *G-I*."

Byrd's eyes lit up. "Oh shit, I get it. Damn, Moon was smart as hell for coming up with that!"

Kole nodded and looked for a *GI* in Moon's contacts. Sure enough, he found it.

"Can I get paid?" he asked Byrd as he dialed the number.

Byrd placed Moon's other phone on the bar and dug a hundred-dollar bill from his pocket. He sneered as he slid it across the marble.

"Don't be getting an attitude," Kole told him. "You the one wanted to bet."

The voice who answered Timber's phone was immediately on edge. "Who dis?"

"It's Kole. Is this Timber?"

"How you get this phone you calling me from?" was the gruff reply.

"You know who I am," Kole said.

"I know who *Kole* is, but how I know you him?"

"For now, you gon' have to take my word for it. I got Moon's phone from his wife. I'm calling 'cause I need your help with a little issue in Dallas."

By then, Timber seemed to have recognized his voice. "Yo, sorry to hear about what happened to your boy. I didn't believe it at first. Moon was a stand-up guy."

"He was," Kole agreed.

"Y'all know who did it?"

"That's what I'm working on right now," Kole said. "That's why I called you."

"I don't know nothing," Timber said right away.

"I'm not asking for a lead. I already got one. Wanted to see if the name sounds familiar to you."

"What's the name?"

"Nero."

After a pause, Timber said, "Yeah, I know him."

Kole's mouth went dry. He licked his lips but couldn't come up with any moisture. "He a hitter?"

There was another pause before Timber said, "He is, but I ain't no snitch. Everybody know that."

"And I ain't the law."

Timber didn't say anything.

"Is there another dude Nero be hanging with?" Kole asked. He gave him the description Lewis provided: "He bald-headed, kinda skinny. Tall, with a full beard."

"Yeah, I know him too," Timber said.

Kole's body went numb. He had to take a deep breath before he spoke again. "Can I get a name?"

"You think they had something to do with Moon's killing?"

"You want me to answer that, or you wanna remain neutral?"

Timber chose the latter. "That other dude, his name is *Damon*."

Kole stared unblinking at Byrd, who watched him with the same intensity.

"You got an address on them?" Kole asked.

"What's it worth?" Timber asked.

"Five G's."

"I can get it."

"Can you call me on this phone when you do?"

"Yeah."

"Alright, holler," Kole said and disconnected. He took another deep breath and let it out slowly.

"He know 'em?" Byrd asked.

"Yeah. The second guy's name is Damon."

"Did he say he had an address?"

"He said he can get it."

"We rolling tonight if he do?"

Kole nodded. He stuffed Moon's cellphone in his pocket and rose from the stool. "Come on. I'll take you back to your car."

They exited the club, and Kole turned to lock up. His body tensed when Byrd warned him to, "Watch out."

Kole turned in time to see a sedan with tinted windows pull into the parking lot. A quick burst of adrenaline made him reach for his weapon, rather than choose flight as an option. As the car neared, the passenger side window began to descend. Kole recognized the occupant. It was Ice, of the MMG set. Ice didn't have a weapon exposed, but that didn't mean this wasn't a hit. Kole withdrew his pistol but held it at his side. He stepped in front of Byrd, who had also reached for his piece.

"Yo," Ice called when the car came to a stop.

Kole approached the vehicle warily. By then he could see the driver, who was also unarmed. He couldn't tell if there was an occupant in the back seat. He decided to let them have it if the back window rolled down, even an inch.

"Got some news," Ice called, as Kole drew within ten feet.

"What's that?" Kole said.

"Word is it was some white boys who killed Moon," Ice informed him.

The news made Kole's brow furrow. "Oh yeah? Where you get that from?"

"Don't worry about where I got it from," Ice said. His disdain for Kole hadn't ebbed one iota since last year. "I'm delivering this message because Brass told me to. After this, we ain't got nothing to do with y'all. Don't come around asking no more questions. Whatever you got to do, leave us out of it."

Kole nodded, half his attention still on the back window. "Alright."

Ice raised his window, and the sedan got moving again. The car made a U-turn in the parking lot before leaving the same way it had come.

When they were out of sight, Kole locked eyes with Byrd. Byrd didn't have anything to say about the *white boy theory* that was picking up steam. He shook his head slowly.

CHAPTER 26

WHEN HE GOT home, Kole was grateful to see Dana's SUV in his garage. She greeted him in the kitchen when he walked inside. She stood uneasily, with uncertainty eating away at her like termites. Kole felt guilty for putting her through this, but there was nothing he could do to alter their current path.

Despite the tension between them, it felt good when she stepped closer and wrapped her arms around him. Kole never thought he'd be the type to appreciate a hug when he got home, but her embrace alleviated a good deal of the stress he'd been carrying. He hugged her back, and she sighed softly.

He released her and asked, "You working today?"

It was a quarter till two. Her shift started at two-thirty. It was unlikely she was going, considering she wasn't wearing her scrubs.

She shook her head.

"You called-in?" Kole asked.

"I'll probably be ready to go back tomorrow," she offered.

"I don't like the idea of you taking these days off for my drama." He stepped past her.

Dana followed him down the hallway. "It's not just your drama," she said. "Moon was my friend too."

In the bedroom, Kole took a seat on the bed. Dana sat next to him and placed a hand on his thigh. He put his hand over hers and squeezed comfortingly.

He said, "You need to go on with your life and stop worrying about me."

Her heart froze. Tears filled her eyes as she stared down at their hands. "You, are you breaking up with me?"

Her heart didn't beat while she waited for him to respond.

Finally he said, "No. But I don't want you taking off work, worrying about me all the time. I don't want you to be here waiting on me every day. You got a life. You got a son, stuff you need to do."

"I'm taking care of everything I need to," she assured him. "Tariq's fine. I talked to him this morning. He's not a child anymore. He's not even home half the time."

Kole shook his head. "This ain't healthy. The stress you causing yourself..."

"I wish I could stop worrying about you," she said. "I wish this was all over, and things were back to the way they used to be. I know you want the same thing. I can't stop worrying about you till I know you're safe. I'd rather wait here for you, than wait at my place and not even know when you get home."

Kole's formidable shoulders rose and fell as he sighed. Realizing he wasn't going to get what he wanted, he dropped the subject. He reclined on the mattress, with his legs hanging over the side. Dana did the same. They stared at the ceiling in silence.

After a while she asked, "Did you hear anything about Moon?"

"Yeah," Kole said. "I think we're getting close."

He told her about the meeting with Lewis, cracking the code on Moon's cellphones and the tip he received from Ice. Dana had a lot of follow-up questions. Kole responded to them honestly. One of the last questions she had was about Ice.

"You went by that MMG club?"

"I did yesterday," Kole said. "Me and Byrd."

"Don't they hate you," she wondered, "after what happened? They didn't try to hurt you?"

"I had a lot of guns on me," Kole admitted. "If they wanted me dead, it would've been the perfect time."

"Were you armed?"

"Yeah, but I didn't reach for my gun. They prolly would've killed me if I did."

"Why – how could you do that? You don't care about what happens to you?"

"I do. But it – it's not that simple. I know they hate me, but we all have to live by the code."

"What's that?"

"It's an unwritten set of rules," Kole explained. "Like when you get arrested, you don't say nothing. Never steal from your homies. Don't get high off your own supply or do dirt where you lay your head. Stuff like that."

"The code says your enemies can't kill you if you don't reach for your gun?"

Kole chuckled. "I wish. Me and MMG have a truce, ever since that incident last summer. I didn't go over to start shit, so the truce stands, even if we hate each other."

"I don't think I'll ever understand all this gang crap," Dana said.

"Good. It's not for you to understand. I prefer you stay safe and *square*."

She sighed, and they were quiet for a minute.

She asked him, "Have you eaten anything? Want me to make something for lunch?"

Kole hadn't had much of an appetite since Moon's death. He knew he should put something on his belly. Without food, he might not have the energy to act when the time came.

He told her, "Yeah, I'm a little hungry."

Dana rose from the bed. "I'll find something to eat. I'll call you when it's ready."

CHAPTER 27

SHE MADE PANINIS with waffle fries for lunch. Afterwards they went to the den, where Kole had movie theater style seating and a huge projector screen. They tried to get into the latest Tom Cruise flick, but they were both distracted and exhausted. After a while, Dana asked, "Do you wanna go lay down?"

Kole said he did.

In the bedroom they did more talking than napping, but that was fine. Lying in bed with him, Dana started to feel a sense of normalcy. They cuddled and discussed things unrelated to murder. Dana was surprised to hear that Moon had a longtime girlfriend. She found Carla's reaction to the news appropriate.

"How long were they married?"

"About sixteen years," Kole said.

"That's coldblooded. And you knew about the other woman?"

"Don't tell me you finna put me through that again. Trust me, Carla already let me have it."

"Good."

"What you mad at *me* for? I'm not the one who was having an affair."

"Yeah, but you knew about it."

"Knowing about something doesn't give me power over it."

"You could've told him not to."

"Damn. Here we go again."

"Did you even try?"

"Look, I'll tell you like I told Carla: I told Moon she was a good woman, and she was the only woman he needed. Aside from that, I had to let that man live his life. Whatever he decided to do was his business."

"If he was cheating for that long, does that mean you're cheating too?"

"I swear you and Carla must've talked before I got home."

"I haven't talked to Carla. Did she ask you that?"

"Yeah."

"*And...*"

"And what?"

She slapped his chest. "Boy, you better quit playing."

Kole chuckled. "You know you my only girl. I made it this far in my life with *no* girlfriend. Now that I got one, you think I'm ready to take on *two at the same time*? Hell naw. You a handful."

She slapped him again. "I am not."

He reached down and palmed her kitty. The move was so unexpected, she gasped.

"You are a handful," Kole muttered as he caressed her genitals.

Dana swallowed and couldn't formulate a response.

CHAPTER 28

KOLE DIDN'T GET a lot of calls that night. While he had unofficially taken over as the head of The Organization, most of the members didn't know this. They continued to reach out to Byrd for a status update. Dana considered the lack of news *good news*. An ominous chill ran down her body when she heard a ringtone she didn't recognize. Kole must have felt the same way, because he hopped out of bed to take the call, rather than simply roll over, like he'd been doing.

"Yeah."

"Yo, it's Timber."

"What you got?" Kole asked him.

"Address for Nero and Damon. Far as I know, they at these spots right now."

The contents of Kole's stomach shifted. The panini he'd eaten felt like a large, cold stone.

"You coming to Dallas tonight?" Timber asked.

"Yeah. I need them addresses."

"I can meet you. I'll give 'em to you when I get my ends."

Kole didn't like the idea of taking his men that far without knowing their destination beforehand, but to get the information he sought, he had to play by Timber's rules.

"At least tell me what side of town they on," he said. "I prolly gotta scoop 'em up and take 'em somewhere private, while I talk to 'em. I wanna make sure the spot I pick is close to where they are."

"They both on the south," Timber said. "That's where I'll be too."

"Where we gon' meet?" he asked him.

"Call me when you on the road," Timber said, "before you hit the city limits. I'll let you know where I'll be. What time you think you'll make it over here?"

Kole checked the time. It was 5 pm. "Not till after dark. We'll probably leave here at nine."

"A'ight," Timber said and disconnected.

Dana had sat up in bed by then. Kole turned her way while he placed a call to Byrd.

"What up?" his friend answered.

"Timber got addresses for the two in Dallas."

"Both of 'em?"

"Yeah."

"What's the play?"

"Gather the troops," Kole said. "I don't think we need more than fifteen, twenty. We'll roll out at nine. You know somebody in the D who got access to a warehouse and don't care what happen to it?"

Byrd didn't have to think too hard before saying, "Naw."

"Can you find one in the next few hours?"

"I'm sure I can. What part of Dallas?"

"South side."

"A'ight. I'll handle that. We meeting at The Moonlight?"

"No. It's too hot over there. Send the guys to south Dallas. Tell 'em to find somewhere to post up till I get the addresses. Me and you can ride together. I'll pick you up."

"Got it."

Kole disconnected and fixed his eyes on the woman in his life. Dana was so apprehensive, her chest rose and fell visibly.

She asked him, "What happened?"

Kole's expression was hard now, his eyes serious. He didn't look like the same person she'd been cuddling with for the past few hours.

He told her, "I gotta take care of some business tonight."

Dana knew full well what that business entailed, and it was horrifying.

"Why do you have to go?"

"Because I have to."

"There's hundreds of men in The Organization," she said knowingly. "Why does it have to be *you*?"

"I'm not going by myself."

"I know Kole, but why do you have to go at all? Let Byrd take care of it."

"It would still be me calling the shots," Kole stated. "In the eyes of the law, I'd be responsible for whatever went down."

"I don't care about the law. I'm worried about something happening to you while you're there."

Dana was only vaguely aware of how far she'd regressed. A year ago, she didn't want him to commit murder at all. Now she was okay with it, as long as he didn't get harmed while carrying it out or in the possible retaliation.

"I have to go," he insisted.

Her eyes filled with tears. "I know you feel like this is something you have to handle personally, but it's not. Why would you want to get your hands dirty?"

"*That's my brother*," he growled.

"*But you don't have to!*"

"*Yes, I do!*" he roared, advancing on her. "*Don't tell me what I have to do!*"

She recoiled, bringing a hand to her mouth. Kole had never seen her respond to him that way. He didn't realize he had stepped within a few feet of her. The look in her eyes made him feel like a monster. The demons dancing on his shoulders told him that description was accurate.

"If you wanna be with me, then you have to accept me for who I am."

"But this isn't who you are, Kole – not anymore!"

"It's who I am now," he said, his teeth clenched. "It's who I am till I find out what happened to Moon."

Dana's lips trembled, but she refused to break down in front of him. Maybe later, when she got home, but not now. After a few seconds, Kole turned and walked out of the room. From the den, he listened to her gather her things. She did not look for him before leaving the house.

CHAPTER 29

KOLE PICKED UP Byrd from an apartment on the west side of town at 9 pm. They hit the road again, this time headed for Dallas. Both men were prepared for the treacherous work that lie ahead, despite having little information about their destination.

"Who's the connect for the warehouse?" Kole asked as he pushed a 2021 Corolla exactly 70 miles per hour on the dark freeway. The car was *borrowed* and the plates were stolen. The last thing they needed was to get pulled over and ticketed on a ride like this.

"A friend of my uncle," Byrd replied.

"He cool?"

"Yeah. But it don't matter no way. He moved to Louisiana a few years ago, told my uncle to check on the place ever so often. Ain't nobody been in there since he left."

"What's in it?"

"A welding shop, but most of the equipment is old or broke."

"No cameras?" Kole asked.

"My unc said there ain't none."

"Got a key?"

"Nope. It's only one padlock on the door. Got some bolt cutters for that."

"What about the businesses around it?"

"It's kinda isolated," Byrd said. "Won't nobody hear nothing going on in there tonight, especially if we gag 'em."

"Think it'd be safe to be there for a few days?"

Byrd frowned at that. "I haven't laid eyes on it, so I can't say. You think we gone need it longer than tonight?"

"Depends on how long it takes them to talk," Kole said. His tone was casual. He wore black jeans with black sneakers and a long-sleeve black thermal, despite the warm weather. He had a pair of black gloves in the glove compartment.

"I don't think it'll take that long," Byrd said. "They got nothing to gain by holding onto the name of whoever hired them."

"You'd be surprised," Kole said. "Some of these hitters take that code of honor shit to the grave."

"That would make it more fun for me," Byrd commented. "Either way, I'm sure we'll get the name tonight."

Kole nodded slowly.

The men were mostly quiet for the next twenty minutes as they passed through Arlington and Grand Prairie. The moment Kole entered Dallas city limits, he placed a call to Timber. The informant gave him the address to a Valero gas station.

Fifteen minutes later, Kole exited Pearl Street and made a left on Flora. He pulled into a gas station near Booker T Washington High School and spotted a black Range Rover parked next to the dumpsters. He approached it slowly and rolled down his window as he came to a stop. The Range Rover had one occupant. The man turned on his headlights and pulled out of his parking spot. Kole allowed him to pass and got right behind him.

He followed the SUV to the main thoroughfare and kept up with it for another three minutes, until it turned onto a quiet street in a bad neighborhood. The SUV pulled into the driveway of a vacant house. Kole parked behind it and exited his vehicle.

Despite the favorable history Timber had with The Organization, Kole had never laid eyes on him. This was Moon's connect. Prior to tonight, Timber preferred to do business with

Moon alone. He rolled down his window as Kole approached the driver's side. Timber was an average-size man in his late thirties. His skin was dark, his hair shaved low.

The informant checked him out warily before asking, "You got my issue?"

Kole produced a stack of 100 dollar bills, secured with a rubber band. He handed it through the window.

Timber placed the cash on the passenger seat without counting it.

"You got a good memory?" he asked Kole. "'Cause I ain't writing none of this down, and if you smart, you won't either."

"I got a good memory," Kole told him.

The informant gave him an address for Nero and a different one for Damon. Neither was very far away.

With their business concluded, Kole asked him, "Is it okay if I give your number to Byrd? He'll be taking over, with Moon gone. He might need some of the same work Moon did."

"Is that him in the car with you?" Timber asked.

Kole nodded.

"It's cool, long as word don't get back to me that somebody's calling me a snitch. If I hear something like that, it's gon' be trouble."

Kole didn't like being threatened, but he knew Timber didn't have enough gunmen to pose a threat to The Organization. He understood why the man wanted to maintain his reputation.

"Nobody will ever hear that from my people," Kole assured him.

Timber nodded and rolled up his window.

Kole returned to his vehicle and disappeared into the night.

CHAPTER 30

THREE CARLOADS OF men from The Organization had already arrived in D town. Before calling to give them instructions, Byrd asked Kole, "You wanna hit both spots at the same time, to make sure a warning don't get out?"

Kole did want that, but, "I wanna be there when we get both of them. Why don't you send a crew to the second address, and they can sit on him till we get there? If he try to duck out, they can take him."

Byrd nodded. He called the driver of each crew while Kole drove south, to meet a man named Nero.

On the outskirts, South Dallas didn't appear as bad as the rumors that made it all the way back to Overbrook Meadows. But Kole knew better. Any city that was a frequent flyer on murder shows like *The First 48* had to play host to many evil deeds on a daily basis. Kole felt no qualms about adding to the city's woes tonight.

As he drove deeper in to the neighborhood, the graffiti bore witness to the crime and gang activity. Like the south side of Overbrook Meadows, the area was littered with dopefiends, prostitutes and other degenerates. Thankfully, the address Timber gave for Nero wasn't on a highly populated street. Things may have been different on a Friday or Saturday night, but this was

Tuesday. Most of the residents appeared to be tucked in for the night. Kole spotted two nondescript vehicles parked on either side of the road.

He asked Byrd, "Them our boys?"

Byrd nodded, his eyes on the hitman's home.

Kole pulled to a stop a few houses down. By then, he could almost taste Nero's blood. Two years ago, he made a vow to never kill again. He knew he'd backslide tonight, and he didn't feel one bit guilty about it.

Byrd looked over at him. In the dark confines of the car, Kole's eyes were the only thing that shone brightly.

He asked him, "How you want this to go down?"

Kole kept his eyes on the killer's house. The lights were on in the front room, but the porch light wasn't. Kole had to assume it might have a motion sensor. There was one car in the driveway. Kole's heart revved when he saw that it was a gray Sonata; the same car crackhead Lewis had described. There was no question this was the right place, and apparently Moon's killer was inside.

"You wanna see if the car has an alarm?" Byrd asked. "If we set it off, maybe he'll bring his dumb ass outside to check on it."

"You think it's late enough for that?" Kole asked. "What if somebody else come outside to see what's going on?"

The clock on the dash read 10:23 pm. Kole noticed lights on inside some of the neighbors' houses.

"You right," Byrd said. "We can wait a couple of hours, till they go to sleep."

Kole was normally a patient man, but the thought of waiting out there for that long felt like torture. He told him, "The hell with that. I'm ready to run up in there and snatch his ass right now."

Byrd grinned. "What about whoever else is in there? We gon' lay 'em down?"

Kole had murder on his mind, but there was no need to wet an innocent. "Naw. We can duct tape and hog tie 'em."

"What if it's some kids?"

The possibility of harming a youngster brought his bloodlust down another notch. He sighed. "You know I don't wanna hurt no damn kids."

"You can wait in the car," Byrd suggested. "I'll do it."

"I don't want you to either."

"We ain't gotta hurt 'em, if they shut up and let the boys tie 'em up."

Kole frowned and ran the possible outcomes through his mind. There were no bicycles or toys in the yard. With only one vehicle in the driveway, it was safe to assume Nero wasn't a family man.

"I don't think it's no kids in there," Kole decided. "I'm ready to do this."

Byrd nodded. "You leading the charge?"

"Yeah. I'ma knock on the front door," Kole said. "When he comes to see who it is, I want four guys to breach the back. While he's distracted with that, I'll kick in the front. I want two men in the bushes over there. They'll follow me in. I want one man to stay in each car. Once everyone's inside, we'll tie him up, haul his ass outta there and throw him in the trunk."

"The trunk of which car?"

"This one."

"You sure you wanna ride dirty like that?" Byrd asked, knowing Kole would face a lengthy prison sentence if they got pulled over with a bound and gagged man in the trunk.

Kole barely considered what that would mean for him and Dana before saying, "Yeah. I'm sure."

"Where you want me?" Byrd asked.

"I need you to get behind the wheel when I get out," Kole stated. "Back into the driveway and pop the trunk. Be ready to roll out when we get him, in case we gotta hightail it outta here."

"I don't wanna wait in the car," Byrd complained. "I wanna go in with y'all."

"I need it to go down just like I said," Kole replied, and the matter was settled.

Byrd nodded. He called his men and relayed the M.O.

CHAPTER 31

KOLE INITIATED THE infiltration by casually walking up to the front door and knocking as planned. The porch light came on before he made it halfway up the steps, but Kole was sure his gloved hands weren't visible from the vantage point of the peephole.

It was hard to maintain his composure when a male voice yelled, "Who is it?" a moment later.

Somehow Kole managed to keep his expression neutral. "I'm looking for Nero," he announced.

After a moment, the person on the other side shouted, "Who the fuck is you?"

Kole's nostrils flared. *It was him*! The man who laid his best friend out in front of his wife and family was standing less than five feet away. Kole began to tap his right foot.

Once.

Twice.

Three times.

He waited.

Five seconds later he knew his signal had been picked up. There was a loud boom at the back of the house. In his mind's eye, Kole saw their target turning towards the sound. He stepped back and delivered a forceful kick to the front door, right next to the door knob.

BOOMP!

The door flew inward, taking jagged shards of the frame with it. Kole didn't plan to hit the target with the door, but Nero didn't rush to the back immediately. The door collided with his shoulder, and he took a few stumbling steps back. He stared into the doorway with wide, fretful eyes.

The next two seconds felt like a whole commercial break.

Kole saw that Nero wore only a pair of boxers. He was a caramel-colored man, with a struggling beard and skinny arms. Rather than a pistol, the hitman toted an assault rifle. If it was a handgun, he might have had a chance to defend himself from the ambush. But the rifle was too big and bulky. By the time his panicked brain told his arms to raise the barrel and point it at the boogey man in the doorway, Kole was on his ass.

He exploded with another solid kick, this time catching the target on the arm and stomach. The force of the blow threw Nero backwards. He crashed into the wall and squeezed out a surprised yelp as the rifle fell from his hands. By then four men had invaded the house from the back. Two more squeezed by Kole and entered through the front. They all converged on the scene in time to see Kole throw a right hook that caught the target squarely on the jaw. Nero's head snapped to the right at what looked like a lethal angle, and spittle flew from his mouth. The hitter's eyes floated in opposite directions before his whole body went limp, as if someone hit the off switch on a robot. He fell slowly, bumping his head against the wall on the way down

No one had to fire a shot.

Kole never even pulled his gun.

CHAPTER 32

OTHER THAN THE target, the house was empty. Kole thanked God for small favors and then caught himself. God had no hand in any of the night's mischief.

Nero was extremely pliable while sleeping. The crew had no trouble tying his arms and legs. Kole wasn't too keen on gagging an unconscious man, out of fear that he might end up choking to death. But he'd rather risk that than worry about someone hearing screams coming from the trunk while he idled at a stop light.

Since no one appeared to have noticed the commotion, Kole altered his plan at the last minute. He let one of the crews take Nero to the warehouse, while he, Byrd and the other four men set out to apprehend the second hitman. According to Timber, they'd find Damon at an apartment complex with his girlfriend, less than ten miles away.

When they arrived at the location, Kole was not happy to see an abundance of nightlife. He was, however, delighted to spot Damon was among a handful of misfits milling about. The crowd was no stranger to gunplay, so they suspected robbery was the motive when six armed men swarmed them, barking orders like a SWAT team.

"Get down on the ground!"

"Hit the floor, bitch!"

"That way! Face that way!"

"Close your eyes! Look at me one more time, playa! I dare you!"

With five men face down on the pavement, all of them fearing a bullet to the back if they didn't comply, Kole stepped forward wearing all black.

He said, "Get up, Damon."

The dummy was foolish enough to push up on his arms before thinking better of it.

Kole approached from behind and grabbed the back of his collar. He yanked him to a standing position, nearly strangling him in the process.

"Yo man, what the fuck?" the hitman squealed. *"What I do?"*

Kole turned and pushed him forward, in the direction of his car. His squad kept guns trained on the others. Damon scrambled like a scarecrow, barely managing to maintain his balance. Kole confirmed his physical description; tall and skinny, bald-headed with a full beard. This was definitely the guy.

"Get moving!" Kole ordered. "You coming with us."

Damon's eyes darted wildly. He saw Byrd standing at the rear of the Corolla. Byrd popped the trunk as they approached. Damon looked back at Kole, his eyes even wider than before.

"I can't get in the trunk!" he cried. *"Please, man! Anything but that!"*

"Shut up and get yo ass in the trunk!" Kole barked.

"No! Please! I'm claustrophobic!"

Despite the high stakes drama, Kole took a moment to consider the absurdity of that comment. Anyone who planned to put you in the trunk of a car clearly meant you harm, up to and including murder. But this idiot was more concerned with his claustrophobia. It was one of the most bizarre reactions he'd ever witnessed.

"A'ight, man," he said. "You can get in the front seat."

145

"For real?" Damon looked back at Byrd.

When he turned Kole's way again, he barely noticed the behemoth's eyes narrow, before the lights went out. Kole caught him with a beautiful left hook, right on the temple. For the second time that night, Kole dropped their target with relative ease.

"Come on," he said to Byrd as he bent to lift the man from the pavement. "Help me get him in the trunk."

"You couldn't have knocked him out *after* we got him in the trunk?" Byrd asked. He put his pistol away and grabbed the man's legs.

"You heard what he said," Kole replied. "He was gon' put up a hell of a fight before we got him in there."

"You could've at least got him *closer* to the trunk."

"Quit being lazy," Kole admonished him. "I swear you youngsters don't appreciate a hard days' work."

CHAPTER 33

THIRTY MINUTES LATER, the hitters found themselves in an abandoned warehouse with no overhead lights, just a few battery-operated lamps brought in by members of The Organization. The place smelled of dust, mildew, gasoline and stale oil. A strong scent of fear and sweat leaked from the captives' pores. The men were bound to folding chairs with duct tape around their ankles, arms and torsos. Their heads were free to look from side to side, up and down.

Before them stood a dozen men, all dressed in black. Their captors no longer toted firearms. They all wore varying looks of anger, satisfaction and disgust. The presumed leader of the group stood mid center. He was not the tallest, but he was the largest. Even with long sleeves, the muscles in his arms and shoulders were massive. Neither Nero nor Damon remembered being hit, but they both knew it was the juggernaut who had thrown the punch. It was hard to believe he was so quick, given his size. It was not hard to believe he had the power to take them down so effortlessly.

Nero wore only his boxers when he was abducted. His outfit had not changed. The duct tape would leave serious chafes on his skin if it was snatched away, but the likelihood of him being freed from his bondage while still alive was bleak. Given his lack of pleading, Kole suspected he knew this, as did his accomplice.

Standing before them, Kole found it hard to believe these wastes of life had taken away so much. Everything Moon was and ever would be was snuffed out in a matter of seconds by two men who were ill-equipped to defend themselves from retaliation they should've seen coming a mile away. It was embarrassing. Kole knew Moon was watching over him. He wondered what his friend thought about the incompetence that took his life.

Kole stepped forward, taking in the hitters' bruised faces and altered mind state. It was clear neither of them expected their nights (and possibly their lives) to end like this. Finally he spoke:

"The man you killed, the one you probably know as Moon, was named Benjamin Cummings. I've known him for more than twenty-five years. He was closer to me than my family."

Kole watched how this information affected them. Nero's eyes dilated. A bead of sweat rolled down Damon's forehead. Nero licked his lips and shook his head, most likely to deny he played a part in the murder, but Kole shook his head, silencing him.

"My name is Kole," he said. "Kole Stone. I ran The Organization with Moon for most of those twenty-five years. I retired a couple of years ago and left it to him. These men," he said, looking from his right to his left, "are members of The Organization. Byrd is their leader now." He nodded in his direction. "His real name is Kelvin Broaddus."

Damon's eyes widened. Nero swallowed hard. His face and chest glistened with sweat. They both knew there was only once circumstance under which Kole would reveal so much information.

But in case they were as dim as they looked, he told them, "You men will die tonight. None of us are wearing masks now. It doesn't matter if you know our names or see our faces."

The men backing him up looked menacing; eager to do what they had come there for.

"I can give you the name of every one of them," Kole continued. "The information will not help you in the slightest. I know y'all are contract killers. I understand you were paid to do a job, and you merely followed instructions. I've done similar things, so I don't fault you for that. The problem is you accepted a job for the *wrong target*. If you didn't know who Moon was, you should've done your research and turned down the assignment. If you *did* know who he was, you're both fools for carrying it out."

"*I didn't do nothing*," Nero pleaded. "Man, I don't know what the fuck you talking about!"

Kole nodded. "It's okay. I don't expect this to be easy for you. I know you don't want to turn over the people who hired you, and even more than that, you don't want to die. But rest assured, both of these things will happen. We didn't pull your names out of a hat. I know for a fact you killed Moon. Now, the only question is how long it will take for you to talk; how long we have to burn you or cut you or how many pieces of you we have to send to the people you love. I'll yank out every one of your teeth, one at a time. Don't make me none."

The killers looked from Kole to one another. Both had trouble breathing when their attention returned to the man who was speaking.

"I would actually prefer you hold out for a *long time*," Kole stated. "I hope it takes *days*, because the way you took my brother from me hurt to the core. Every man in here would love to inflict as much bodily harm on you as possible. We'll shoot you up with speed, so you can't even pass out from the pain. But what I really want is the man who ordered the hit. That's the one who matters the most. You're just the instrument he used to carry it out.

"So here's my offer," Kole said. "The first one of you to give me the pertinent information will receive a bullet to the head. No pain. No suffering. The one who holds out will receive plenty of pain. *Lots of suffering*. I'll burn your foot to a crisp, and then move on to the other one. Either way, both of you will die. It's just a matter of how you go."

This news caused Nero to hyperventilate. Damon's eyes filled with tears. They spilled unabashedly.

"How, how I know you'll take me out quick?" Damon wanted to know.

"Because I'm a man of my word," Kole said. "But I ain't finna spend all night trying to convince you of that. You gon' have to take my word for it."

"I'll, I'll tell you," Damon breathed. "Can you prom— cuh, can you promise you'll give a message to my peeps, my daughter. Can you tell her something for me? I just want her to know I love her, and I'm sorry."

Kole nodded and told his cohorts, "Move this one to the other room."

Four men stepped forward and hefted the whole chair with the occupant included. They quickly moved him to another part of the warehouse.

"Gimme them pliers," Kole told one of his other soldiers.

The man handed him the tool. Kole approached the remaining captive, his expression hard and focused.

"*Wait! I'll talk too!*" Nero blurted.

Kole stopped but said, "I already got one of you talking. I don't need both."

"*You never gave me a chance!*" Nero cried. "*You didn't give me a chance!*"

Having both of them talk was Kole's goal all along. It was the only way to ensure the information they gave him was accurate. But he appeared disappointed about not being able to follow through with the torture.

"Fine," Kole breathed with a show of frustration. "Tell me who hired you."

"A white man," Nero squealed. "His name is Trey. He from Overbrook Meadows. He all tatted up. He in one of those skinhead gangs. I don't know nothing else about him. *I swear!*"

This was the third person who had brought up white men as the culprits. As with the first two instances, the information left

Kole baffled. The Organization had very few interactions with white gangs and had made no enemies with any of them. Kole wondered if *Trey* was the same man who had come to Carla's restaurant and harassed Moon during dinner. More importantly, he wanted to know why he felt it necessary to take Moon out.

"What'd he say it was for?" he asked the hitman.

"*I don't know!*" Nero cried. "*We don't never ask why. We just do what they pay us to do!*"

Kole believed that. A hitman didn't need to know the what's and why's. They only needed to pull the trigger.

"Did you know who Moon was when you got the assignment?"

Nero's breathing became more erratic. After watching him squirm for ten seconds, Kole realized he wasn't going to answer the question. He snorted and approached him with the pliers again.

"*Okay, wait!*" the hitman shouted. "*Yes! Yeah we knew!* But he offered a lot of money; twice as much as we normally get. *I'm sorry, Kole! Please don't hurt me!*"

"*I'm gonna hurt you to the fullest!*" Kole bellowed. "*Your ass is gonna die tonight!*"

"*But don't torture me, man! I'm telling you everything I know. You promised! You gave your word!*"

"You ain't told me shit!" Kole replied. "I wanna know how the man contacted you, where you met, who he was with and what kind of car he drive. I wanna know every little thing you can think of when it comes to that motherfucker. If you do right, you'll get the bullet to the head. If I think you holding out *one time*, we going to plan B. And once I start mutilating you, ain't no going back."

Nero trembled so badly, his teeth rattled. "Oh, okay, man," he breathed. "Okay. I'll tell you everything. I swear. *I swear I'll tell you everything!*"

CHAPTER 34

IT TOOK HALF an hour to get the full story from the men. Their information wasn't always specific, but it was sufficient. Kole learned a white man named Trey, accompanied by more white men, met with the hitmen before the murder and gave them partial payment and pertinent information about Moon. They met with them again for the remaining payment. The white men all appeared to be members of an Aryan prison gang.

Despite their obvious racist inclinations, the white men were respectful of Damon and Nero. They had no qualms about hiring black men to kill another black man. The white men drove a red pickup. Trey was the only one they could describe well. He was in his early thirties, tall and not too muscular. He wore a goatee. His hair was shaved short but not completely bald. He had a full sleeve of tattoos on both arms. One of his forearms had a noose scrawled along the length. The other forearm had the word WOODS in bold, block letters.

Kole was disgusted that Damon and Nero would follow orders from someone who obviously hated people like them, but he was a man of his word. He instructed his men to bring Damon back to the room with Nero. The killers cried like girls when Kole hefted a gasoline can and doused them.

"You said you wasn't gon' torture us!"

"I'm not," Kole said. He continued to wet them from head to toe. "I'm not gon' light you up until *after* I kill you."

"*But why you gotta do that?*" Damon cried. "*I want a regular funeral*! You said if we talked–"

"*I'm not gon' torture you*!" Kole said again. "I'm burning this whole warehouse down. You included. This is about destroying evidence, not your sorry ass."

The men continued to plead while Kole's men drenched the rest of the warehouse. Their cries fell upon deaf ears. Everyone from The Organization hoped Kole would burn them alive. The hell with a promise made to a couple of dead men. But Kole's word was his bond.

He executed both men personally with a gunshot to the head.

He hadn't killed anyone in a few years, but the numb rush of power and damnation was all too familiar.

He sent his men home before he lit the place up and fled the scene with Byrd.

PART FOUR
LEMON

CHAPTER 35

Gracious and dear, consistently loving
Pillar of wisdom, comforting – nothing
Stands test, nor time, nor pain or fire
As does your love. How I desire
To see you rise – from this dust, your lowly
Relationship – And stand, and slowly
Lift your head and see me smile
Your eyes now gleaming at your child

DANA HAD COMPOSED herself by the time she got home, but the stress remained. All she wanted was a quiet night alone. Her chances of that happening fell flat when she saw Brendon's girlfriend's car in the driveway. Thankfully he parked on the right side, leaving room for her to enter the garage on the left. She sighed as she pulled in next to her son's SUV. She took a few moments to check her features in the visor mirror before she entered her home.

She heard the ruckus from Tariq's company when she stepped into the kitchen. Neither of their girlfriends was loud or disrespectful, but with both couples in the living room, the get-together was boisterous.

The teens were watching a standup comedian on Netflix. They were all in good spirits, with Tariq and Sabrina on one sofa and Brendon cuddling his main squeeze on the other. The coffee table was littered with snacks. The smell of pizza made Dana's stomach churn.

Kole was the only thing on her mind when she tried to walk past them. She said, "Hey, Tariq," to her son but didn't want to dally long enough to entertain the other three.

"Hey, Miss Dana," Brendon called.

"Hi," Sabrina, Tariq's girlfriend said. "How was your day?"

"It was fine," Dana replied, without looking the girl in the eyes. "Hi, Brendon," she said lethargically. She tossed Brendon's girlfriend another, "Hey." She didn't remember that girl's name or care to think about it at the moment.

She heard Brendon ask, "Yo, is she alright?" as she continued down the hallway. If Tariq responded, he did so quietly. When she got to her room, Dana closed the door to block out their chatter. She lie on her bed without turning on the lights or undressing. Less than thirty seconds later, there was a knock on her door.

"Can I come in?" Tariq asked.

Dana took a few heavy breaths before she rolled over and sat up. She told him, "Yeah."

Tariq opened the door. In the darkness, his silhouette was tall and manly. It was amazing how fast he'd grown. Soon he'd be gone away to college, and she would be alone. Dana used to think she'd have Kole to counter the yearning for her son. Now she wasn't so sure.

"Can I turn on the light?" he asked.

"Go ahead," she told him.

He did so and stepped inside. He closed the door softly. He watched his mother for a few beats, took in her sullen features and puffy eyes.

He knew the answer but asked, "Is everything alright?"

"Yeah. I'm fine."

Tariq couldn't bring himself to call her a liar. "You didn't work today?" he asked instead.

She shook her head. "No. I might go back tomorrow."

"You take off because of what happened to Moon?"

Technically that was true. She nodded. "Yeah."

He watched her for a second and then asked, "How's Kole?"

Dana looked him in the eyes. "He's okay."

Tariq brought a hand to his mouth and nibbled one of his nails. Normally she would've asked him to stop, but Dana had bitten most of her nails in the past couple of days. Who was she to judge?

"What's he gonna do about Moon?" the boy asked.

She asked him, "What do you mean?"

Tariq looked back at the door, as if to make sure it was closed. "I, uh, I know what he did for us last summer, when that gang was after us. I figured if he'd do that much for us, and he didn't even know us that well, he'd probably do a lot more for Moon, since that was his best friend."

Dana wasn't surprised by the conclusions he was jumping to. She knew this conversation was coming.

"What are you asking me?"

Tariq cocked his head slightly and then spit it out. "Is he gonna hurt somebody because of what happened to Moon? Is that why you're upset?"

She shook her head. When did her child become a man? Eighteen years was not enough time to prepare her for the transition.

"You have company," she told him. "You need to go tend to them."

He frowned. "I need to know what's going on with you."

"You can't come in here and talk to me about this stuff while you have company," she countered. "We can talk tomorrow."

"But Mama."

"I'm serious, Tariq. The conversation you want to have is *personal.* I'm not talking to you about it while you have guests. Go be with your friends, and we'll talk tomorrow."

"Mama—"

"*I'm not doing this right now,*" she said more forcefully. "*Go be with your company, and we will talk tomorrow.*"

He took a deep breath, his bird chest rising and falling slowly. He turned and exited the room. Despite his temper, he did not slam the door.

Dana lie back on the bed. She was pissed that he didn't turn the light off, but she didn't feel like getting up to do it herself.

She was even more pissed when he knocked again five minutes later.

"Can I come in?"

"What did I just tell you?" she grumbled.

He opened the door without her permission. Dana sat up and glared at him.

"I don't have company anymore," he explained. "I told them to go home."

She frowned at him. "I didn't tell you to do that."

"You told me we can't talk while I have company. Now they're gone."

He came and sat on the bed next to her. "Can you talk to me now?"

Dana reached and rubbed her forehead. She didn't think Tariq had ever forced a conversation like this. She stared at him, noticing how prominent his Adam's apple was. The hairs on his chin were not as sparse as they were the last time she checked.

"Tariq, I don't know what Kole's gonna do about Moon," she said. "I assume he wants revenge, but I don't know that for sure. I don't know what you want me to tell you."

"Revenge means he'll kill someone?"

For the life of her, Dana couldn't understand why she was entertaining this discussion. No matter how many hairs Tariq had on his chiny-chin-chin, he was still a child. He was *her* child. He didn't need to know anything about the complexities of her relationship.

"I don't think it'll come to that," she lied.

"But it could," he said. "He used to kill people. Why wouldn't he do it now?"

"Tariq, this is a lot more complicated than you think. Kole isn't the same man he was back then."

"So he's not gonna hurt anybody?"

She scowled. "I don't know."

"You gonna stay with him if he does?"

Her eyes widened. "I don't wanna talk to you about this. I don't know what's gonna happen with Kole, but it's really none of your business."

"You said we could talk when I didn't have company."

"That was before I knew you were gonna ask all these crazy-ass questions."

"It's not crazy cause I wanna know if my mama is gonna stay with a man who kills people."

"*No one said Kole is gonna kill anyone*," she nearly shouted. "I know you think you know everything, but you don't, Tariq. Not this time."

She felt guilty about lying to him, but he left her no choice. Admitting that Kole planned to commit murder was not something she could do. Not to her son. Not to anyone.

Tariq backed down. His shoulders slumped. His eyes were softer when he told her, "Mama, you're a good woman. I love you."

Dana's expression softened as well. "I love you too, baby."

"I appreciate everything Kole did for us," he stated. "But I'm starting to think you deserve better."

Dana was surprised by the comment. "Kole is a good man," she countered. "He treats me good. We never have problems."

"He is a good man," Tariq agreed. "But if he does something to try to get revenge, he could go to jail, or end up getting killed. I don't want you to be with somebody who goes to jail. You can be with a regular guy – not a thug."

This was the most candid conversation they ever had about Kole. Dana knew he was telling her right, but things weren't as black and white as he made it seem.

"Kole did things in the past that made him a thug," she said. "That was his old life. I wouldn't be with him if he was doing those things now. People can change. You know that."

Realizing she wasn't going to come around to his way of thinking, Tariq had no choice but to let it go.

He told her, "I can go to Texas Lutheran in the fall, if you want me to."

Her mouth fell open. "Why would you do that?"

"So I'll be here for you, if something happens."

His compassion made Dana's eyes water. "You're going to Florida," she said. "Don't think about changing that because of me. I'm fine, Tariq. Trust me."

"But what if–"

"If Kole and I break up," she said, cutting him off, "or whatever else you think might happen to him, it doesn't change your future. I won't let it. If I had been single for the past year, I'd still want you to go to the college that suits you best. You can't make decisions like that based on me needing you around."

"But–"

"Even if I was *unhealthy*," she stressed, "I'd get a nurse to come to the house to take care of me before I'd ask you to change your college plans. I love you, Tariq. I appreciate that you care so much about me, but it's time to live your life. You're still at an age when I make sacrifices for you – not the other way around."

She leaned closer and wrapped an arm around him. Tariq reciprocated the hug. As she stared over his shoulder, Dana fiercely fought an urge to break down and tell him everything.

CHAPTER 36

AT THIRTY MINUTES past midnight, she awakened with an overwhelming sense of urgency.

And *heat.*

She sat up in a panic, not realizing that she had dozed off and not understanding why she was so hot. Sweat not only beaded on her forehead, but her whole face glistened with perspiration. Her pillow was damp. Her heart pounded, as if struggling to free itself from her rib cage.

She reached for her phone as she struggled to make sense of the heat and her sudden state of agitation. Kole had not called her. She wiped her face and then held her hand against her chest, feeling her heartbeats.

Gradually she reclined on the bed, lying on her side. The sweat on her pillow had cooled. Initially it felt good against her hot skin, but after a minute it only felt wet. When she reached to turn the pillow over, an unexpected odor invaded her nasal passage. It was faint but unmistakable.

She smelled gasoline.

She sat up and brought the pillow closer to her face. It was damp, but the smell wasn't there. She sniffed under the pillow, her hands, her sheets. She didn't smell anything at all now. She had to accept that she never had.

BACKSLIDE 2

It was hard to believe she'd *dreamed* a scent, especially while awake, but there was no other explanation.

CHAPTER 37

SHE HADN'T MANAGED to return to sleep when Kole called an hour and a half later. Dana felt completely drained. But upon seeing his number on the caller ID, she was alert within an instant. She sat up, her stomach tight, her mouth dry.

"Hey," she breathed.

Kole told her, "I'm back. I'm home."

Dana's heart hammered. That was good news, but it was woefully inadequate. "What happened?" she asked.

"Do you remember what we talked about earlier?"

She hesitated. They had spoken about so much. After a moment she said, "No."

"Plausible deniability," he said. His speech was concise and emotionless. She might as well have been talking to a robot.

"I wanna know," she said. She checked to make sure her bedroom door was closed. It was, but that didn't mean Tariq wasn't ear-hustling on the other side.

"Everything's been taken care of," Kole informed her.

Her heart froze. Dana swallowed roughly. When her heart started to beat again, it was with a sickeningly slow pace. Every one of her organs felt like it was dying. She thought she might vomit.

Everything's been taken care of.

Did that mean Kole pulled the trigger himself? Even if he didn't, he told her that if he gave the orders, he'd still be responsible, as far as the law was concerned.

When she first met Kole, he told her about the bad things he'd done in the past. Dana accepted him, because that was his past, and he had changed. During the time it took for him to save her and Tariq from the MMG gang, Kole had to wield The Organization's manpower and firepower once again. But he made it through that harrowing chapter of their life without a single death.

Now Moon was dead, and the men responsible had been *taken care of*. Kole had taken it upon himself to become their judge, jury and executioner. In doing so, he could be arrested at any moment. Even if he stopped there, and he and Dana attempted to return to their normal lives, he could be apprehended twenty years from now. There was no statute of limitation for murder.

Hot tears rolled down Dana's cheeks. Was she prepared to look over her shoulder forever? Did she deserve this?

"Is it over?" she asked, her voice trembling.

"No," Kole said immediately, still robotic and without empathy. "I told you those men were only carrying out orders. Now I have to find the man or men who gave the orders."

Dana's heart skipped a beat. Her tears flowed even harder. "When, when you find them, will it be over?"

She squeezed her eyes closed. Jesus, was she making a deal with the devil? Kole had just killed an unknown number of people tonight. Why was she accepting this? Would she stay with him if he stopped after just one or two more? Where the hell would she draw the line? Five, six bodies?

"It should be over then," he said.

Dana didn't respond, but her breathing revealed how tormented her soul was.

Kole sighed and said, "I understand if you don't wanna be with me anymore. You're a good woman. You deserve better."

Dana's expression crumbled into something that resembled a sad clown face. Kole had just confirmed what Tariq said. But she didn't need either of them to tell her something she'd known all along. She didn't think she'd ever been more conflicted. She couldn't make a decision at that moment. She continued to cry softly but otherwise did not speak.

"I don't want you to come to Moon's funeral tomorrow," Kole said. "The people who killed him, they're still out there; in this city. I still don't know why they targeted Moon. They know The Organization will be at the funeral, and they might try something. I don't want you around that."

Despite it all, Dana found his need to protect her endearing. It was this need that had brought him into her life in the first place.

He told her, "I gotta go. Try to get some sleep."

Dana still couldn't find her voice.

Never one to handle emotions very well, his or hers, Kole told her, "Bye," and abruptly disconnected.

CHAPTER 38

KOLE WAS NOT surprised when Dana approached the first pew at Ebenezer Baptist Church the following afternoon. He sat next to Carla, who wore all black, including a veil. To her right was a host of other family members. Kole held Carla's hand as she stared straight ahead at the closed coffin less than twenty feet away. For the moment, she was composed. Beneath the veil, her skin was ashen, her eyes zombie-like.

Dana stood, unsure of herself. By comparison, she was beautiful, even with a dark, unflattering dress and no makeup. Kole wore a black suit, as did all of the men from The Organization. There were over two hundred of them in attendance. They were all armed, though the bulges beneath their suits were mostly imperceptible. They all wore the same look of anguish mixed with anger.

Kole didn't know if Dana's presence meant she had decided to stay with him, despite the blood on his hands, or if she was only there to pay her respects to Moon. He rose to his feet and reached for her hand. Her eyes watered as she offered it. He pulled her into his arms and embraced her fully.

They sat together, with Dana on his left and Carla on his right. Kole held both women's hands. It was unlikely his grip could stop their worlds from falling apart, but Kole's hands were large and very strong. He could certainly try.

CHAPTER 39

THE FUNERAL WAS beautiful.

The pastor was excellent, and he had been paid very well. His intonation alternated between commanding and whisper sweet during his sermon. He spoke about how God's grace and mercy was enough to save even the mightiest sinners. By the end of his speech, Kole believed his best friend really was up in heaven smiling down on them, rather than agonizing in hell due to Moon's many transgressions.

None of the bullets that took Moon's life had struck him in the head, so there was no question his casket would be opened. The funeral director stepped to Kole beforehand, because Kole had told him he did not want to bear witness to that portion of the service. He believed the image of his brother lying in the plush coffin would haunt his dreams for decades. Kole knew Moon was dead, and he did not need to offer his final goodbye to a lifeless body.

He and Dana were the only ones to leave the church at that moment.

Walking down the aisle hand-in-hand, with everyone seated and watching them, Dana had the eerie feel of a wedding – except rather than white, she wore black. And the spectators shed tears instead of offer cheers. She squeezed Kole's hand, and his grip around hers tightened.

She had come to the funeral to support him, but as usual, it was his unwavering strength that got her through an emotional freefall.

CHAPTER 40

IN ADDITION TO the motorcade that would lead the way to the cemetery, there were several police cars parked outside of the church. Kole wasn't too concerned about them. If they were detectives working on a racketeering case, they would've been in unmarked cars. They would've been taking pictures surreptitiously. That still might have been happening, but Kole was confident his men never left enough evidence for an indictment. No member of The Organization had ever been coerced to testify in court.

As for the black and whites, Kole guessed the police were there to keep the peace. They knew many of the mourners were angry; looking for an outlet for their frustration. Also, if Moon's killers did want to strike again, they'd be less likely to try anything with police on the scene.

Kole was quiet and contemplative during the procession to the cemetery. They rode in Dana's car, with him behind the wheel. There were many questions on Dana's heart, but she didn't think any of them were appropriate at the time. It would've been selfish to discuss their relationship while Kole was burying a man who meant more to him than anyone else.

Rather than focus on her dilemma, she asked, "Are you alright?"

Kole looked over at her as he followed the slow-moving taillights before him.

She placed a hand on his thigh. He put his hand over hers but didn't respond to her question. Dana didn't speak again for the rest of the ride.

CHAPTER 41

KOLE WAS NOT a pallbearer at the church, but he stepped to the back of the hearse when they arrived at the cemetery. Dana thought his suit fit him to a T. His shades were as dark as his sports coat. Beneath the dappled sunlight, he was clean and sharp, freshly shaved. He looked strong enough to carry the casket all by himself. The other pallbearers were dressed almost identically. Together, the six of them looked like the secret service.

Tempers began to boil over at the gravesite. Away from the holy grounds of the church, Dana heard mean cursing under their breath, vowing to avenge their fallen leader. As she stood shoulder to shoulder with Kole, Dana realized they looked to her man for guidance. She thought he'd leave her to offer them instruction, but he remained by her side throughout the final portion of the funeral.

The only time he excused himself was when a Hispanic gentleman approached, after they'd lowered Moon's casket into the grave. The crowd had started to disperse by then. Dana saw that the stranger was short in stature. He didn't wear a suit, but he had slacks with a tie. His button-down was a little too big. Dana could tell he wasn't the type to get dressed up very often. She saw a few tattoos poking out above his collar.

172

"I'll be back," Kole said before walking away with the man.

Dana turned and saw that Carla had not left her seat on the front row of the gravesite. There were family members comforting her. Dana was compelled to join them. As she approached the grieving widow, she couldn't help but look back at Kole. He led the newcomer away from the crowd; towards a large shade tree.

Kole had known Cres "Slimey" Ortiz for more than a decade, though their factions rarely worked together. Slimey was the leader of Tango Blast, a gang that originated in Texas prisons. His crew wasn't very large, only about fifty strong, but they were notoriously vicious. They had the backing of larger Tango Blast sets throughout the state.

Under the copious leaves of a maple tree, Kole turned to face him. Slimey had dark skin and a thin moustache. He was in his early thirties.

"What's up?" Kole asked him.

Over Slimey's shoulder, he saw Byrd watching them in the distance. He knew Byrd was skeptical of the Mexican gangster and would be there in an instant if things went awry. Further away, Kole saw a few police cars idling, with the officers behind the wheel. He paid them no mind. If they had come to arrest him, they would've done so by now.

"Yo, sorry about what happened to your boy," Slimey said.

Kole nodded, eyeing him warily. "Yeah. Me too."

"You heard something about it yet?" Slimey wanted to know. "You know anything about who did it?"

"I heard a few things," Kole said, unwilling to show his hand. "Why? You know something?"

"I don't know who pulled the trigger," Slimey replied, "but I know who ordered the hit."

"Oh yeah?" Kole's eyes narrowed. "And who might that be?"

"*The Woods*," Slimey said. "Guy named Trey running 'em."

Kole felt his temperature rising. One of the dead hitmen told him Trey had the word tattooed on his forearm. "What the hell is *the Woods*?"

"It's a gang," Slimey said, "Aryan nation, skinhead assholes. Think it's short for *peckerwoods*."

Kole wasn't surprised a white gang turned what was meant to be a slur into a term of endearment, because black people had done the same with the n-word.

"They ain't been in Overbrook Meadows that long," Slimey continued. "They was lowkey at first. But they been trying to expand. Trey, he wants to take over all the meth in the city. Been trying to push everybody else out. I heard he went to Moon and told him he didn't want nobody in The Organization selling meth. Moon told him to go to hell, and that's why they did him."

Kole shook his head slowly. He didn't doubt Slimey's story. It fit perfectly with everything he'd learned thus far. But he couldn't believe a racist faction had taken Moon out over something as negotiable as *turf*, and Moon never told anyone he was having trouble with them.

Had he been informed, Kole would've had his friend's back to the fullest, even if it meant going to war. He would've relished the opportunity to put a racist gang in its place.

"How you know that's why they killed Moon?" he asked Slimey.

"Because Trey told me the same thing," the OG said. "That was about a month ago. I told him to get the hell on, just like Moon did. He said he'd give me some time to reconsider. I put my boys on alert, waiting for that fool to try something, but he never did.

"I was hoping them white boys would go against us straight up, 'cause we got 'em outnumbered for sure. But they didn't play it like that. Trey hired somebody to kill Moon. He a coward for that. But at the same time, it let us know he serious about his little threats.

"I'm thinking, I prolly got a price on my head too," Slimey said, subconsciously looking over his shoulder. "If that fool would go after Moon like that, ain't none of us safe. Them white boys can't stand niggas or Mexicans. They think we gon' roll over now. But we, you know, we gotta stick together."

With every sentence, Slimey revealed more of the ugly truth behind Moon's death. And it was clear he wasn't delivering the information for noble reasons. This was all about self-preservation. Slimey feared for his life, and he knew there was safety in numbers. But Kole could care less about what happened to him or his gang. He would go after Trey – and whoever chose to stand with him – because of what he did to Moon. Period. Slimey had better learn to protect himself.

But since he had so much information, Kole hoped the Mexican OG could fill in the last piece of the puzzle.

"You know where I can find Trey?"

Slimey nodded. "Yeah. They got a dope house over by Camp Bowie. It's a duplex. They sell coke and meth outta there."

Kole's heart knocked. "Please tell me you know how to get there..."

Slimey grinned. "Yeah. I do."

Kole took the information and went to speak to Byrd before returning to Dana. She was eager to know what the stranger had told him, but Kole was tightlipped.

"I'ma catch a ride with Byrd," he said. "You need to go home, spend some time with Tariq. I know he's been worried about you."

Dana nodded but didn't immediately head to her car. Kole put an arm around her waist and walked her in that direction.

"You gon' be alright?" he asked as they stepped across the lush cemetery lawn.

"I'm more worried about you," she said. "I don't know what's going on anymore."

"When are you going back to work?" he asked.

"I told them I'd be there tomorrow."

He nodded.

When they made it to her car, Kole pulled the door open. He wrapped both arms around her before she got inside. Dana had been longing for his touch for so long, she nearly melted. She rested her head on his chest and locked both arms around his torso.

As they embraced, Kole watched the last of the mourners. Byrd was speaking to high-ranking members of The Organization. They all stole glances at Kole, waiting for him to give their fury direction.

"Will I see you tonight?" Dana asked him. She felt his muscles tense beneath her hands.

"I don't think tonight will be good for us," he replied. His voice was flat, without compassion. "Just got another lead on Moon's killers. I'ma try to find them tonight."

Dana's heart skipped a beat. Since last night, she found it impossible to come to terms with her conscious; what she knew about right and wrong, good and evil. Accepting the fact that the man she'd fallen in love with was a cold-blooded killer rocked her foundation. All she wanted was their old life back. But what if this new Kole was here to stay?

"Tell me it's over after this," she stated. "Please tell me this is the last of it."

Kole sighed. He was blown away by her loyalty, but it hurt to see how far she'd backslid. To be with him, she would accept the ugliest, bloodiest things he had to offer. She was no longer willing or able to tell him he'd crossed the line.

He backed away suddenly. He steeled his heart and looked her in the eyes.

"I don't think you should come by the house tonight." His eyes were as cold and sharp as icicles. "I don't know why you can't see it for yourself, but I ain't no good for you. Not right now. Maybe never."

He abruptly turned to rejoin his comrades.

An avalanche of emotions pummeled Dana as she watched him go. The most prevalent was anger that he would walk away from her like that. She didn't want to make her announcement at that time – certainly not at that location – but if he was going to shun her, he needed to know exactly how much he stood to lose. She didn't think she spoke loudly enough for him to hear her, but Kole stopped dead in his tracks when she said, *"I'm pregnant."*

He turned slowly, his eyes as frigid as they were a moment ago. But now the irritation was singed with doubt. He stared into her fierce, brown eyes for an eternity before returning to her. His intensity made Dana back further into her car. Her heart thundered.

Kole sneered when he asked her, "Why you saying that shit?"

Dana had envisioned a myriad of responses when she revealed the news to her boyfriend, but that comment was nowhere near her radar. Then again, she didn't expect to tell him at a cemetery, after his best friend had been laid to rest, and Kole had his mind set on bloody murder.

She pushed off the car and met him head on. Her nostrils flared when they were chest to chest.

"You said you're no good for me," she snarled. "So I thought you should know."

Kole's hot breaths singed her forehead. His look of disgust intensified.

"Is this your way to stop me? You lying to get me to back down?"

Dana stood her ground. "Why the hell would I lie about something like that?"

Kole took a deep breath and exhaled roughly. She continued to stare deeply into his eyes. What she saw made her question every intimate moment they shared in the past month. Kole not only looked like he didn't want to be a father, but he appeared angry enough to reach into her womb and destroy the new life by hand if he could.

177

"How–" His mouth snapped shut, biting off his words.

Dana suspected he was going to ask how she managed to conceive naturally at the age of forty. But Kole never finished the statement.

Instead his face hardened again. He shook his head and told her, "Don't make no difference. I'm still doing what I gotta do for my brother."

Dana knew he'd say that. She couldn't formulate a response before he turned and marched to his men, who congregated near the gravesite. He did not check to see if Dana got in her car, but some of his soldiers did. They looked away when they saw the rage in her eyes; the raw fury.

Dana had to fight her way through a whirlwind of disappointment and desolation before she got in her car and fled the cemetery.

CHAPTER 42

Explosive
Miraculous
Molecular fusion divides
One soul from another
As our DNA combines
Bringing forth the most beauty
This world can provide
Without question
I know this child is mine
And this woman
Has steadfastly stood by my side
Though my demons
Surround me
They claw and they bite
Through clenched teeth
I fight them
Blood pressure on the rise
Sword in hand
I yearn for peace
Knowing each day I might die
Surely I'm cursed
But this blessing
Comes from the Most High
Will I survive
Or never look upon

This precious new life?

AFTER SPEAKING WITH his men, Kole slipped inside Byrd's car, riding shotgun. Byrd had been studying his friend's mood since Kole spoke with Dana at the cemetery.

Now that they were alone, he asked him, "You good, man?"

Without looking at him, Kole nodded. "Yeah."

Byrd knew he was hiding something, but he didn't push it. As far as he knew, Kole only shared his innermost thoughts with one person. That man just happened to be in a brand-new coffin.

Instead he asked, "You wanna swing by the church to pick up your ride?"

Kole nodded. "Yeah. And then we need to go change, get out of these suits."

"You got some news?" Byrd asked. He drove slowly down the gravelly path leading to the cemetery's exit.

"Slimey had some info," Kole stated as he loosened his tie. He relayed everything he learned from the Mexican gangster.

When he was done, Byrd said, "Damn. He know everything."

"Yup," Kole agreed. "Now we got a location."

"We headed that way after we change?"

Kole nodded.

"You don't wanna wait till it gets dark?"

Kole shook his head. "I'm not gon' have a shootout in broad daylight. If we spot Trey, we'll follow him, hopefully get him somewhere secluded."

"But we don't know what he looks like."

Kole's solution to that was simple. He barely gave Dana's news any thought as he said, "I got no problem laying 'em all down."

His demeanor lit a fire in his cohort's belly. Byrd loved it when they didn't have to be careful about who got shot.

"What if Slimey trying to play us?" Byrd cautioned.

"You think he'll tell Trey we coming for him?"

Byrd shrugged. "Wouldn't be the first time that fool pulled a double-cross."

"That's why we gon' take it slow," Kole replied. "What time is it now, three o'clock? I got nothing better to do than sit on that duplex all day. If they're expecting us, we'll see 'em getting ready."

"And then what?"

"We'll bring *more* guns and more men and massacre all of 'em. Then we'll wait a few weeks and pay Slimey a visit."

Byrd's nostril's flared. He could already smell the gun smoke. Moon had been an excellent leader of The Organization, but he and Kole didn't have the same tenacity when it came to murder and mayhem. Byrd missed the days when Kole was in charge. He became quiet and contemplative as they exited the cemetery.

"They sent him off pretty good though, didn't they?"

Kole's eyes narrowed. His jaws clenched before he said, "Yeah. They did. The church, funeral home, they took care of him. If I die tonight, I want the same thing for me."

Byrd blinked back tears before saying, "Yeah, man. Me too. I want it just like that."

CHAPTER 43

BYRD DROPPED KOLE off at the church with instructions to pick him up from his home an hour later in a car they could get *dirty*. To acquire this vehicle, Byrd had several sources who would make a car accessible to "steal" and not call the police until Byrd abandoned it after their mission.

When he got home, Kole had time to ponder the news Dana had given him and how it would factor into his actions that night. He did not believe she was lying to him. Ever since he came clean about his involvement in The Organization, honesty had been the cornerstone of their relationship. At the moment, he considered her pregnancy a remarkable stroke of bad luck, rather than a blessing. But he sensed that opinion might change in the months to come.

For now, his options were simple: Stay home and be a responsible future-dad or risk his life and freedom to avenge Moon.

Simple.

As simple as trying to decide whether to cut off his right or left leg.

"*Fuuuuck*!" he shouted as he marched to his bedroom.

He was forty-two years old. He'd gone his whole life without producing a seed. Now he was set to have an infant in his arms at forty-three. He'd be 61 when the child graduated high school. If Kole ate right and remained fit, he'd see his son or daughter through college, marriage and a first grandchild before he checked out.

He caught himself and shook his head dismally. The fact that he was calculating all of this meant he was mentally preparing himself for fatherhood. If so, he should stay home tonight. Even though Moon wasn't there to give his advice, Kole could hear his best friend's voice.

Listen, man. Don't be doing all this shit on my account. Let Byrd and them handle it. It's plenty of them. Byrd knows what he's doing. You got an address. Pass it on and step back. You done got your hands dirty enough already. Last night went like you wanted, but flatlining niggas two nights in a row is pushing it.

Those words sounded so much like Moon, Kole's heart bled all over again.

And then it hardened, as did his eyes.

He stepped into his closet and quickly replaced his funeral garb with black jeans, a black tee and a long-sleeved black thermal. The thermal immediately felt too warm for the summertime temperature. But Kole would always prefer to err on the side of caution, rather than fashion. If tonight's stakeout led to gunplay, his gunshot residue would be on an easily-discarded garment, rather than on his forearms.

Mindful of evidence, Kole selected his favorite murder weapon; a Smith & Wesson center fire revolver with a 6 ½ inch barrel. The pistol kicked like a mule, but when it came to stopping power, few handguns could compare. Plus with a revolver, there would be no shell casings left at the scene.

His outfit complete, Kole went to the front room and sat silently. He thought about Moon but would not allow thoughts of Dana and her pregnancy to enter his mind and cloud his judgment. Five minutes later, he peeked through the curtains and saw an unfamiliar sedan parked in front of his home. He pulled his cellphone from his pocket and texted Byrd.

That you?

His friend replied, Yup

Kole exited the house and climbed into the passenger seat. He was pleased to see Byrd dressed similarly in all black.

"How many men you got on standby?" Kole asked as he secured his seatbelt.

"Shit, all of 'em," Byrd replied.

Kole nodded his approval and settled in for the ride.

CHAPTER 44

UNLIKE THE SOUTH side, the west side of Overbrook Meadows was mostly upscale. The stretch of Camp Bowie Boulevard that ran from Merrick Street to Arch Adams was one of few thoroughfares in the city that was still paved with bricks. Old-fashioned street lights in the area furthered the warm glow of vintage city life. On either side of the road, high-end strip malls and eateries paid top dollar to maintain their leases.

A dozen miles west of the historic district, Las Vegas Trail offered a completely different view of the west side. There, more than half of the residents lived below the poverty line. Drugs and violence ran rampant. Kole didn't have many connections in the neighborhood, because it was mostly white. But when it came to criminality, he was as much at home there as he was on the south.

Following Slimey's directions, Byrd drove casually past the duplex in question. It was located on the corner of a four-way intersection. That left four paths for interception and four avenues of escape. Byrd drove two more blocks before performing a U-turn and pulling to a stop on the opposite side of the street. The house he parked in front of appeared to be vacant. The men were quiet as they surveyed the scene.

The duplex wasn't much to look at. It was in need of fresh paint, and the lawn was a little overgrown. Two rusted bicycle frames decayed in the middle of the yard. The shades on all of the windows were drawn. There was a blue pickup parked in front of one of the garages. There wasn't much pedestrian or vehicle traffic at the time, but Kole suspected that would change by nightfall, if the duplex catered to the local junkies, like Slimey reported.

"What you think about this house?" Byrd asked, eyeing the residence on their right.

"Looks vacant," Kole replied. "You thinking about posting up in there?"

"You don't think it's a good idea?"

Realizing they could monitor the duplex perfectly from that location, Kole nodded. "Yeah. That's good thinking. But if the electricity's not on, it'll be hotter than a sauna."

Byrd looked over Kole's outfit and said, "Yeah, you'd be sweating your ass off."

"I ain't worried about no sweat," Kole stated. "I'm worried about passing out from dehydration."

"I got a guy who can turn the electricity on, if it's off," Byrd said.

Kole wasn't surprised by that. "You got a guy for everything. It's no wonder Moon liked you so much."

Byrd grinned at the compliment. "This dude," he said, "he works for the electric company. If you ever need him to rig your meter at home, let me know. Me and my girl was getting free electricity for a year before they caught on."

"I might take you up on that," Kole said. He checked out the duplex again before returning his attention to the vacant house. "Let's kick the back door, see if anybody's home."

CHAPTER 45

KOLE KICKED THE door in on his first attempt. He knew the place was vacant the moment they entered; the heat was so stifling. But they checked every room anyway, to make sure no crackhead had fallen asleep and possibly succumbed to the heat.

They met up in the front room. Both were already sweating.

"It's so hot in here, don't make no damn sense!" Byrd complained. "It stinks too!"

Kole agreed on both accounts. The June temperature was over a hundred that day. It was at least 30 degrees hotter inside the house. The place was unfurnished, and the last residents had left their mark in every room. The carpets were soiled, probably permanently. There were trash bags left behind, assorted debris on nearly every surface.

"I'll call my man," Byrd said, "but I think we should wait in the car."

"I sure as hell ain't waiting in here," Kole agreed.

On a whim, he flipped one of the light switches on the way out. Both men were surprised when an overhead lamp came on.

"Would you look at that," Kole muttered.

"Guess this is meant to be," Byrd said, returning to the front room. He found the controls for the AC and turned it on. A few seconds later they heard a mechanical hum as the unit came to life.

"I'm still waiting in the car," Kole told him.

"I'm right behind you," Byrd said, wiping his brow.

It took thirty minutes for the AC to push enough Freon to get the house somewhat comfortable. While they waited, the men didn't see any activity at the green and white duplex. Not one visitor or even a stray dog crossed the lawn.

When they returned to the vacant house, Kole found a paint bucket and lugged it to the front window. He took a seat and confirmed he could watch both sides of the duplex with only one blind parted. He rose to his feet and met Byrd in the kitchen.

"Water running?" he asked.

Byrd shook his head. "No, but I got a guy..."

"Don't even worry about it," Kole said with a chuckle. "Why don't you call some of the boys over? I was gonna wait till later, but now that we got this place..."

"How many?" Byrd asked, reaching for his phone.

"A carload should do for now."

"Bet."

"Tell 'em to bring some water," Kole said. "Lots of it. And some food too. No telling how long we gon' be here."

"A'ight."

"And I need you to move the car," Kole ordered. "I don't care where. See if you can make it back through that alley." He gestured towards the back yard.

Byrd nodded. "Anything else?"

"Just steer clear of that duplex. Don't wanna get them boys nervous."

"Naw," Byrd agreed. His smile was sinister. "We wouldn't want that."

CHAPTER 46

TWO HOURS LATER, the sun had mostly relinquished its hold on the warm skies above Overbrook Meadows. The vacant house sitting catacorner to the green and white duplex brimmed with anxious energy. Kole and his crew were well fed and well-armed. They all sported the same outfits; black pants, black tops and black gloves. Each man was pissed and eager, after receiving positive news from the surveillance.

With sunset, the neighborhood had sprung to life all around them. There were children playing in nearby lawns. They heard people shouting, music from some of the passing motorists.

Even better, the duplex was bustling with activity. Kole had seen well over a dozen people enter the property, either disappearing inside the unit on the right or the one on the left. Each visitor concluded their business and exited within five minutes. Twice Kole had seen men exit one duplex and disappear inside the adjacent one. Both of these men were white. Even from a distance, their description matched what Kole would expect from a white supremacist gang.

"They running both houses at the same time," Byrd noticed, peering over his shoulder.

"Not a bad set up," Kole said. "I wonder if they slanging the same product from both."

"You can't tell by the customers?"

"Coke heads and meth heads look the same to me," Kole stated. "I know they're not selling to *dealers*. Everybody going through there looks strung out."

"You haven't seen any cars, other than that blue truck?"

"Nope. And it hasn't moved. I been waiting for them to re-up. I know somebody's gotta go get the new supply – unless they get it delivered."

"How many you think we need to take 'em?" Byrd wondered. He was squatting now, looking Kole in the eyes.

Kole looked back at the other three men in the room. There was a fourth soldier elsewhere in the house.

"I think we need at least four men per door," he told Byrd. "I don't think it's very many of 'em in there. I've seen two of them. The one on the right, when he goes to the other door, he hurries back, so I think he's alone. The other one, he stayed on the right side for thirty minutes, so I know there's a third guy on the left. Maybe more.

"What we need is more intel," Kole said. "We can hit the place, but if we miss our chance to get Trey, I ain't gon' feel good about none of this. We need to scoop up one of them fiends." As he spoke, another junkie rounded the corner and headed for the duplex.

Kole looked back and locked eyes with a thug he'd known for years.

"Yo, Lemon."

The lanky gangster stepped forward, eyes bright, ready for action.

"You see that gal over there?" Kole asked him.

Lemon leaned down and peered through the cracked window blind. "Yeah. What's up with her?"

"I need you to snatch her, find out who in that house, if she know anything about Trey."

"Fa sho."

"You might have to hold onto her, till we get ready to run up in there."

"A'ight." Lemon asked one of the men he arrived with, "Yo, where the keys?"

A goon named Head tossed them to him.

Before Lemon took off, Kole told him, "Don't hurt her. I know you tend to go overboard sometimes."

He was thinking of the last mission he and Lemon were on. No one was supposed to get hurt when they robbed a couple dozen MMG dope houses, but Lemon found cause to shoot a man in the stomach. The victim survived, but Kole heard he'd wear a colostomy bag for the rest of his life.

Lemon laughed, reading his mind. His gold teeth gleamed in the dimly lit home.

"You know that wasn't my fault, Kole. Dude reached. What was I supposed to do?"

"Well, that fiend don't weigh 80 pounds soaking wet," Kole said. "Shouldn't be nothing she can do to make you go ignant."

Lemon continued to grin at him. "Hmph. We shall see," he said and headed for the back door.

Kole shook his head and returned his attention to the window. Somewhere behind him Byrd chuckled.

Kole had eyes on the duplex when the junkie exited the unit on the left and disappeared around the corner. It didn't take ten minutes before he got a call on his cellphone.

"Yeah."

"It's me," Lemon said. "Got her."

Kole could hear his hostage whimpering in the background. Before he had to ask, Lemon told him, "She alright, just a little shook up is all. Ain't you?"

The girl pleaded with him. *"Please let me go. I don't know anything else!"*

"Calm down, yuck mouth," Lemon told her. "I told you I'ma let yo ass go." To Kole he said, "Everything's like you think. Them Woods been running this house for about three months.

191

They selling coke out the door on the right, meth out the left. She say it's only three of them in there. They armed, but they not ready for what we got coming. Shouldn't be no trouble."

Kole's breaths came quick and hot.

"She said Trey's not there," Lemon went on. "But he'll be here tonight to collect the money and drop off more product. The way they moving it, she said it shouldn't be more than a couple of hours."

Kole checked his phone display. It was almost 10 pm. He asked him, "She know what Trey's driving?"

"A red truck," Lemon informed him. "What is it about white boys and pickups?" he wondered. "How the hell you gon' bring a crew, if some shit go down?"

Kole was too apprehensive to find humor in that. "She'll know the truck when it gets here?" he asked.

"Say, you'll know that fool's truck when it gets here?" Lemon asked his new friend.

"*Yes*," she bawled. "But I can't stay with you the whole time. I'll be back. I got, I gotta drop this off, before my boyfriend come looking for me."

"Naw, baby, you ain't going nowhere," Lemon told her. "If I let you go, and you snitch, I'll have to come looking for you. You know you don't want that."

"*I swear I won't tell!*"

"Hush up with all that." Lemon's voice was surprisingly tranquil. "You gon' sit right there till Trey gets here. After you point him out, I'll turn you loose."

"*Please, sir! I won't tell! I swear!*"

"*Gal, please close your mouth*," Lemon implored her. "You ain't got one good tooth left. Gon' make me throw up."

"Ask her if Trey usually comes alone," Kole instructed him.

Lemon repeated the question. Kole heard the girl's response: "No. He usually comes with Less."

"Just one guy?" Lemon asked.

"Yeah," the girl said. "Usually just them two."

"You heard her?" Lemon said into the phone.

"I heard her," Kole confirmed. "You cool with keeping her till they get here?"

"Yeah, I'm good," Lemon said. "I'm parked down the street. If somebody get too close, I'll push her head down in my lap. I'm sure won't nobody bat an eye, if it looks like she giving me head."

"What about the laws?" Kole asked. "I ain't seen none pass through. You?"

"Naw," Lemon said. "That's weird, ain't it. By my house, they everywhere. Nigga can't even blow his nose without getting hemmed up. But over here, they letting these white folks get away with *anything*. Thought it was supposed to be a crackdown."

"Look like the crackdown only applies to brown people," Kole surmised. "Holler at me if you lay eyes on Trey before we do."

"No doubt," Lemon responded.

In the background, his informant continued to go against the grain. "*Pleeeease, sir*. I promise I won't tell nobody. Just let—"

"Hey, now, I done promised my homey I wasn't gon' hurt you," Lemon said away from the phone. "But if you keep it up—" He disconnected before Kole could hear the rest of his threat.

Kole returned the phone to his pocket and turned towards his crew. He relayed the information Lemon had given him.

"No laws, huh?" Byrd said. "Sounds like an easy in and out."

"Don't get too confident," Kole cautioned him.

"Wanna bring in more guys?"

Kole nodded. Counting him and Byrd, they were six deep. If Trey brought the man named Less with him, the opposition would only have five men. Another carload on Kole's side should guarantee success.

He told Byrd, "Four more should do it. Tell 'em to bring some gas cans. We gon' need plenty gas..."

CHAPTER
47

Thunderous
Murderous fury
Volcanic
Hot lava
Like cocaine in the veins
He who planned it
Shall suffer a fate worse than those condemned to hell
Where the weeping and gnashing of teeth serves them well
Pray tell
Who did it?
Who foolishly awakened this beast?
Dark and vicious
Dead eyes like a wolf as he creeps
Through this portal
That separates the blessed from the damned
Breath like fire
Much closer to Satan than man

THE NEXT COUPLE of hours passed dreadfully slowly, like watching a spider spin an enormous web. The second crew arrived an hour after Byrd made the call. They came equipped with assault rifles, bad attitudes and several cans of gasoline. With nine killers in the house, the AC couldn't put out enough cool air to override the testosterone.

None of the men from The Organization were overtly racist, but hearing that a white-power gang was responsible for Moon's death stoked their black pride. They couldn't wait to kill every *cracker* inside the duplex. Kole told them patience is a virtue, and their emotions could be a hindrance. They had to handle this assignment with the same discipline they always practiced – even more so, because this hit was sure to generate a lot of attention.

Kole designated one soldier to be the *burn man*. If the detectives who came to investigate the homicide were any good, they would realize the vacant house was a base of operations. At midnight the burn man soaked every room in the house with gasoline, excluding the living room and the kitchen. By then Byrd had opened every window, but the fumes were still heavy. When they left to raid the duplex, the burn man would hang back and douse the remaining rooms before lighting the fire. Till then, most of the soldiers retreated to the kitchen, where the backdoor was open, and the breeze was fresh.

At 12:45 Kole finally got the call he'd been waiting for.

He answered with a gruff, "Yeah."

"This him coming up the street," Lemon reported.

Sure enough, two headlights illuminated the street on Kole's left. The beams were followed by a rumbling motor and finally a red pickup. The truck had both windows down. Kole could see the occupants well enough to confirm they were both white, but not much more than that.

"You can see us from where you at?" Kole asked Lemon.

"I got eyes on the truck and your spot."

"You can cut your friend loose and fall in line when you see us roll out," Kole instructed him.

"Save some for me," Lemon said.

Kole disconnected without promising he would.

He returned the cellphone to his pocket, his full attention on the red truck. Byrd crouched next to him, peering through the opening in the blinds.

"That's him?" he asked, his voice hushed.

Kole nodded. "That's our boy." His blood ran ice cold. He had to force himself to take deep, slow breaths. "Divide the team, so we can hit both units at the same time," he told Byrd.

"How long we waiting?"

"We can head out as soon as they go inside."

"Which side you going in?"

"You know who I'm following," Kole said, not looking at him.

Byrd rose to his feet and went to corral the troops.

Kole remained at the window a while longer, long enough to get a look at Trey before Moon's killer disappeared inside the duplex. The man didn't look to be more than thirty-five. He was tall and thin, with a buzzcut and a full sleeve of tattoos on both arms. He didn't look like much, not powerful enough to take out someone like Moon, but there was no doubt he had done just that.

Kole backed away from the window for the last time and joined the men at the back door.

CHAPTER 48

THE NIGHT AIR was humid when Kole and his team left the vacant house, marching low and quickly, ski masks pulled down. Half of them crossed the street immediately, while the other half remained on the right side. Many of the houses on the street had interior lights on, but thankfully no one was chilling in the front yard.

There were pedestrians up ahead; some near the duplex and some beyond it. They would be alarmed when The Organization drew near, but by then it would be too late to send a warning.

Kole was near the front of his line, but he was cognizant of things going on in the rear. He stopped and turned at the sound of hurried footsteps. He started to raise the barrel of his weapon when he saw a dark figure approaching. But the man was dressed like them, and he smoothly fell in line. Kole wasn't certain it was Lemon until the newcomer grinned, flashing a mouthful of gold.

Both units in the duplex were identical, with a front door and another around the back. They had two stories but no balconies or breezeways. Kole's men divided a second time when they reached the building, with half going to cover the exits. In the alley behind the duplex, a sudden scream cut through the silent night.

It was female, and it was loud.

Kole suspected some of his men had surprised one of the locals. Whatever the case, they shut her up quickly. But the damage was done. Before Kole reached the door on the left, he saw the curtains part on the window directly ahead. The face that appeared in the opening was white. Two baby blue eyes widened to the size of dinner plates when he saw the destruction headed their way. The man scarcely had time to shout a warning to his partners before Kole gave orders of his own.

"Go! Now! Hit it!"

He led the charge, slamming into the door with the force of a linebacker. A dozen possible scenarios flashed through his mind as he breached the entrance. Kole could've encountered more men than expected, dogs, children. He could've come face to face with the barrel of a shotgun. In an instant, he decided none of that mattered. Despite cautioning his soldiers against their emotions, Kole's rage was blinding. He looked every bit like the boogeyman when he crashed into the house with a horde of legions behind him.

He roared as he raised his weapon, but neither of the pale faces standing before him was Trey. Kole spotted the skinny punk making a run for it. Up the stairs his target bounded, taking them three at a time. Kole was right on his ass. He barely noticed the gunfire erupting all around him. He did not feel the blood splatter from the Woods' first casualty, even though he was within three feet of the victim when he got hit.

On the upper level, Kole saw the house was barely furnished. Trey's breaths were hot and audible as he scrambled around a corner and disappeared inside one of the bedrooms. Below them, gunfire continued to ring out loud and free. Kole knew there were only two enemies left down there, and they probably hadn't made it to a weapon. He didn't fault his men for the overkill.

Kole heard a loud crash of glass up ahead. He knew his target had thrown caution to the wayside in an attempt to escape his destiny. Sure enough, when Kole entered the bedroom he found it empty. The window on the far side was shattered, with most of the blinds hanging outside of the jagged orifice. Kole gave no forethought to the artery-slicing glass as he gave chase. He dove headfirst, creating an even bigger hole as he smashed through.

On the other side, the atmosphere was hot again, much hotter than before. Somehow the sun had descended directly atop the chaotic street. Kole heard more shouts and gunfire, coming from both units. He hit the ground with a **THUD!** and allowed his momentum to roll him forward. He was on his feet immediately. So was his prey. The white man sprinted full out, both hands empty. His tattooed arms cut the air like an Olympian. Within seconds Kole was gaining on him, so he didn't bother shooting him in the back.

To his left, Kole saw the unnatural sunlight was actually the house he and his men had vacated. He knew the burn man had doused it with gasoline, but he didn't expect it to erupt so quickly. The house looked like it had been on fire for hours, rather than seconds. Huge orange flames licked the night sky, creating dark plumes of smoke that blocked the moon.

Trey screamed when he heard the footsteps draw nearer. He made a quick left and leapt a chain-link fence with hardly any effort. Kole reached for him but couldn't snag his shirt before he went over. The fence gained Trey a three second advantage, but Kole cut the distance again when he made it to the other side. He reached again. This time he snagged the back of Trey's collar, just as they reached an overgrown alley.

Kole halted his forward progress with a ferocious yank. The white man squealed, both out of surprise and the sudden loss of oxygen. Trey's arm's flailed wildly as he fell backwards. He landed hard on a pile of twisted branches and debris. Kole brought up a foot to stomp his face, but the man rolled quickly to the left, and Kole's sneaker struck the ground. He was amazed when Trey sprang to his feet. He was even more surprised when the man took a swing at him, but Kole's shock didn't dull his reflexes. He rolled away from the punch and caught him with a picture-perfect counter; a right hook to the jaw.

Trey's knees buckled. Kole was on him before he hit the ground. He delivered two more strikes to the head and fully mounted him when he fell. Rather than continue to pummel him, Kole's hands snaked around his neck and clamped down with the strength of a vice. He thought he'd rendered his foe unconscious, but Trey fought valiantly to free himself. He bucked his hips. He twisted his body in awkward, contortionist angles. He threw punches at Kole's face, but the angle was off. His blows were useless. With each swing, his strength steadily drained.

"Ack!"

Finally panic set in, as Kole drove the back of his head into the hard earth. Trey's eyes bulged. Bright red blood vessels filled the whites of his eyes like spider veins. Kole snarled as he watched them burst. Trey slapped at his forearms, clawed at his gloved hands. He reached around for an object, a weapon.

Anything.

But all he found was small twigs and grass.

"This is for Moon," Kole growled. It was important for his enemy to know that, before he reached his final destination in hell.

With Trey's eyes already bugged, it was hard to tell if he reacted to the news, so Kole said it again.

"This is for what you did to Moon, you sorry sonofabitch!"

Trey's mouth fell open. His tongue lolled. His nostrils flared, frantically seeking one precious breath of air. But all he received was the demented stare of his killer. Kole was as black as the night. The whites of his eyes and his bared teeth were the only thing visible. His heart roared at the same pace as his enemy's.

He squeezed.

Hard enough to bend a pipe.

Much harder than necessary.

"Ughk!"

He had killed many, but this was only the second time Kole choked a man to death. The feeling was surreal.

Powerful.

He stared into Trey's eyes as the movements beneath him gradually came to a stop. He felt the cold touch of death approaching. He felt the lightning in his foe's chest, the muted thunder as his heart accepted its fate. He felt everything the man ever was and everything he ever would be escape his body by way of a grief-stricken ghost.

Kole inhaled deeply, taking Trey's soul into his chest.

Thirty seconds later, he could not bring himself to release the grip on his throat. He could see Moon's killer was lifeless. The whites of Trey's eyes were completely red, matching his purplish face. Three thick veins snaked across his enemy's forehead like tree branches. All four of his limbs were limp, flat on the ground.

Trey was as dead as the legend he murdered, but Kole didn't release him until Byrd and Lemon grabbed his gorilla-size arms and pulled him off the corpse.

"Come on," Byrd told him. "We good. Got 'em all. Time to go."

To his recollection, Kole had never blacked out in the midst of a battle. But for the life of him, he couldn't recall how he made it out of that alley and into the waiting getaway car.

All he saw was fire; flames so intense he thought he was entering hell – and smoke so dark it blackened the whole sky.

CHAPTER 49

Raw
Unnatural
Untamed and unkempt
Plunging to the depths
Of her heart
And her soul
Dark passion blossoms
To the height of this tragedy
Tearfully longing for more
Yet resistant
Dueling spirits
Fully conscious of this calamity
Stretched and bent
Face down
He annihilates the surface
Of her desire
Her labia
A cocoon of safety
Purposefully
He breaks it
Her essence
Is her dowry
Greedily
He takes it
Submission

The only option
All willpower
Forsaken

KOLE WAS NOT pleased to see Dana's car in the garage when he finally made it home at 2:30 am. He pulled in next to her and sat behind the wheel for a while after the garage door descended behind him. With a deep sigh, he exited the vehicle and stepped inside his home.

His muscles were weary. He was sore in more places than he could count. No more than five minutes passed between the time he burst into the Woods' duplex and the moment Byrd pulled him off Trey's twisted body. But in that time span, he had jumped from a second-floor window, sprinted full out and fought a man to the death. There were cuts and human scratches on his arms and back. He felt more bruises on his neck and face.

Instead of the black outfit he had on when he left the house that night, Kole wore a white tee-shirt with blue jeans. Every item of clothing he wore during the raid was now burnt to a crisp, most likely still smoldering in a car fire on the west side of town.

Kole stepped stiffly through his home and encountered Dana in the front room. She sat on the couch wearing scrubs, so he knew she'd been to work that day. Her eyes were glued to the television. When they swam in Kole's direction, they widened as she took in his demeanor and battle scars. Kole made eye contact with her before walking to the bar. Dana's eyes were red and puffy from crying. They filled with more tears as she stared at him.

She didn't ask any questions, and Kole didn't volunteer any answers. He rounded the bar and selected a bottle of aged whiskey. Rather than heft the bottle to his lips, he placed a drinking glass on the bar and poured three fingers. He downed it as Dana watched him. He refilled the glass with the same amount.

On the television, Channel Six's star reporter Chad Collins sat behind his desk with breaking news. The handsome reporter's tone was as grim as the developing story. Kole was interested in what he had to say. Gradually, Dana's attention returned to the television as well.

"So far, five bodies have been recovered from what police are saying is one of the most gruesome crime scenes in recent memory," the reporter said. "We have Gabriella Sands live at the scene..."

Gabriella was a fair-skinned Hispanic woman with dark, curly hair. She stood strategically at an intersection with a firetruck in the background. Beyond the firetruck was the remnants of a home that had been completely destroyed by fire. The charcoaled remains were still smoking. Firemen and other investigators collected evidence from the scene.

Gabriella was poised, her voice confident. "Chad, I'm standing at the twenty-seven hundred block of Tinsley Lane; a normally quiet neighborhood, but tonight neighbors were awakened to the sound of gunfire at approximately 12:45 am."

The camera feed switched to an interview of one such neighbor; a middle-age woman with thick glasses and dirty-blonde hair.

"It sounded like a war was going on – right outside my window!" the woman exclaimed. "First I heard a scream and then a lot of gunfire. I looked outside and saw a bunch of people, had to be twenty of them. They were all dressed in black. They were running from that house on the corner," she said and pointed.

Her eyes widened when she said, "They had *ski masks* on! They had guns; *big ones*. They did all the shooting, at whoever was in that house over there. Then they run off, all in the same direction. I didn't see what kind of car they got into. By then I saw the fire across the street. The whole house was lit up like a bonfire. I think they had something to do with that too!"

After a pause, the view returned to Gabriella on the scene.

"The house she's referring to is the one right behind me," the reporter stated. "This house was still on fire when the first responders arrived on the scene. The shooting occurred at the home across the street."

As she spoke, the camera panned in that direction. Dana saw a green duplex with white trim. There was a blue truck and a red one parked outside. The place was crawling with police and crime scene investigators. Bright lights from emergency vehicles had the place lit up like it was midday.

"Multiple witnesses have confirmed the shooters were dressed in black," the reporter went on. "They wore ski masks, and there was at least a dozen involved. Most of the victims were found inside the duplex. The police are saying this was definitely a targeted attack, but at this time they have not identified a motive or the identity of any of the victims."

The camera swam back to the attractive reporter, and she said, "Some of the neighbors, who requested not to be identified, have told us the duplex is known for drug and gang activity. The police have declined to confirm that information or speculate as to whether that played a part in tonight's shooting.

"At this time investigators are also unwilling to provide information about the fire that appears to have occurred at the same time as the shooting. The first firefighters arrived at 1 am and found this home fully engulfed in flames. Police officers arrived minutes later and made the grisly discovery across the street.

"We spoke to one witness who says she was near both crime scenes at the time of the shooting. We were not able to conduct a full interview before she was taken to the police station for questioning. But she did give us *some* information.

"According to the witness, she encountered a group of men in the alley behind the duplex before the first shot rang out. She said she was frightened, and she screamed. One of the masked gunmen looked her in the eyes and told her to run away. Less than ten seconds later, she said gunfire erupted behind her. She did not look back to see what was going on."

The view switched to a split screen of Chad in the newsroom and Gabriella at the crime scene.

"This is a horrible story," he told her. "With so many shooters involved, this certainly sounds like a well-orchestrated effort."

"That's one thing the police have acknowledged," Gabriella replied. "This shooting was definitely planned. The house fire might have been a diversionary tactic. Investigators are not saying if the fire was caused by arson. But as I stand here now, Chad, the smell of gasoline is strong. It certainly appears these two crime scenes are connected."

"Thank you, Gabriella," Chad told her. To the viewers, he said, "We'll have more on this story as it develops."

They went to commercial, and Dana's attention returned to her man. He was pouring more alcohol into a glass that seemed to have no bottom. She didn't realize it when he first entered the room, but the smell of gasoline had followed him from his late-night endeavors. Kole's skin was dark, his eyes low and red. Dana saw faint bruises on his face and arms. Her heart skipped several beats as she rose from her seat. She felt lightheaded. Her legs didn't want to cooperate, but she got them moving in Kole's direction.

Her eyes blurred when she approached the bar. She wiped the tears away, so she could see him clearly. She reached and pressed a hand against her chest. She didn't think her heart had ever beat this wildly for this long.

Kole's hair was unkempt, with a few blades of dead grass embedded. He had scratches on his neck and arms. Some had started to form long welts. A closer examination revealed the majority of the scars were actually cuts; from a knife or possibly glass. One laceration ran from the corner of his mouth to the side of his neck. None of the cuts were very deep, but the sheer volume made him look like he'd been tortured.

Kole's eyes were unreadable and without compassion. One of his large hands gripped the bottle of liquor. The other brought the glass back to his lips. He swallowed the intoxicants down without a grimace. Dana reached to stop him when he started to pour more.

He looked down at her hand covering his and then looked her in the eyes. He didn't appear angry or distraught. His barrel chest rose and fell slowly.

Finally he said, "Move your hand."

Dana swallowed hard. It was hard to maintain eye contact, but she did. She didn't respond or do as he told her.

Kole took another slow breath before saying, "I buried my brother today. I can't have a drink?" His voice was deep and grumbly.

Dana blinked away her tears but couldn't stop her heart from racing. She asked him, "Are you drinking because of the funeral or because of what happened tonight?"

Kole was surprised by the question. His eyes narrowed. He told her, "Both."

Dana frowned, but she slowly withdrew her hand. Kole continued to stare at her, rather than pour another drink.

She asked him, "Are you drinking because you messed up tonight? Did something go wrong?"

Kole's look of confusion intensified. He shook his head slightly.

"What does that mean?" Dana said. "Did you mess up tonight or not?"

He let go of the bottle and rubbed his forehead. When he withdrew his hand, his frown remained. "Why you asking me that?"

"Why do you think I'm asking you," she nearly snapped. "I'm worried about you, Kole. What, do you think I'm the police or something?"

He started to respond. Instead his mouth hung open. After a few moments, he said, "Didn't we already talk about this – *plausible deniability*...?"

Flustered, Dana said, "Kole, I don't give a damn about that right now. I need to know if you're okay. I wanna know if you screwed up tonight."

He found it hard to get over her directness, but he managed to respond to her question. "I didn't mess up tonight. Everything went like it was supposed to."

"There's a lot of witnesses," Dana breathed. She wanted to be as strong as her words but couldn't stop her voice from rattling. "Are you sure they didn't see anything?"

Kole shook his head vacantly. "They only saw what we wanted them to see."

"No one saw you get in a car – after?" she pressed.

Kole sighed and poured more liquor. He needed it to get over her transition from Miss Goody-Two-Shoes to Miss Pregnant to the new role she wanted to play as his accomplice.

After draining the glass, he told her, "Even if they did, the cars are burned."

"Wh, what about these marks?" She traced a finger along one of the scars on his arm. "Did you get in a fight?"

"That's a cut from glass," he said, no longer attempting to avoid this interrogation.

"This one's not," Dana said, moving her finger to a shorter scratch.

"That one's from a fight," Kole conceded.

"Someone got your DNA under their fingernails?" Dana asked, her heart knocking again.

He shook his head. "I had long-sleeves on. If anything, they got fabric from my thermal."

Dana relaxed a little and continued to look him over. Noticing the bruises on his face, she asked, "You had a ski mask."

Kole nodded.

"What if they find the clothes?" she wondered.

"It's all burnt up," he reported. "Look, I appreciate you being concerned and all, but this ain't my first time. I know what I'm doing."

"Well, this is *my* first time," Dana countered. "So if it's alright with you, I need to know that everything is okay." Her eyes watered again when she said, "I don't want the police to come looking for you."

Kole couldn't believe she'd adapted to his lifestyle so quickly and so thoroughly. If she was willing to make that move, the least he could do was be as forthcoming and comforting as possible.

"The police aren't coming," he assured her. "We covered all our tracks."

"Wh, what about the other people?" Dana wondered. "I don't want them coming for you either."

"They all dead," Kole stated. "Ain't nobody left to come for us."

"Are–" Her throat caught. When she could speak again, she said, "Are you sure?"

Kole shook his head. "Can't never be sure, when it comes to stuff like this. But even if it is some more of them, they not gon' know who took their people out, just like the police don't know."

He didn't feel 100% comfortable telling her that. The streets *always* knew more than the police. But to the best of his knowledge, the Woods didn't know The Organization was after them.

Dana sighed. She bit her bottom lip before asking, "Do you want to get cleaned up? You, you need some alcohol. And Neosporin. I – I can help you."

Kole's frown returned as he nodded. "Yeah. Let me..." He started to pour another drink but thought better of it. He took the bottle to the head instead, taking three long pulls.

When he returned it to the bar, Dana took his hand and led him to the bedroom. Midway down the hallway, she stopped cold when he asked, "The baby... You keeping it?"

She turned and eyed him seriously. "Yes," she stated, her voice sure and steady now. "Since you been drinking, I'ma give you a pass for asking me that."

BACKSLIDE 2

She stared at him for five long beats, to see if he had a rebuttal. He did not. They continued down the hallway, hand-in-hand.

CHAPTER 50

SHE HELPED HIM undress and shower.

When he got out, she led him from the restroom and instructed him to lie on the bed. The liquor he'd consumed had taken its effect by then. Kole's eyes were low. His movements sluggish. He lie on his stomach, while she returned to the bathroom for first aid supplies. Most of his bruises were superficial, but there was a cut on his shoulder that could probably use a dozen stitches. Instead it got alcohol, antibacterial ointment and two Band-Aids.

She massaged his neck and shoulders before turning him over. The scratches on his face were light. She thought they'd heal within a few days. In the meantime, they made him look even more handsome, in a rugged, dangerous sort of way.

She noticed him growing erect as she tended to his wounds. She ignored it, as she had grown accustomed to doing with his morning wood. Even with all of his dark, chocolaty muscles beneath her hands, arousal was the last thing on Dana's mind. She was more concerned about the cops kicking down the door at any minute and the fact that her boyfriend (and soon-to-be baby-daddy) was a mass murderer, and somehow she was okay with it.

When she finished caring for him, she gathered the supplies and started off the bed. Before her foot hit the floor, Kole sat up suddenly and reached for her with a speed that belied his inebriation. He snagged her scrub pants and dragged her back to him. Surprised, Dana couldn't stop a startled whimper from escaping her as the medicine fell from her hands.

She landed in his lap. Before she could react or even look back at him, Kole scrambled from beneath and pushed her further onto the mattress. Dana found herself on all fours. Her eyes were wide, her breaths uneven. Strong hands that were really more like claws gripped the waistline of her scrub pants. He tried to yank them down, but rather than elastic, there was a drawstring. It held firm.

Kole blew hot fumes from his nostrils and yanked harder. Dana cried out with nervous excitement as the fabric dug into her skin. Then there was an audible **RIIIIP!** and the fabric was torn away. She realized he had ripped her panties as well when she felt cool air on her backside. She looked back at him, her jaw unhinged, eyes confused. She gasped when she locked eyes with the beast. Dick in hand, he looked as threatening as he must have when he murdered five men a few hours ago.

Dana lowered her chest and buried her face in the pillows, bracing herself for the unbridled passion. Without seeing him, it was easier to give in to the sinful pleasure.

Another **RIIIIP!** and her pants fell away from her thighs. One more yank, and he was able to pry her legs apart. Dana gripped the mattress with both hands. Her heart rattled against her sternum. She couldn't breathe. But her body responded to him; coating her walls with lubrication, even before he rubbed his hard piece against her opening.

Her ears were ringing, but she heard an inhuman growl when he entered her, slamming all the way in on the first thrust. She squeezed her eyes closed and screamed into the pillow. Kole pumped his hips, hard and fast. He gripped her hips and drew her to him with each thrust. Dana could hardly hear their thighs clapping over the sound of her own cries for more.

Her body greedily beckoned him. Her walls gripped him, milked him. His dick slammed in and out of her with the speed of a piston. Her clitoris awakened and rang like a school bell. She barely managed to catch her breath before an ear-splitting orgasm cracked her spine like a whip, causing her to howl even louder.

On one level she understood that in the past two days, Kole had fully given in to Satan. And she had accepted every one of his flaws, lowering her standards to a point of no return. But in the here and now, as her orgasm ricocheted off every one of her bones and had them harmonizing like a xylophone, Dana only knew that this was her man, and she was his woman, through thick and thin.

She would follow her soulmate anywhere. Hopefully there were better days ahead, but she was equally prepared for the gates of hell.

PART FIVE
RIDE OR DIE

CHAPTER 51

WHEN SHE GOT home the following afternoon, Dana felt a little uncomfortable when she saw her son's SUV in the garage. That was an odd feeling that made her even more unsure of herself. Tariq was the only family she had. She never wanted to be self-conscious around him.

But her initial reaction was reinforced when she went inside. As she stepped down the hallway, she heard the television in the front room. It was tuned in to Channel Six. Their star reporter offered an update on last night's murders. Dana hesitated in the doorway. She saw Tariq sitting on the couch with his eyes glued to the screen.

He looked over at her with an expression that was so judgmental, Dana felt like her whole life had been laid bare. It felt as if he knew everything that was going on between her and Kole, even the rough way he made love to her in the wee hours of the morning.

She wanted to continue to her room and avoid whatever might be swirling around in that brilliant brain of his, but avoidance wouldn't do with Tariq. He loved his mother and would never stop wanting the best for her. Even though she was conflicted at the moment, Dana considered that one of his most endearing qualities.

She entered the room and took a seat next to him on the couch. They watched the remainder of the news story together. The police still didn't have any leads – at least none they were willing to share with the reporters. The only new information Channel Six had was the detectives now believed the fire at the vacant house was used to destroy evidence from the men responsible for the murders. Although no one saw the shooters inside the house, witnesses spotted the men heading from that direction prior to the shooting. Witnesses also indicated the killers arrived on foot, which would make sense if they were set up in the vacant house.

Kole already revealed all of this to Dana. She was relieved the police hadn't discovered anything he didn't want them to know. Her relief fizzled when Tariq turned the TV off and looked her in the eyes.

With no pretense, he said, "That was Kole, wasn't it?"

Dana sensed the question was coming, so she was able to minimalize her shock. "What? Why would you ask me that?"

"I know his friend got killed," he said. "The funeral was yesterday. And now all of these people getting killed. I know he had something to do with it – if he didn't do it himself."

Dana shook her head. "Tariq, people get killed all the time. You can't point fingers at Kole, just because someone close to him was murdered."

"You didn't say he *didn't* do it," her son noted.

Dana didn't bat an eye. "He didn't do it."

Tariq studied her features, hoping for some kind of tell. Dana didn't have one. She was as convincing as she was when she told him about the Tooth Fairy and Santa Claus.

"Would you tell me if he did?" the boy wondered.

Dana shook her head. "No, I wouldn't."

He frowned. "Why not?"

"Because despite your age, you're still my child. And Kole's my boyfriend. I'm not going to talk about a lot of things that go on between us."

"But this is different," her son argued. "If he did that, he could go to jail."

"Kole could've gone to jail for some of the things he did to help us last summer," Dana reminded him. "Things he did to help *you*."

"So, you're saying he did it."

"I just told you he didn't."

"And you said you wouldn't tell me if he did."

"Then you should see how pointless this conversation is," Dana stated. She was growing irritated, but she suppressed that emotion. Tariq had a right to ask these questions.

He shook his head in disappointment. "I can't believe you, Mama."

"I know you're upset," she told him. "But don't let your attitude lead you to disrespecting me. You don't have to like my decisions, but you will respect me."

"I'm not disrespecting you. I just don't understand why you'd put up with something like that. I told you, I like Kole. He a good dude. But you don't need to be with nobody that's gon' be getting in trouble like that. He could get *you* in trouble. You deserve better, Mama. I feel like, I don't know... Maybe you don't think you can do better."

She considered what he told her and nodded. She confused him by asking, "Do you remember what I told you about your father?"

He frowned. "Yeah. I mean, you never said too much about him."

"What do you remember?" she asked.

Tariq shrugged. "You said his name was Rodney. Y'all went to college together, and he broke up with you after you got pregnant. You said you didn't want anything to do with him after that. Never sued him for child support. You said he's one of the reasons you left Chicago."

Dana nodded. "I didn't tell you he was a GD?"

Tariq's frown deepened as he shook his head. "What's that?"

"A Gangster Disciple. It's one of the biggest gangs in Chicago."

The boy's mouth hung open. "My dad was a banger?"

Dana nodded. "Yeah. He was."

"Why you didn't tell me?"

"Because you were young and impressionable. I didn't want you to follow in the footsteps of a man you never met, just because you thought it was in your bloodline."

He shook his head. "I wouldn't have done that."

"Good," Dana said. "Then no harm done."

"He was in a gang while y'all were dating?"

"Oh, most definitely," Dana recalled. "Rodney was a mediocre student. Actually, it was the gang that made him stay in school. They said they wanted some educated brothers in the ranks. I think they would've beat Rodney up if he tried to drop out."

Tariq's eyes were wide. He absorbed this new information like a sponge.

"Rodney got in fights," she told him. "Never on campus. But when we'd go out, he'd run into his enemies sometimes. He wouldn't let anyone disrespect him, especially when he was with me.

"I remember one time he took me to his parents' house for Christmas. It seemed like every time we went to his old neighborhood, he ended up getting into it with somebody. That Christmas was the worst, and it was the closest I ever came to getting hurt because of him. We hadn't made it to his parents' house yet when some guys started talking noise at a red light. Like I said, Rodney never backed down from anyone. But when they pulled a gun, he had enough sense to take off."

Tariq barely blinked as he listened to the story.

"They chased us," Dana told him, "for, I don't even know how many blocks. They started shooting. Hit the car a few times.

I don't think I've ever been so scared. Rodney told me to duck down, but I already had my head between my legs. I wasn't no fool. Anyway, Rodney lost them somehow, and we made it to his mother's house and had our Christmas dinner like it never happened."

She shook her head at the memory. "His mother's dressing was *terrible*."

The teen considered everything she told him before asking, "Why you telling me this now?"

"Because I want you to know I'm not as green as you think I am, Tariq. I don't make a habit of dating *bad guys*, but if I do, you need to know they're not taking advantage of me. I know what I'm doing. If I choose to stay with Kole, despite anything he's done or anything you *think* he's done, that's my choice. I'm loyal, when I'm in love. The main thing I'm concerned about when I'm with a man is how he treats *me*, not how he treats the rest of the world. I'm sorry if that bothers you, but this is my decision."

Tariq was quiet for a while. Finally he sighed and said, "Okay."

Dana gave him a hug before rising to her feet. "I gotta get ready for work. Want me to make you something to eat?"

"Can you order a pizza?"

"No, but I can give you the money, and you can pick it up. You'll save money on the tip. Plus they put a surcharge on deliveries."

"Okay, you can pay for the pizza," he said. "I'll pay the surcharge and tip with *my* money."

Dana shook her head, but she was grinning. "Boy, you too lazy for your own good."

CHAPTER 52

AT WORK, DANA found it increasingly difficult to escape her beau's evil deeds. Moments after arriving for her 2 to 10:30 shift, her coworker Courtney greeted her with the latest news.

"Did you hear about those killings last night?"

Dana hadn't even put her purse down yet. She approached her workstation and stowed it in the drawer before responding.

"Yeah, I heard about it. It's all over the news."

"One of those firemen was here," Courtney informed her.

"Here, where?" Dana asked. "At the hospital?"

"Yeah," Courtney said, nodding. She sat on a swivel chair with a bag of Cheetos in hand.

Other than them, the department was empty. But they had several X-rays scheduled within the next hour.

"What happened to him?" Dana wondered. Kole hadn't mentioned any harm done to civilians. She took a seat on a chair opposite her friend.

"He got burned when they were putting out that house fire," Courtney reported.

Dana's heart shuddered. Though she wasn't responsible for anything Kole did, she felt culpable because she continued to support him.

She asked, "Is he alright?"

"Yeah, I think so," Courtney said. "He only got burned on the arm. You know those fire suits protect them from most stuff."

Dana sighed inwardly. "He didn't get admitted?"

Courtney shook her head. "No, they treated him in the ER and released him. It was some reporters down there, trying to get an interview. White folks been going crazy, since they found out it was some of them that got killed."

Dana frowned. "They released the identity of the victims?"

"No, but they said they were all members of a white-power gang."

This was news to Dana. She wondered why Kole had kept that from her. "*A white-power gang?*"

Courtney chuckled. "Yeah. They were all racist, you know, like skinheads. And the guys that killed them were black. So this could be like, the start of a race war or something."

Dana couldn't stop her eyes from widening. "How do you know the shooters were black? I thought they had on masks."

"They had on ski masks," Courtney confirmed. "But you know those masks leave the eyes and mouth open. Everybody know they was black – they just not saying it on the news yet."

Dana's pulse raced, as if identifying the race of the killers brought the police closer to arresting her boyfriend.

"You okay?" Courtney asked, noticing her discomfort.

"Yeah," Dana said. "You just, talking about race wars and stuff..."

"Girl, I don't know if it's gonna come to all that," Courtney said. "I'm just saying, how often is it that black people murder white people like that? And they didn't go after *regular* white folks. They killed some *skinheads*. Everybody be wanting to do that, but they actually *did it*."

"Everybody wants to kill skinheads?"

"You never saw 'em marching on TV, with their torches and confederate flags, and wished somebody would bust a cap in they ass?"

221

"I wished they would go home," Dana told her. "I don't think I ever wished someone would kill them."

"Girl, you lying. What about when they killed that lady in Charlottesville – or when that punk killed those people at that church?"

Dana couldn't lie about her feelings regarding Dylann Roof. "I did want him to get killed," she admitted. "I still do."

"Well, five of 'em got killed last night," Courtney boasted, "before they had a chance to do something bad. I know you think I'm wrong, but I'm glad they got took out, and I'm glad it was some black folks who did it."

Dana didn't like the tone of this conversation, but she was grateful for the motive her coworker proposed. If people thought the killings were some form of racial justice, maybe the police wouldn't link it to Moon and The Organization.

"Oh, hell, here they come with this shit," Courtney muttered as the doors to their department swung open.

Dana looked back and saw a transporter wheeling a patient in on a wheelchair. Any other day, Dana would've found it amusing that her friend referred to their job as *this shit*. At the moment, she was just happy for the break in the conversation.

"Is this one yours or mine?" she asked Courtney.

"*Yours*," her friend said without hesitation.

"Of course," Dana said, and she rose to her feet. She approached her X-ray table and told the transporter, "You can bring him over here. Sir, are you able to stand on your own...?"

CHAPTER 53

KOLE WAS NOT the type to contact her at work simply to see how she was doing, so when Dana got a text message from him that said, "Call me when you can," she headed to the breakroom at her earliest convenience.

The breakroom was occupied by a couple of slacking PCT's, so she opted for a single-person bathroom instead. It was a quarter till nine. She'd been watching the clock since eight o'clock and was glad she only had an hour and a half left in her shift.

She stood before the mirror and dialed her boyfriend's number. The reflection staring back at her revealed the toll the past few days had taken on her.

"Hey," he answered. "You somewhere you can talk?"

Dana was instantly on edge. "Yeah," she told him. She looked back to confirm the bathroom door was locked. "What's going on? Is everything okay?"

She heard him sigh heavily, which made her even more anxious.

"Kole, tell me what's going on."

"I think we might be getting a little blowback," he said. His voice was as deep and steady as ever, but it was also filled with concern.

"Wha, what kind of blowback?"

"The thing that happened last night – looks like those boys were more connected than we thought."

Dana's eyes narrowed. "Those were white supremacists; the people that got killed. You didn't tell me that."

"I didn't think you needed to know."

She shook her head. "Kole, if we're in this together, then you have to start acting like it. After all those questions I asked you, why would you leave that out?"

"You was acting different yesterday," he said. "You never came at me like that. Caught me off guard. I didn't know what to tell you."

"How about the truth," she said. "Starting right now."

Her heart pounded. Her eyes remained glued to her own reflection. As she continued to follow her man down this rabbit hole, the woman in the mirror was becoming more of a stranger.

"They call themselves *The Woods*," Kole told her. "It's short for *peckerwoods*. They're a white gang, like the skinheads or Aryan Brotherhood. If I was going after them for any other reason, I would've taken the time to see what kind of backing they had. But after what happened to Moon, I didn't. It didn't matter.

"Now we gotta deal with the repercussions. I'm sorry, baby, but I think you and Tariq need to law low for a while. We all do. Word on the street is somebody's watching me. Some say they were watching me before they went after Moon. If so, they've been watching you too. I got a safehouse. I want you to come here when you get off work."

Dana's eyes widened. Her heart sank to the pit of her stomach. *Again?* She'd gone into hiding with Kole before – her and Tariq. She didn't doubt he could keep them safe, but she didn't want to believe things had come to that. Unlike last summer, neither she nor Tariq had done anything wrong.

"Who do you think is watching us?" she breathed.

"The Woods, they're not that big in Overbrook Meadows. But in prison, they're a big deal. All those white-power gangs are.

224

They don't like what went down last night. Supposedly, they been having meetings, and some of them are coming down here, from as far away as Oklahoma and Louisiana. They wanna retaliate. Until I figure out how best to deal with them, I'm not taking any chances – especially not with you."

Dana brought a hand to her mouth. Her eyes watered. "But – but you said everything was taken care of. You said you were safe."

Kole kicked himself for not being completely honest with her last night. He grunted and said, "Look, when it comes to things like this, it's two levels you gotta look at. I told you we was cool, as far as the police. And that's true. But them other people, we gotta take that as it comes. If some out-of-towners put the greenlight on Moon, then they probably know who took their people out. If they don't know yet, it's only a matter of time."

Dana felt her bones rattling. She couldn't believe things had gotten so convoluted. "Wh, what are you gonna do when they find out?" She knew The Organization was a force to be reckoned with, but if they went to war with multiple white gangs, they might actually start the race war her friend was hoping for.

"We'll talk about that later," Kole told her. "First thing I need to do is make sure you and Tariq are safe. I'ma text you the address to where I'm at. I need y'all to come here tonight. Don't worry about going home for your clothes or nothing like that. I don't wanna risk it."

Dana's pulse was steadily on the rise. "Okay. I'll, we'll come. I'll call Tariq and have him meet me there."

"If I'm not around when you get there, there's a spare key on top of the porch light."

"Okay."

"Where do you park at the hospital?" Kole asked. "Are you in a garage or an open lot."

The hairs stood on Dana's arms. "Kole, you're scaring me."

"I'm sorry," he said. "I don't mean to. I just – I need you to be safe. You're carrying my baby."

225

That was the first time he'd referred to the new life as *his*. She'd been worried, but Dana now believed he would love and cherish their child as much as she would. Her heart glowed, despite their predicament.

"I park in a garage," she told him. "It's only for employees. No one else can get in there."

"Good," he said. "I wanna come to the hospital and walk you to your car. But if they're on to me, I'd be leading them right to you. Do you think you can ask someone in security to walk with you when you get off?"

She shuddered. "Kole, do you really think someone's coming for me?"

"I underestimated them the first time," he admitted. "That's something I won't do again. If you don't wanna call security, I'll send someone to walk with you."

As distraught as she was, the thought of an unknown member of The Organization showing up at her department was even more unsettling.

"I'll call security when I get ready to leave," Dana said. "I promise."

CHAPTER 54

AS INSTRUCTED, DANA called security ten minutes before she clocked out and asked if someone could walk her to her car. She had to provide a reason, so she told them, "My boyfriend's ex has been threatening me. She knows where I work."

She wasn't surprised when her coworker's eyes widened. Courtney rushed to her side.

"Girl, what's going on with you?"

"It's nothing," Dana told her. "Just some woman being immature."

"How long has this been going on? Is that why you won't post pictures of Kole on Facebook?"

"Sure, whatever," Dana said. She loved her friend, but sometimes Courtney got on her nerves.

"I told you he was probably married," the woman said. "I know *he* said that's his ex-girlfriend, but that might be his *wife*!"

Dana didn't have the patience to entertain this. What she and Kole were facing might be life or death. Courtney was stuck on a Jerry Springer drama.

"Leave me alone about this, okay? I got enough to deal with, without you running your mouth."

She spoke more firmly than she intended, but she got the desired result. Courtney's mouth snapped shut, and she didn't speak to Dana for the remainder of their shift, not even to say, "Goodnight."

The security department sent a portly guard who probably couldn't run two blocks without getting winded, but Dana appreciated his company. The trek from the main building to the parking garage never felt so long. The night air was thick with fear of the unexpected.

But Dana made it to her car without incident. She forwarded a text message to Tariq and called him as she rolled out of the garage.

"Mama," he answered, "what's this address you sent me?"

"Are you at home?"

"No, I'm at Sabrina's house."

"Are you spending the night?"

"No, I was gonna go home in a little bit. Why? What's up?"

She took a deep breath and girded herself for his attitude. "I need you to go to that address when you leave. Don't go home. We might have some trouble."

After a long pause, during which Dana listened intently to her son's breathing, he said, "This got something to do with Kole, with what happened last night, doesn't it?"

"We'll talk about it when you get there."

"Naw, Mama. We need to talk about it now."

"*I said we'll talk about it when you get there, Tariq*! This is not a conversation I wanna have over the phone, and I'm damn sure not having it while you're over Sabrina's house. I'm telling you not to go home, and that's all I can tell you right now."

She thought he'd get the message when she raised her voice, but her son could be an insolent brat.

"You lied to me. I asked you about this today, and you looked me right in the eyes and lied."

Dana was so angry her hands trembled. She wanted to reach through the phone and wring his skinny neck.

"I'ma do a lot more than lie to you, if you don't hang up and do what I told you to do. *Do not go home tonight*! When you leave Sabr–"

She brought the phone away from her face and stared at it in disbelief. Damn if the little booger didn't hang up on her.

CHAPTER 55

DANA PLUGGED THE address Kole had given her into her GPS and set off in that direction. The safehouse was on the far east side of town. According to the GPS, she would arrive in a little over twenty minutes.

While she drove, she fretted over how Tariq would respond to Kole once he got there and how Kole would react to her son's insolence. She didn't worry about her own safety until a cursory check in the rearview mirror revealed a pair of headlights that seemed to be travelling in the same direction as her, despite how many turns she made on the darkened streets.

Dana's mouth went dry, but panic didn't set in just yet. The vehicle in question was six car lengths behind her. Due to the sparse traffic, there were no cars in between them. Dana went against her GPS' directions and made a right on one of the random streets ahead. The street was more desolate than the thoroughfare she turned off. Sure enough, the car made the same right and followed at a steady pace. This time Dana saw that it was a sedan, either white or gray. It was too dark, and the car was too far away to make out the occupants.

Dana's GPS urged her to make a couple of lefts and return to Rosedale Avenue. She was eager to do so, and get off the residential street, but she thought the move would be too telling.

If she was being followed, her pursuers might know she was on to them.

She gritted her teeth and continued straight instead. Worry lines creased her brow. She nibbled one of her fingernails and finally made a left after several blocks. She fought a strong urge to floor it, once she was out of the sedan's line of sight. Maintaining the posted speed limit was one of the most difficult things she'd ever done. She didn't make it two blocks on the new street before the same headlights swam into view behind her. The sedan continued its pursuit methodically and patiently.

Dana's features melted into a frown so severe, tears sprang to her eyes. She took deep breaths and tried to pull herself together as she reached for her cellphone. Between watching the road ahead of her, the car behind her and her cellphone's bright display, she didn't realize she was approaching a speed hump. She hit it so hard her front axle emitted a pained crunch that jarred everything in the car. The sudden shock caused Dana to scream and drop the phone between her legs. She cursed herself as she scrambled for it.

The phone couldn't have gone too far, but she came up empty when she pawed for it blindly. The thought that she might have to turn on an interior light or pull over to search for it fried her nerves even more. Her heart thundered as she raked her hand from right to left, her eyes barely over the top of the steering wheel. Finally her fingers came in contact with the device. She held it in her lap and turned on her blinker before making a right at the next intersection.

She pulled up Kole's number when the sedan was no longer in sight. She watched her rearview mirror and saw the car make the same turn, just as Kole answered.

"Hey," he said. "You alright?"

"*No!*" she sobbed. Her head was spinning. She squeezed the steering wheel so tightly, her fingertips were cold. "*There's somebody following me.* They've been behind me since I left the hospital."

Kole's voice didn't register alarm when he asked, "Are you sure?"

"*Yes!* I turned off Rosedale, and they did too. I drove for a while and made a couple more turns, and they're still behind me."

"I'm on my way."

Dana could hear he was on the move.

He asked, "What street are you on?"

She told him the upcoming intersection.

"I need you to get on Hemphill," he said, where there's more traffic. Judging by the increase in his breaths, she knew he was moving faster now. He told someone, "Come on, we gotta go."

"*I – I don't know how to get to Hemphill from here*," Dana nearly bawled. She was so stressed, she could barely see straight. "Do you, you want me to go to the safehouse?"

"No," Kole said. "Try to calm down. *Breathe.*"

She heard more rustling on his end, and then she heard an engine start. She had no idea how far away he was, but knowing he was on his way alleviated some of the pressure. She heeded his advice and tried to work on her breathing.

"If you're headed south, you should be able to make a left and go straight to Hemphill," he deduced. "You think you can do that for me?"

"*Yes*," she cried. She hated to sound so weak and defenseless, while he was calm and assertive.

"I'm not gonna let anything happen to you," Kole promised. He sounded 100 percent sure of himself. "You believe that, don't you?"

His declaration should've made her feel better. Instead her tears flowed harder. As she watched the car in her mirror, her thoughts kept returning to the burgeoning life in her womb.

"*Oh – okay*," she said. "I – I'm making a left right now."

"Good," Kole said, and Dana heard something that did make her feel better. He was driving so fast, his engine *screamed*. "Tell me what street you're on now."

She said, "Allen."

"She's on Allen," Kole reported to whoever his passenger was. "You got that pulled up yet?"

"Yessir," a man said.

"Is he still behind you?" Kole asked Dana.

By then the sedan had made the same turn as her. She told him, "*Yes.*"

"Ask her if she made it to College Ave yet?" Kole's passenger said.

Kole repeated the question.

Dana wiped her eyes with the back of her hand. "It's, yeah, it's coming up." She was surprised they had pinpointed her location so quickly. But the headlights on her ass took precedence over any relief she might have felt.

"Hemphill's three blocks from College," Kole informed her. "When you get to Hemphill, make a right. Is he still behind you?"

"*Yes.*"

"Do you know what kind of car it is?"

"*No,*" she cried. "I just know it's white. It's a sedan."

"Have you seen who's in it?"

"*No. It's too dark.*"

"Do you know if they're white or black?"

"No. I'm sorry – I can't... *I can't–*"

"It's cool," he said. "You doing good. Try to stay calm."

In the background, it sounded like Kole was doing quite the opposite. She heard his engine roar even louder.

"Do you think it's those people?" Dana asked. "*The Woods?*"

"I don't know if it's them or one of the new gangs that came to help," Kole said. "I confirmed they had eyes on me before they went after Moon. They figured I'd step in when he was out the picture. I don't know why they backed off their plan to take us both out, but they fucked up now. Should've got me when they had the chance. Now I'm coming for 'em."

The irony of that statement was not lost on Dana. As far as she could tell, the pissed off white-power gangs were on the offense.

"*Where are you?*" she wailed.

"I'm close, baby. You staying calm?"

She knew he could tell she was not. She was unarmed and most likely outnumbered by shady individuals with murder on their minds.

"You made it to Hemphill yet?" Kole asked.

"Yeah, I'm, I'm almost there. It's a red light."

"Good," he said. "Any cars behind you, other than the white one?"

Dana checked her mirror. "Nuh, no."

"When you stop," Kole said, "they'll have to stop behind you. I want you to turn on your blinker and wait for the light, like you normally would. When they get closer, tell me everything you can about them and the car. Can you put me on Bluetooth, so they won't see you're on the phone?"

Dana only had to press a couple of buttons on her dash to make that happen. But every move she made seemed ten times harder. "Okay, hol, hold on."

She tossed the phone to the passenger seat and had to flip her blinker, because the intersection was drawing near. When she came to a stop, she afforded herself a few seconds to set up the Bluetooth before her eyes moved to the rearview mirror. The sedan was approaching, but it had slowed, much more than it should have for a stop at the light.

"Kole, are you there?"

"Yeah." His deep voice boomed through the speakers now. "You stopped at the light?"

"Yeah. But the car slowed down. He didn't pull over, but I think he's stalling, till the light turns."

"I'm close," Kole assured her. "*Real close.* Is there a lot of traffic?"

"No. Not a lot. I think the light's about to turn green."

"I need you to tell me everything you can about that car," he repeated.

"There's no cars coming," Dana said. "Should I turn right?"

"I need you to wait."

"*There's no cars.* It'll look weird if I don't turn."

"How close is he?" Kole asked. "Can you see anything?"

"No. *He's driving so slow!* Kole, the light just turned green."

"I need you to wait."

Dana had to fight with her own instincts to keep her foot on the brake. *"I'm sitting at a green light."*

"That means they gotta get closer."

Dana understood why he'd want that, but it was the exact opposite of what she wanted. She felt like he'd asked her to stick her hand in a beartrap.

"Oh – *okay,*" she said, her voice quavering. "He's coming now. It, it's a Mitsubishi. I don't know what kind. It's white. It's new. It's – it's a white man driving! White man in the passenger seat. They..."

Dana didn't mean to lock eyes with the driver, but he was staring straight at her rearview mirror.

"Oh, God, Kole, they're looking right at me!"

"Okay, go," he said, still not expressing the apprehension she expected. "Make your turn."

Dana was so eager to get moving, she gave her car too much gas and darted into the intersection. She had to jerk the wheel hard to make the turn.

Kole heard her tires squeal and asked, "Is that you?"

"Yes," she cried. *"I'm sorry!"*

"It's okay, baby. You're doing great."

Dana knew that was a lie. She appreciated him trying to placate her. "I never been followed before," she explained. "I know these people are dangerous."

"For someone who's never been followed before, you're doing a helluva job," he said. "What are they doing now?"

"They're still behind me," she reported, and then her eyes widened. "They're not hanging back anymore, Kole! *They're right behind me!*"

"That's cool," he said. "We're real close. Speed up, and tell me what they do."

The speed limit on Hemphill was 40 mph. Dana pushed her ride to 50. The Mitsubishi stayed on her bumper.

"*Kole, they're coming for me! They're speeding up too!*"

"How fast you going?"

"*Fifty. Fifty-five,*" she said after checking her speedometer.

"Alright. Slow down and tell me what intersection you're at."

Dana took her foot off the gas but didn't hit the brakes. Her car began to lose momentum on its own. In her rearview mirror, the white faces in the Mitsubishi were agitated and focused. Dana had to force a lump down her throat before she told Kole, "We're about to pass Cantey."

"Good," he said. "That light on Berry red?"

"*What?*" Dana looked ahead a couple of blocks to see what he was talking about. Sure enough there was a red light on the horizon at Berry Street. "Who, how do you know that?"

"I told you I was close," Kole stated.

"You want me to run the light?" she asked.

"No. I want you to stop at the light, like normal."

Dana checked her mirror again. Her eyes bugged when she saw the Mitsubishi making a move. "*He's switching lanes! He's gonna pull up next to me!*"

"I see him," Kole said, as cool as ever.

Dana looked around frantically but didn't see *him* anywhere. "What do you mean? *Where are you?*"

"I'm catching up."

Dana had one block to go before she reached the light. *"You want me to stop?"*

"Yes, like you normally would."

By then the Mitsubishi had moved to the lane on her left. With the reduced speeds, the driver easily pulled alongside her. Dana risked a glance in that direction and nearly wet her pants when she saw two tatted-up thugs inside the vehicle. The passenger window was down. They were now close enough for Dana to see everything clearly. Both men were watching her. Stopping at the light was the absolute last thing she wanted to do, especially when the passenger's arm came up with a flash of steel in his hand.

Dana relied on blind faith, because she had nothing else. If Kole didn't save her, she was a goner either way. There was no way she could outrun the Mitsubishi, and she sure as hell couldn't outrun bullets, if they started to fire at her.

"*Kole!*" she screamed as her car came to a perilous stop at the light. "*He got a guuu-*"

CREEAAKK!!

The sudden sound of heavy metal slamming into more metal cut through the night like gunfire. Dana's eyes were as big as doorknobs. She barely saw what had transpired. One moment she was staring at the passenger in the Mitsubishi. The next second, the car was gone. It took her eyes a moment to catch up with the blurred movement. She turned towards the intersection and saw the back of Kole's car. Twisted fiberglass and shattered glass was everywhere. Ten yards ahead of him was the Mitsubishi. Kole had plowed into it so hard, the sedan's trunk looked like it was the back seat.

Dana's mouth hung open. She hadn't seen Kole approaching. Surely the occupants of the Mitsubishi were also caught unaware. Dana had no idea what she expected in the form of salvation, but Kole using his car as a weapon was definitely not on the list.

All around them, cars screeched to a halt to avoid the accident. Kole's Infinity didn't move. Neither did the Mitsubishi. Dana didn't have time to express relief. Kole's wellbeing was the only thing that mattered. She couldn't see the front of his car, but if it looked anything like the Mitsubishi, he could be seriously injured.

"*Kuh, Kole*?" she said, her voice hushed.

Her audio system hummed, but there was no response. A terrible chill enveloped her. *Oh God.* She wanted him to come to her rescue, but at what cost?

"*Kole*," she said again.

Still no response. She knew this could be because he dropped his phone during the collision – How could he not? But the lack of communication might also mean he was incapacitated.

Dana's eyes filled with tears. She began to hyperventilate when the light turned green. She took her foot off the brake and slowly rolled into the intersection. Bits of glass crackled under her tires. By then other drivers had left their vehicles to render aid. As she pulled alongside the battered Infinity, Dana saw that both front airbags had deployed. She recognized the man in the passenger seat. It was Byrd. His mouth was bloodied. It took a moment for his eyes to focus, as he looked over at her and nodded.

Past him, Dana saw two strong arms push against the driver's side airbag. Her heart froze. She stopped her car completely, ignoring the other traffic. Kole shoved his door open and staggered out of the Infinity. He turned and locked eyes with his woman over the roof of his car. He was shaken, but otherwise appeared to be uninjured. Dana knew he and Byrd had time to brace for the impact, unlike the occupants of the Mitsubishi. So far no one in that car had stirred.

Despite the bone-rattling accident, Kole had the wherewithal to wink at Dana; to let her know he was okay. A wave of relief struck her like a tsunami. Her blood ran ice cold. She half-smiled at him. Her eyes glistened beneath the streetlights.

Kole gestured with his head for her to get out of there. Dana didn't want to leave him, but she understood he always had her back, and Kole knew best, even when his methods left her in the dark.

Her eyes filled again as she continued through the intersection. This time they were guardedly happy tears.

CHAPTER
56

Said the eagle to his father
I can fly to the moon!
My wings are strong enough to do
Whatever I want to!
Said the eagle to his son
You cannot fly to the moon
Stay home
That flight is not destined for you

Said the eagle to his father
Pa, I'm battered and bruised!
I should've stayed home
And listened to you!
Said the eagle to his son
I will always love you
You cannot learn without failure
Let me tend to your wounds

KOLE CHECKED ON the passengers of the Mitsubishi, like any concerned citizen would. Both airbags had deployed in the sedan. But as he suspected, the occupants were blindsided by his attack. The driver had his seatbelt on, but the passenger did not. The passenger was unconscious, bleeding profusely from the face.

The driver was awake but very disoriented. He could do no more than moan incoherently.

The man behind the wheel looked to be in his early forties. The passenger was in his late twenties. Both men had tattoos on their arms that were quickly identifiable as racist. Kole noted the double lightning bolts that were reminiscent of Hitler's SS military force and had been adopted by Neo Nazis. Other less obvious tats were the numbers 88, which represented the phrase, "Heil Hitler," with *H* being the 8th letter of the alphabet. The number 14 on the passenger's neck referred to a 14-word mission statement popular among white-power groups: We must secure the existence of our people and a future for white children.

Kole didn't see the gun Dana spoke of, but due to the collision, he suspected it had fallen from the would-be killer's hand. Hopefully the paramedics would find it when they removed the men from their mangled car.

"Did you even try to stop?"

Kole turned and glared at a bystander who had left her car to gawk at the wreck. The look in Kole's eyes made her back down and back away.

"Are, are you alright?" she asked instead.

"I'm pretty shook up," Kole replied. He had a role to play, and this was a good time to get started on it. He reached and rubbed the back of his neck, which actually was sore. A dull throbbing between his eyes made him wonder if he'd sustained a concussion.

The woman couldn't take her eyes off his bulging triceps as he massaged his neck. She blinked a few times and decided he was friendly enough to try her question again.

"Did you even try to stop?"

"I did," Kole stated. "I don't know what happened. I think my brakes went out."

The woman checked out the remains of his brand-new Infinity and appeared doubtful. "If you were texting, they'll see it in the red-light camera," she warned.

"I wasn't texting," Kole said. He stepped away from her, so he could check on his friend.

Byrd had another set of civilians attending to him. They instructed him to, "Stay in the car. Don't try to move." Byrd was against that advice, but he had a role to play as well.

Windshield fragments crunched under Kole's feet as he drew nearer. The smell of gasoline was strong. He wasn't sure if it was safe to stand so close to the trashed Mitsubishi. Cars didn't normally blow up after every wreck, like they did in the movies. But sometimes they did.

"You alright?" he asked his partner in crime.

"Yeah," Byrd responded. He pushed against his deployed airbag. "If I can get this thing out my face."

"That thing saved your life!" one of the onlookers said.

Byrd sighed and rolled his eyes at him.

"My lips busted?" Byrd asked, rubbing his swollen mouth.

"Yup," Kole said. "Not that bad though."

"What about them?" Byrd asked, gesturing towards the Mitsubishi.

"Oh, they're way worse," Kole said. "One of them wasn't wearing his seatbelt."

Byrd wanted to grin at that, but with so many eyes on him, he restrained.

"You hit the hell outta that car!" another bystander told Kole. "Looked like you were still on the gas when you ran into 'em."

"Shit happens," Kole said with a shrug. "I think my brakes failed."

"They're gonna sue the shit outta you!" the bystander predicted.

"Yup," Kole agreed. "I reckon they will."

CHAPTER 57

THE POLICE WERE a lot more suspicious. After declining an ambulance ride to the hospital, Kole and Byrd should've been cited and released. At the very least Byrd should've been allowed to go on his way. He was only a passenger. Instead both men were taken downtown for questioning. They weren't under arrest and could've refused, but Kole wanted to allay the officer's suspicion, rather than deepen it.

Once separated, the men were grilled for nearly an hour. Kole played dumb when asked, "Do you know who was in the other vehicle?"

"Did you know they were armed?"

"Do you have an affiliation with any gang?"

He finally drew the line when they started questioning him about the shooting at the green and white duplex.

"Man, what the hell is this about?" he asked indignantly. "How you go from asking me about an accident to trying to tie me to that bullshit?"

"We're not trying to tie you to anything," one of the detectives stated. "I just asked if you were aware of the murders."

"Of course I'm aware of it. Every time I turn on the news, that's all they talking about."

"Don't you find it coincidental that two members of a white supremacist gang just *happened* to get run down by you, after what happened. Witnesses are saying you ran into them on purpose."

"I had a goddamn car accident!" Kole barked. "You already gave me a breathalyzer. I ain't drunk, so you can leave me out of all that other shit you talking about. You ain't finna hem me up, just because you can't find nobody to arrest for that shooting."

"No one's trying to hem you up, Mr. Stone. Even if you didn't have anything to do with the shooting, we have to ask you about it because of the men you ran into. A white power-gang got attacked last night, and it looks like more of them got attacked tonight. Checking to see if there's a connection is routine."

"Yeah, I seen how your routine questions go," Kole countered. "One minute you being all friendly. The next minute you pin a life-sentence on a nigga. But I ain't the one. Either arrest me for whatever you trying to cook up or turn me loose. I ain't answering no more questions without a lawyer!"

As was always the case when the cops had no evidence and were hoping an idiot would snitch on himself, the "L" word shut everything down. Kole stepped out of the police station ten minutes later. He called for a ride, and they waited another five minutes for Byrd to get out.

"They try to ask you about that other shit?" Kole asked him as they drove away.

Byrd nodded. "Yep. I told 'em to gone take me to jail and let my lawyer answer they questions."

Kole smiled at that.

"You know this about to come to a head," Byrd warned. "Them white boys can get your name and address from the police report."

"They already got my name and address," Kole stated. "That's how they found Dana."

"So what's the next move?"

"Not sure," Kole admitted. "But you know I'd rather play offense than defense."

Byrd nodded. His busted lip couldn't stop him from grinning.

CHAPTER 58

KOLE HAD HIS associate drop him off at a lot where he had another car stashed. He hadn't spotted anyone following him, but he kept his eyes out for a tail as he drove to the safehouse. Dana hadn't called while he was with the police. He appreciated her patience, knowing she must be a nervous wreck. He called her when he got on the freeway.

"Kole." Her voice was filled with concern. "What happened? Are you okay?"

"Yeah. I'm fine. I'm headed your way now. How's–"

"What happened with those people?" she asked. "Did the police come? Are you hurt? Did you have to go to the hospital?"

"I didn't go to the hospital," he told her. "I'll talk to you about the rest when I get there. Did you talk to Tariq? Is he there?"

"He is," Dana said. She blew out a pent-up breath.

"What's wrong? Is everything okay?"

"Hold on." Kole heard her move to a different room. "He's got a problem with us being here," she told him. "He's upset with you. I don't... I don't know how he's gonna react when you get here."

Kole gave that some thought and said, "I guess we'll find out in a few minutes."

"Please don't take it personal," she said. "He's been acting like this ever since I told him we had to come. This place is amazing. I appreciate everything you're doing for us. I know Tariq does too. Even if he doesn't say it."

"Your son's grown," Kole said. "He's old enough to speak for himself. If he's got something on his mind, I'm ready for it. Did you tell him what happened tonight?"

"No. That would've made it worse."

"Okay. I'll be there in about fifteen minutes."

Dana rubbed the worry lines on her forehead. The upcoming confrontation between the two men in her life made her as nervous as she was when she realized the Mitsubishi was following her.

"Don't be mad at him," she pleaded. "He doesn't know what he's saying."

"Don't worry," Kole said. "I'm tired. The last thing I wanna do when I get there is argue."

CHAPTER 59

KOLE'S SAFEHOUSE WAS bigger than Dana's home. It had three bedrooms, a jacuzzi in the master bathroom and a pool in the backyard. Kole was pleased to see Tariq and Dana's cars in the driveway when he pulled in. He wasn't sure how she'd done it, but his life had come to revolve around her happiness. Never before had he looked forward to simply coming home to *hold* a woman.

The warm sentiments didn't last. Kole stepped into the front room and found Dana and Tariq waiting on the sofa. The television was tuned into the news, but they were both scrolling through their cellphones. Tariq looked up at him – rather *glared* at him – and stuffed his phone in his pocket. Never one to avoid a conflict, Kole came to a stop in the center of the room.

Tariq surprised him by rising to his feet and stomping forward. Dana shot to her feet as well, but Kole shook his head at her and motioned for her to back off. Tariq stopped a safe three feet away. That was still too close for someone Kole planned to have a physical altercation with, but he was fairly certain it wouldn't come to that.

"*You killed those people!*" Tariq shouted. "Now you got people coming after my mama! *Why don't you just leave us alone*? You ain't been nothing but trouble, ever since she hooked up with you!"

The boy's fair skin grew more crimson by the second. The veins stood out on his neck and forehead. Kole noticed he had his fists balled as well. He wondered if the boy would take a swing at him after all. The outcome of that would be iffy. Kole outweighed him by 60 pounds of rippling muscle, but he couldn't lay hands on his woman's son. Even wrapping Tariq up in a bear hug might be too much.

He folded his arms over his chest and stared down at him. Kole couldn't have created a more imposing figure. His dark presence overpowered everything in the room.

"What you know about it?" he asked the teen.

Dana's eyes widened. She thought his comment would escalate tensions, rather than vice versa. But she remained seated and kept her mouth closed. So far Kole had never led her astray.

"I know you killed those people, and you can't say you didn't!" Tariq spat.

"Okay. I killed them," Kole admitted. Dana sucked air between her teeth. She lost her breath completely when he said, "Maybe they deserved to die."

Tariq didn't expect that response. His chest rose and fell as he fought to maintain momentum. *"But you don't get to decide!"*

"Who said I don't?" Kole asked him. "When you was in trouble last year, you didn't have a problem with the way I took care of it."

"That was different!"

"You and your mama were in danger then," Kole countered. "People was coming to your house. They shot up the place. You remember that?"

Tariq's nostrils flared as he filled his lungs. He snorted and said, "That's different! We didn't do nothing wrong. Those people were messing with us for *no reason*. This time you went after them first!"

"They came after me first!" Kole growled. He wasn't aware that a hard sneer grew on the side of his face. *"They killed my brother!"*

"I'm sure he did something to deserve it."

The callous remark almost earned him a slap across the face. Kole only had to look over at Dana to remind himself why he was tolerating this. She appeared ready to jump between them at any moment. But Kole's arms remained folded. He sighed quietly and allowed his anger to dissipate.

"Do you know who was in that house?" he asked. "Those five men, do you know anything about 'em?"

"I heard they was some skinheads."

"So you got no problem with skinheads killing a black man. But if black people retaliate, you don't like it?"

The question threw him. Tariq looked back at his mother to regain focus. "I really don't care about none of that. All I care about is what happens to my mama."

"Well, maybe that's the problem right there," Kole stated. "I know you live in a safe, little bubble where everything is sunshine and rainbows..."

Tariq frowned at that.

Kole kept talking. "But in the real world, there's a lot of ugly stuff going on right under your nose. I ain't saying Moon was a saint. He was a criminal, just like I was when I was with The Organization. Maybe he did some things that should cost him his life. But he didn't die for any of those things. He died because a gang of *racist white men* came to town and attempted a hostile takeover.

"They see us niggas already got a hold of something and figure they can just come take it, like they been taking from us for *four hundred years*. I didn't mean for your Mama to get involved. *You know I didn't.* But for you to sit there and tell me we should've sat back and accepted what they did to us and not raise a hand in defense is ass-backwards, boy. I ain't never been of the Martin Luther King, *let's hold hands and sing kumbaya while*

they throw bricks at us, mind state. When it came to stuff like
that, I would've been rolling with *Malcolm.*

"You can hate me for the trouble I got you and your mama
into. But man-to-man, I'ma let you know I got *no regrets.* I'ma
keep y'all safe, whether you like it or not. And I'ma lay some more
crackers down if I have to, until they decide to *back the hell up.*

"Now that's all I got to say about it. You got something else
you wanna tell me?"

Dana couldn't tell if her son was frightened, shocked or in
agreement, but Tariq stood quietly for a few beats and finally
shook his head.

Kole nodded and told him, "Sorry I raised my voice. You
got me hot, saying my brother deserved what he got."

Tariq wilted visibly, like a week-old bouquet. "Sorry. I
didn't mean it. I'm just worried about my mama. She's the only
person in the world I really care about. I'd go crazy if something
happened to her."

"I would too," Kole said. "That's why I'm not gon' let
nothing happen to her. I'd give up my life to protect her – *both of
y'all.* Deep down, I think you know that..."

Tariq didn't respond.

Kole sighed and turned and left the room. Dana stood and
gave her son a hug before following her man.

CHAPTER 60

IN THE BEDROOM, Kole headed for the closet to see if he had a change of clothes for tomorrow. When he noticed Dana behind him, he told her, "Don't worry. I'ma get some clothes for you and Tariq. Some food too."

"We're fine," she replied, though her eyes were wrought with stress. She took a seat on the bed.

Kole came and sat next to her. He placed a hand on her thigh, and she turned to face him. "I'm sorry," he said. "For everything that's happening."

"It's..." She took a deep breath and blew it out slowly. "It's alright. It's not your fault."

"Yeah, right. Even Tariq knows better than that."

"I mean, I understand why you feel motivated to do the things you do. I just wish it was over. But after what happened tonight, I'm guessing it's not..."

Kole remained silent. He couldn't lie to her.

Dana brought her hands to her lap and wrung them together. Kole placed his bear-size mitt over hers and steadied them.

"Wha, can you tell me what happened after the accident?" she asked.

"Accident?"

"I mean, you know, your traffic accident..."

He grinned. "That's what I've been telling everybody: It was an *accident*."

He told her about the aftermath of the wreck and his trip to the police station. As expected, Dana was more worried when he finished speaking.

"So they're on to you?" She was on the verge of tears.

He shook his head. "No. They were fishing. They wanna solve the case. Anything that's got to do with a white gang is gonna get their attention. I don't think they bought my story about the wreck, but that's on them. They can't arrest nobody because of what they *think* happened."

"But you're on their radar," Dana insisted. "They'll keep investigating you until they find something."

"They got nothing," Kole said assuredly. "Trust me. I been closer than this to getting arrested. They got nothing on me."

"But the white gangs, they know who you are now."

"They already knew, or they wouldn't have found you."

"They're gonna come back," Dana predicted. "This will never end, Kole. Can't we just, can we run? Can't we find somewhere else to live?"

"*Run?*" He frowned at her. "Didn't you hear what I just told Tariq?"

"*Kole, I don't care about that shit.* I only care about you being *alive* – and not in jail. If this is your bravado talking–"

"I'm a man before anything else," he said, cutting her off. "Don't act like you don't know who I am."

But he wasn't too manly to drape an arm around her and comfort her when she broke down. He held her until her tears subsided, and then he laid her back on the bed, so she could get some rest. By then it was after 2 am.

Kole returned to the front room to check on Tariq. The teen was still on his phone, paying half attention to the television. Kole took a seat next to him on the couch. Tariq put his phone aside but was too nervous to look him in the eyes.

He stared down at his hands and said, "Sorry I yelled at you."

"It's alright," Kole replied. "I ain't mad at you."

"I was... That's my mama," the boy said. "I don't want nothing to happen to her."

"I respect that," Kole told him. "It takes a real man to protect his mama like that. You showed me something tonight. I'm proud of you."

Tariq did meet his eyes then. It didn't appear Kole was trying to placate him.

Kole told him, "I appreciate you because this situation, it might not go like I want it to. I'm sure you know these people I'm into it with, they don't want your mama. They don't wanna hurt you either. They would only go after y'all if they can't get to me. So if worse comes to worst, and I don't make it out of this, you two will be alright. I'm cool with that, because I know your mama has you to take care of her, make sure she's okay."

Tariq frowned. "But, but you're gonna be alright though, right? Nothing's gonna happen to you..."

Kole reached and patted his shoulder, which wasn't as bony as it was this time last year. "I'll be fine. There's some food in the fridge," he said as he rose to his feet. "If you're hungry, eat whatever you want. Let me know what clothes or whatever else you need, and I'll get it tomorrow."

Tariq stared after him when Kole exited the room. Having never known his father or believed in superheroes, the teen was conflicted about his feelings towards this larger-than-life human spectacle that had stolen his mother's heart.

All he knew for sure was he did not want Kole to die. The world – not just his mother's life – but *the whole world* was a better place with Kole in it. Of that much, Tariq was certain.

PART SIX
AKA EASY RAWLINS

CHAPTER 61

THE NEXT MORNING, Dana awakened feeling loved and secure, despite the drama of the previous evening. She was accustomed to Kole spooning her as they slept. This time his arm was not merely draped over her. His large hand palmed her belly, as if he was comforting and protecting the new life that would make her stomach swell in the months to come.

Or maybe she was reading too much into it.

Whatever the case, Kole didn't acknowledge it when he opened his eyes and spoke into the back of her head.

"You up?"

"Yeah," she replied. "Wasn't able to sleep much."

"I gotta go check on a few things," he told her. "You and Tariq gonna be alright here?"

Dana appreciated him asking, though the question was somewhat rhetorical. She and Tariq didn't have a choice as to whether they wanted to be there or not. But with the looming danger aside, she found his safe house very beautiful and spacious.

"Yes. We'll be fine."

"I'm sorry about all of this," Kole said. "I don't think it'll take more than a couple of days till your life can go back to normal."

Your life?

"What about you?" she asked. "Nothing's gonna be normal unless you're safe."

Kole rolled over and sat up on his side of the bed. "I'll be fine. Just need to figure some things out."

Dana rolled towards him. In the dimly lit room, his black skin looked like a dark ocean. The size of his torso was as breathtaking as it was intimidating.

"What are you going to do?" she asked.

She wasn't sure if he'd tell her, but Kole said, "I need to find out who went after you last night and who ordered it. They weren't successful, so I'm guessing the hit is still on, if that's what it was."

The thought of having a *hit* out on her was horrifying. Even though she'd seen it firsthand, this sounded like something that was happening to someone else.

"Once you find out, then what?"

"I have to neutralize all threats," Kole said, without looking back at her. He had his cellphone in hand now. He typed a quick message to someone and then rose to his feet. He looked her in the eyes and said, "If I can't neutralize them, I have to eliminate them."

Kole wore only his boxers. He looked powerful enough to prevail over any foe. But Dana worried about him as much as she fretted over her son. She knew there was no way to talk him out of whatever plan of action he came up with, so she simply said, "Please be careful."

"I will. Text me and let me know what clothes you and Tariq need. Plan for three days, but I don't think it'll take that long. Are you okay with being off work again? They not gon' trip?"

"They should be fine," Dana replied. "I've only missed three days in the past year. They know I wouldn't call in unless it was serious."

Kole nodded and headed for the closet. Two minutes later he emerged fully dressed in what Dana considered his norm; black shirt with sneakers and dark jeans.

"When you text me about the clothes, don't forget sizes."

"You going shopping?" she asked.

When not wearing his day-to-day *uniform*, Kole was a snappy dresser. But in the year they'd been dating, she'd never seen him enter a mall.

"I'll send someone for it," he stated.

Dana didn't think she had a reaction to that, but she must have. Kole grinned as he sat next to her on the bed.

"You worried about someone knowing your panty size?"

She grinned too. It was amazing how he always found a way to put a smile on her face, even in the darkest times.

"Are you sending a guy or a girl?" she wondered.

"A girl," he said.

Dana was aware that her eyes narrowed then.

"Don't worry," he said. "It's not someone I know. It'll be a girlfriend of one of the men."

He leaned closer and kissed her on the forehead. "Be back soon."

She placed a hand on his shoulder. "Be careful," she repeated, her expression serious now.

"Always," he said and kissed her on the lips. "Try not to worry."

She kissed him again before whispering, "Yeah right."

CHAPTER 62

KOLE ARRIVED AT The Moonlight a little after 10 am. He didn't try to fight the wave of nostalgia that struck him the moment he walked through the doors. He took a seat at the bar and thought about one of the last conversations he and Moon had there. He smiled wistfully, thinking of how he wanted to slap his best friend upside his big, bald head.

"It's been a year, and you still with that woman," Moon had told him. He had stood behind the bar drying a few shot glasses.

It was summertime, a couple of weeks before his niece's graduation. Kole casually sipped a glass of bourbon.

"It's been a year?" Kole questioned. "Damn, how you know that? You keeping up with my anniversaries now?"

"Hell naw," Moon had said. "Can't even keep up with me and Carla's. I know it's been a year 'cause it was around this time last summer I had to help you out with that MMG situation."

"You helped *me* out?"

"I saved your ass, as usual," Moon recalled. "Brass was putting a whooping on ya."

Kole shook his head, chuckling. "Way I remember it, I had that fool in a chokehold. Put him to sleep in front of his whole crew."

"That's because *I* kept his crew in check," Moon boasted. "You think they would've sat there watching the fight if we didn't have guns on 'em?"

"I know I couldn't have taken care of that problem without you," Kole acknowledged. "What's your point?"

"My point is you always find a way to change the subject when I bring up Dana," Moon noticed. "I was trying to ask what's going on with y'all. You ain't never been known to keep a woman around this long."

Moon was only a year older, but physically, Kole appeared to be ten years younger. Even during his heyday with The Organization, Kole took pride in his health; running a couple of miles whenever time permitted and staying true to a pushup/sit-up regimen at least five days a week.

Moon had been married for sixteen years, and his wife owned a homestyle restaurant. Rather than pushups, he had trouble *pushing away* from the table. But despite his gut, Moon was formidable; with broad shoulders and strong arms. His chest was as big as Kole's, just not as defined.

"Why are you and Carla so concerned about what's going on at *my* house?" Kole had wondered. "Actually, I can understand why *she's* all in my business, her being a woman and all. But what's your excuse?"

Moon shook his head, smiling, rather than taking offense to the comment. "There you go getting defensive again. That means you in love with that woman."

Kole blew him off with a frown and a shake of his head.

"I was just wondering," Moon went on, "is Dana the type of gal who'll jump ship if you don't put a ring on her finger, or is she cool with you being a lifelong bachelor?"

"I ain't buying no rings," Kole had told him, "so I guess we'll find out."

"You retired," Moon continued. "Ain't got nothing holding you back from settling down. What's the problem?"

In a rare moment of openness, Kole had told him, "I ain't never seen a marriage work out. If Dana do get tired of me, it'll be easier to go our separate ways, if ain't no court involved."

Moon thought for a second before saying, "What you mean you never seen a marriage work out? What about me and Carla?"

Kole chuckled. "You mean you, Carla *and* your mistress? You call that working out?"

"*Shiiit*, it's been working," Moon stated. "All three of us happy; living life to the fullest."

Kole's eyes watered as he waited in the deserted club. He wished Moon was there now, so he could bounce a few ideas off him. Moon knew he was against having children. Kole wondered what his friend would say about Dana's pregnancy. Knowing Moon, he'd jump on the opportunity to clown him:

What'd you wait so long for, old-ass nigga? What kind of fool waits till he's damn near **geriatric** *to get into* **pediatrics***?*

Kole still had tears in his eyes when Byrd entered the club. His friend took a seat next to him and studied Kole's sullen features before speaking.

"What's up, man. You alright?" Byrd's bottom lip was swollen from the explosive impact of the airbag last night.

"Yeah," Kole said. He sighed. "Just thinking about Moon."

"I feel you," Byrd said.

In their line of business, a homey could get clowned for expressing emotions. But when it came to Moon, everyone in The Organization felt the same way. They would never fully recover from the loss.

"Anyway, what's the word?" Kole asked, refocusing his thoughts.

"Hell, I guess the word is *white people*," Byrd said, getting down to business. "You seen how they been up in arms lately? I saw a motorcycle gang on the way down here. All white. Rolling through the hood like it ain't nothing. I saw a couple of trucks too, with confederate flags on the back."

"I saw one," Kole said. "Thought it was strange for them to be riding through the hood like that."

"More than *strange*," Byrd said. "If it was just the one, that would be hella reckless, damn near suicidal. But they showing up in numbers."

"Think they just flexing?" Kole asked. "Or it's something more to it?"

"I heard it's something big going down," Byrd reported.

"I know it's a lot of them coming to town," Kole agreed. "But what's their plan? Our people are too spread out for them to do us like we did them."

"People talking about a rally," Byrd told him.

Kole frowned. "A rally? What you mean?"

Byrd shrugged. "A white supremacist rally, I guess. They getting together today for something major. But it ain't happening here. Supposed to be somewhere in the boondocks."

Kole's frown deepened. "What's that gonna solve?"

Byrd shook his head. "I don't know. A show of unity?"

Kole considered that. After what they did to Trey and his crew, it would make sense for the white gangs to come together. But he expected some sort of street-level retaliation, like the way they went after Dana last night.

"Marching down the street ain't gon' do nothing but bring a lot of attention to them," he surmised. "If they planning on getting back at us, attention is the last thing they'd want."

Byrd nodded. "Yeah. I thought so too."

"So maybe the big thing they're planning ain't a rally," Kole offered. "I can see some alt-right nuts pulling that mess. But the people we dealing with are legit bangers. Cops could show up at a rally and arrest all of 'em for outstanding warrants."

Byrd continued to nod.

"I need you to get in touch with our peeps, and tell them to be on high alert," Kole instructed. "You already got our spots shut down?"

"They been shut down since Moon died," Byrd confirmed. "We been losing a lot of money, but it's better to keep everyone safe."

"Alright," Kole said, rising from his stool. "Let me know if you hear anything else about their *big plans*, and I'll do some digging myself. I would love to crash their party, if we can find out what it is and where it's at."

"That's what I'm talking about," Byrd said.

He stood and gave Kole a bro-hug before they went their separate ways.

CHAPTER 63

KOLE HIT THE streets for the next few hours but came up empty on his search for more intel. Frustrated, he picked up the clothing and other items Dana had requested and returned to the safehouse. She and Tariq were in good spirits when he got there, especially when they saw the Chinese food Kole had brought. The threesome watched old reruns of COPS while they dined.

Kole didn't let on how irritated he was until they finished eating and he headed to the bedroom. Dana joined him a few minutes later. She found Kole lying on his back with his legs hanging over the bed.

She sat next to him and asked, "What's wrong?"

He shook his head. "Nothing."

She reclined with him, and they stared up at the ceiling together. "You don't have to lie," she said. "You could just say you don't wanna talk about it."

Kole remained quiet for a few seconds before telling her, "It's a lot of white folks in town. They're planning something, but I can't figure out what it is."

"White folks, like the KKK?"

"Basically. Except the ones I'm seeing ain't hiding under hoods. They're more dangerous; like the prison gangs I told you about. I knew they were coming, but I didn't expect them to be out in the open; riding through the hood, trying to intimidate people."

Dana took a deep breath and blew it out slowly. In her mind, every white face in the city was looking for Kole.

"Don't worry," he said. He sat up and patted her knee. "I'll get to the bottom of it."

He went to an office next to the dining room and remained there for the next hour. Dana returned to the living room and was grateful to find Tariq engaged in his video games. She busied herself with apps on her cellphone but was not able to reach her son's level of comfort.

In the office, Kole got a couple of leads that only left him more confused. A snitch from the west side told him *something major* was scheduled for later that night in Waxahachie. Waxahachie was a Podunk town about an hour away. That confirmed Byrd's comment that *the big event* would take place in the boondocks. Kole pressed the snitch for more details, but he didn't have any.

The second bit of news came from Byrd. He called with an update on The Organization:

"I talked to everybody, told them to keep their head down and be ready for *whatever*. The only one I couldn't get a hold of is Lemon. He missing in action."

Lemon was one of the most reliable henchmen in The Organization.

Kole's eyebrows bunched together. "What you mean *missing*?"

"He ain't answering none of his cellphones," Byrd told him. "His peeps haven't been able to get in touch with him either."

"You think he laid up somewhere with a ho?" Kole wondered.

"Maybe, but that ain't never stopped him from answering his phone before," Byrd said. "He damn sure knows to answer his phone now, with everything that's going on."

"You checked the jails?" Kole asked. "He could've got popped on some old warrant."

"I had my girl call them. If he locked up, they haven't booked him yet."

Kole realized Byrd was on top of things. As hard as it would be to replace Moon, Byrd was a worthy successor.

"Alright, let me know if he pops up. I'ma head to the west side, see if I can't find this redneck I know."

"You going by yourself?" Byrd asked. "I can come scoop you."

"Where I'm going, one black face is bad enough," Kole informed him. "*Two* black faces will prolly get the law called on us..."

CHAPTER 64

ON THE WEST side of town, less than ten miles from the massacre at the green and white duplex, Kole pulled up to a biker bar called the Green Rooster. He exited his vehicle and casually strolled past a row of Harleys on his way inside. It was 6 pm; too early for the rowdy crowd that would congregate at the bar and pool tables till closing time, but not early enough to go unnoticed in an establishment so honkytonk it made you wonder where the "WHITE ONLY" sign was.

Kole collected a lot of stares as he sauntered to a small table. But due to his size and the no-bullshit aura he always carried, no one said anything to him. That didn't mean his presence was appreciated. Some of the cowboys and bikers mad-dogged him openly, muttering easy-to-read comments under their breath or to their drinking buddy. Kole ignored them. He didn't look away, which would've been a sign of weakness. But he didn't glare back at them. He wasn't there to intimidate these people.

Kole perused his cellphone and pretended to be unbothered by the fifteen minute wait he endured before someone came to serve him. The waitress, a former meth addict who looked like she was on the verge of relapsing, reluctantly made her way to his table. She stole glances at the other customers; her eyes apologetic, as if to say the Bill of Rights was the *only* reason she was speaking to the interloper.

Kole knew the woman fairly well. He was not offended when she looked him in the eyes and asked, "What are you doing here?"

"Can't a man get a drink?" Kole asked, putting his phone away.

"I can't imagine you came all the way over here for a drink," the waitress stated, "especially after what happened the other day. Plenty of juke joints on your side of town."

Kole had to smile at that. He sometimes wondered what it was like for the sit-in protesters during the Civil Rights Movement. The atmosphere at the Green Rooster gave him a taste of that.

"Last I checked, a man can get a drink anywhere he wants."

"Yeah, but a man can get messed up if he chooses the wrong bar," the waitress spat back.

If he wasn't on a mission that required diplomacy, Kole would've grabbed a handful of her dirty blonde hair and dragged her halfway down the street for that remark.

Instead he said, "Who gon' get messed up? Bet it won't be me. Your customers might get messed up though, if they try something."

The waitress looked around fretfully. Her customers had Kole outnumbered fifteen to one, but Kole wasn't just anybody. For all she knew, he had a hundred goons waiting outside the door.

"What do you want?" she breathed.

"Jack and Coke," he said. "And John's phone number."

John was such a common name, he could've been referring to anyone. But the waitress knew exactly who he was talking about.

"What makes you think he wants to talk to you?" she asked, her voice low and conspiratorial now.

"That ain't up to you," Kole said. "If you want this hundred-dollar tip, you'll do what you're told."

The woman's thin nostrils flared. She stared at him for a few seconds before returning to the bar. Kole watched her every move, while pretending not to. The other patrons made no attempt to pretend they weren't watching Kole.

The waitress made a call before she prepared his drink. The call didn't last more than thirty seconds. Kole didn't see her write anything down, but when she returned with his order, he noticed a number scrawled on the napkin she placed his drink on. She didn't make eye-contact or speak to him this time. Kole downed his drink in a few gulps and took the napkin before placing his glass on the table. He stood and slid a hundred-dollar bill under the glass.

When he got outside, Kole made the call from his car.

A gruff, southern voice answered with an unwelcoming, "Who is this?"

"This is Kole. Just got your number from Becca at the Green Rooster."

"What the hell you doing over there?" John asked. "Don't tell me your black-ass is still there..."

When it came to racists, Kole liked them out and proud. He couldn't stand in-the-closet bigots who gave him an attitude for no reason and left him wondering if he'd done something offensive.

"I'm still here," Kole told him. "In the parking lot."

"You need to get from there," John replied. "What the hell's wrong with you? After that shit you pulled the other night, you got the nerve to show up at the Rooster?"

"I was at home eating Oodles of Noodles the other night," Kole replied. "You must be mistaken."

"Oodles of Noodles my ass! Hurry up and tell me what you want."

"I need to talk. I think you have some information I need. If not, I know you can get it."

"And what do you think'll happen to me for colluding with one of you's?"

269

"No one has to know."

"You done already told Becca you was looking for me," John said. "You think that bitch ain't no blabber mouth?"

"Just 'cause I got your number don't mean nothing. If anybody asks, you can say you told me to go to hell, for all I care. I'm ready to put a thousand dollars in your pocket right now. All you gotta do is ask a few questions and call me back with the answers."

The older man mulled that over. "What if I take your money, but I don't get those answers?"

"As long as I know you tried, we even," Kole told him.

The white man was silent for a handful of seconds. "I'll take your money," he decided. "But I don't wanna hear no shit if I can't come up with nothing."

"Long as you call me back and tell me the truth, we cool," Kole assured him. "But if I don't hear back from you, we ain't cool."

"Yeah, whatever," John said. He gave Kole the address for a shopping center fifteen minutes away.

CHAPTER 65

JOHN WAS A self-proclaimed redneck in his late fifties. At the meeting point, he refused to get inside Kole's car. Given the recent racial tension in the city, Kole didn't blame him. John leaned in the driver's side window and accepted his payment and instructions.

Kole returned to the safehouse to check on Dana and Tariq. They were doing as well as to be expected. Kole couldn't stop his mind from racing, so he threw all of his attention into making dinner. It turned out great. Initially Tariq balked at the idea of *eggplant parmesan*, but he tasted it and decided Kole was a master chef.

The unconventional family was halfway through their meal when Kole received the call he'd been waiting for. He excused himself and headed for the bedroom.

"What's up?" he answered.

"Yeah, it's me," John said. "I think you owe me more money. Had to drive all the way to Waxahachie to get that info for ya."

A smile lit Kole's features. John had gone above and beyond. Kole knew he didn't do it out of the kindness of his heart or even for the additional money he was requesting. John did it because calling him back with *no news* after he already took the money could lead to his untimely demise.

"I'll take care of you," Kole promised. "What you got?"

John gave him an address on a rural road in the small town. "That's where tonight's festivities is going down," he said.

Kole committed the address to memory. "What's the festivities?" he wanted to know.

"Nobody will say," John replied. "I know it's a few prison gangs involved. They're pissed about what happened to those boys over by Camp Bowie. They wanna show you niggers who's really in charge."

John did not apologize for using the N-word with a hard 'r.' Kole bristled, but he didn't mention it either.

"Alright," he said. "You know what time?"

"Nope. It'll be pretty late, though. After most people done went to sleep."

"Alright. 'Preciate you."

"Just for the record," John went on, "I think you boys need to lay low and leave this alone. Y'all was dead wrong for what you done, and these folks got a right to be mad. You come down here stirring up shit–"

"*I said I appreciate you,*" Kole said, cutting him off. "Now shut the fuck up, before you piss me off."

He disconnected and called Byrd. After relaying the information John had given him, he said, "Get the team mobilized. We leaving after dark, around ten. Hopefully it won't be too many laws patrolling down there, 'cause we'll stick out like a sore thumb."

"How many men you wanna take?" Byrd asked.

"At least a hundred," Kole stated. "Armed to the teeth."

"Bet."

"Still no word from Lemon?" Kole had been thinking about his gold-toothed comrade all day.

"Naw," Byrd replied. "I'm starting to worry about him. You think one of those white boys did him?"

The thought had crossed Kole's mind. "I hope not. If they did, the Trinity River will run red with their blood," he said, referring to Overbrook Meadows' largest waterway. "They'll wish they never heard of me or Moon."

"*Awwwready*," Byrd exclaimed. "We'll be ready to roll out at ten."

"Alright. Be safe," Kole said and disconnected.

Back in the dining room, his mood was somber. Kole quickly wolfed down the rest of his meal. Dana and Tariq watched him silently. When he was done, she followed him to the kitchen.

"Is everything alright?"

Kole put his plate in the sink and turned to face her. His expression was hard, ready for war. "I'm leaving at ten."

Dana checked her watch. That was less than an hour away. She was past the point of hoping he'd back down. Instead, she desperately wanted to help in some way, even if only to alleviate his stress.

"Is there anything I can do?" Her features were downcast, her eyes pleading.

"Pray," Kole said.

Dana found it odd that he would request such a thing.

Before she could question him, Kole said, "Not for me. Pray for *them*."

He left her at the sink and walked out of the kitchen.

CHAPTER 66

Four hundred years
Of bondage so cruel
Blood-drenched soil of the south
Will **never** wash clean
The ghosts of our ancestors
Tormented
Wailing
Celebrated the war meant for freedom
But despite the north prevailing
The confederate's bitter defeat
Brought white hoods
And foul torches
Ominous flags
Burning bodies
From the trees those black bodies
Hung for all to see
Yet
We persist
Sit-ins and walkouts and black fists
Raised
For the basic right to exist
Get over it
They say
But how can we
When Today

That foul hatred's on display
In so many white faces
Some tatted
Most basic
Decades after Martin and Malcolm
They hold fast to absolute abhorrence
For the poor souls
Born with dark skin
In America

IT WAS AFTER eleven when Kole and Byrd made it to Waxahachie in a 2001 Yukon. There were five more men in the backseats; all of them dressed in black and armed with assault rifles. Kole hadn't ridden dirty like this in a while. A random traffic stop could land all of them in prison. The same could be said about the seven 15-passenger vans elsewhere on the freeway. But for Moon, they would eagerly risk their freedom. They would lay down their lives for their fallen leader, if need be.

The mood in Kole's SUV was edgy. Unlike most of their missions, the men had no idea what to expect when they arrived at their destination. Kole worried the city was so small, the vans would be easily noticeable. He instructed the drivers to avoid travelling within a few miles or even on the same street as their counterparts.

Above them, the moon shone dark orange, almost blood red. The stars were bright and plentiful. When they exited the freeway, the country roads were dark, with few streetlamps and even fewer signal lights. Luckily the local police were just as scarce. Kole hadn't spotted a patrol car since they entered Waxahachie's city limits. The occupants of his vehicle were silent, other than Byrd giving directions to the other drivers.

Kole kept a lookout for any obstacles or potential threats as he navigated the mostly deserted streets. The bikers and pickup trucks emblazoned with confederate images were nowhere in sight. As they neared the farm-to-market road where the big event would supposedly take place, Kole was reminded of his upbringing in the equally small city of Texarkana. Like Waxahachie, that town was filled with more potholes than promise, more chickens than people. Kole found the nostalgia unnerving, even more so because of the uncertainties that lie ahead.

The address John had given him led to a paved road with no curbs or sidewalks. The neighborhood offered a mix of large houses, some recently built, as well as long mobile homes; many of which were in disrepair. The houses sat far away from the street with even more land in between them. Most were fenced with horses or other livestock.

When Byrd finally said, "This is it coming up," Kole killed his lights, which impaired their sight considerably. The closest street light was nearly 100 yards away. Kole drove slowly past a nondescript three-bedroom flat that appeared to be vacant. There were no cars in the driveway, and the yard was in need of mowing. There was no fence surrounding the property. No signs of life that Kole could see.

He pulled to a stop twenty yards past the home. Everyone remained quiet as they stared out of the windows on the right side of the truck. Kole broke the silence by speaking into a CB radio.

"We're here." His transmission went out to all seven drivers who were trailing behind. "Doesn't look like anything's going on. Hang back. Find somewhere to chill, while we check it out."

Kole knew that was easier said than done. Seven full-passenger vans parked randomly on those country roads was not an ideal scenario. But none of the drivers questioned his orders. He handed the radio to Byrd and hefted his own weapon, an AR-15, before pulling his ski mask down over his face. His heartbeats thumped hard and rhythmically, but on the outside, Kole was completely calm. Weapon in hand, he looked like a one-man SWAT team.

"You ready?" he asked his second in command.

Byrd hefted his rifle and pulled his ski mask down. He nodded.

The duo crept from the car like goblins and almost immediately became one with the night.

CHAPTER 67

AS KOLE SUSPECTED when they first arrived at the location, the address John had given him was vacant. The porchlight was missing a bulb as was a floodlight that would've illuminated the gravel driveway. Kole and Byrd crept alongside the home, not taking anything for granted. When they reached the back porch, Kole mounted it and tried to gain entry through the back door. It was locked. He pressed his ear to the wood and listened intently. Not a creature stirred inside.

As his eyes adjusted to the darkness, Kole could barely make out Byrd at the bottom of the steps. He rejoined him. The porch was made of old wood that creaked beneath his weight, but no dogs were alerted to the sound.

Speaking softly, Kole told his friend, "I don't think anyone's lived here in a while."

"Think we got sent on a wild goose chase?" Byrd wondered.

Kole doubted John would do that to him. Even though they weren't friends, the informant was loyal to the almighty dollar. He shook his head, looking towards the backyard. It was so expansive, Kole doubted if he'd be able to see from one end to the other, even if the sun was out. In the distance, he made out a dense tree line that appeared to be on the same property.

Following his gaze, Byrd asked, "You think we should check it out?"

"We're here," Kole replied. "Might as well."

The pair stuck together, moving through darkness that seemed more overwhelming with each step. The deeper they trekked into the backyard, the taller the grass was; leaving them susceptible to a number of pitfalls; anything from a coiled rattlesnake to an uncovered septic tank.

It was Kole who first noticed something odd underfoot. He risked a peek with his flashlight and then squatted to get a better look. He ran his fingers along the ground and motioned for Byrd to check out his find. His assessment was the same as Kole's.

"Tire tracks?"

Kole nodded. "I ain't no tracker, but I think they're pretty fresh. You see how the grass is laid down?"

Byrd nodded. Kole swam his light back towards the house and confirmed the tracks had originated in that direction. He flashed his light to the right and left of where they were standing.

"More of them," Byrd said.

"A lot more," Kole concurred, his heartrate kicking up a notch.

"So they did come through here," Byrd deduced.

Kole nodded. He shone his light towards the tree line. "You think they went way the hell back there?"

"Where else could they have gone?" Byrd asked, looking around.

By Kole's estimate, they were a couple of miles away from the trees. He calculated the risks and said, "Why don't you and me head there on foot, have the rest follow us in the vans? We can scout ahead, let 'em know if we run into any fences."

"Sounds like a plan. Want me to call it in?"

Kole nodded. "Yeah. If them white boys can drive through here, we can too."

Byrd snatched the radio from his belt and gave the instructions. When he was done, he noticed Kole staring straight ahead, sniffing the air.

"What's up?" Byrd asked him.

Kole tilted his head as he looked back at him. "You smell something burning?"

CHAPTER 68

THE LEADERS LED the way on foot, with an SUV and seven vans trailing slowly behind. The passenger vans weren't ideal for the rough terrain, but it hadn't rained in a while, so there were no muddy holes or soft patches of earth for them to get stuck in.

Initially Kole and Byrd followed the tire tracks, turning their flashlights on ever so often to make sure they were on the right path. But as they drew closer to the tree line, Kole found that he could follow the scent of fire just as well. It wasn't uncommon or even illegal to burn trash piles in the country. But given the hour and the mystery of whatever the white gangs had going on, the acrid smell of wood and debris was ominous.

Kole's stomach churned when they finally made it to a dense line of oak trees and could see smoke in the distance. It rose thick and dark, blotting out the moon at times. Kole strained his other senses, and he faintly heard voices. Some appeared to be laughing. He and Byrd continued, until they spotted a cluster of vehicles. Kole gave orders for all of their men to kill the engines on the vans and proceed the rest of the way on foot.

As Byrd and Kole crept forward, more vehicles came into view. Most were trucks, but Kole saw half a dozen motorcycles as well. All in all, he counted 23 vehicles. Even if some of the trucks had arrived with a couple men sitting in the beds, he was confident his team outnumbered them.

By then he and Byrd were flanked by dozens of darkly clad men, all wearing ski masks. They moved quietly, crouched with their weapons at the ready. They trailed through the enemy's vehicles like army ants. They could all smell the fire now. They heard voices; rednecks for sure. Loud and boisterous. Some were drunk. All were pleased at what they had accomplished.

Kole's eyes blazed fury even before they made it to a clearing. The anticipation of what these men had done – *were doing* – made his blood flow like lava. If not for the men who depended on him, he would've charged in, all fury and no game plan. But The Organization was much bigger than him, bigger than whatever foul things the racists had in mind that night.

So Kole practiced patience. He told his men to fan out around the opening in the woods. As they inched closer, they could see the fire. A huge heap of mostly wood was fully engulfed. Thirty-five to forty men crowded around, as if celebrating the Burning Man festival. Some had drinks in hand. None wore robes, but plenty of them had tattoos. They were laughing and lively. And why shouldn't they be? They had just accomplished every white supremacist's dream.

Or maybe they hadn't.

Kole's breaths were hot and ragged. His breathing stopped altogether when he noticed a smaller crowd separated from the other revelers. These men, a group of four, held the only black face amongst them by the arms, which were tied behind his back. Their prisoner was beaten to a bloody pulp, but even by the light of the fire, he could tell it was Lemon.

He exhaled roughly and became lightheaded. Kole was relieved to see the rednecks had not yet commenced the evil deed. But as he watched, he realized the men weren't merely holding Lemon. They were dragging him towards the fire, which was really more of a pyre. Lemon fought valiantly, but it was clear his strength had been sapped. With both legs limp, his captors drug him effortlessly towards his demise.

"*Go!*" Kole hissed to his right and his left. "*Everybody, go! Now! Goooo!*"

Word traveled fast down the line. The Organization burst from the trees simultaneously, guns up, teeth bared. They barked orders at the white men as they increased their half-circle advantage to a full circle.

"HANDS UP!"
"DON'T MOVE!"
"GET ON YOUR KNEES! NOW!"
"DON'T REACH, MOTHERFUCKER!"
"ON YOUR KNEES!"

Stunned, the white men surrendered within a matter of seconds.

All of them.

Kole hadn't instructed his men to avoid gunfire, but they were disciplined soldiers. None of the rednecks had fired on them, and despite the horrific scene they'd interrupted, no one from The Organization pulled the trigger. They held them all at gunpoint; with the fire in the center, a ring of racists surrounding it and a ring of masked men encircling them.

Kole rushed to Lemon and gun-butted one of the men holding him. The white man grabbed his mouth and blood gushed through his fingers. He fell to his knees spitting teeth and gore.

"*Let him go!*" Kole shouted a second too late.

Hearing his savior's voice, Lemon staggered towards Kole. He tried desperately to open his eyes, but they were swollen shut. He fell to his knees and leaned forward, with his bruised face pressed against Kole's thigh.

"*Shoot 'em!*" he squealed. "***Kill 'em! Kill 'em all!***"

Kole desperately wanted to fulfill that request, but as he looked around, he realized the folly of the move. Forty dead racists sounded good on paper, but the aftermath could spell doom for The Organization. Retaliation from the gangs these men belonged to would be the least of their worries. With a massacre that large, the feds were sure to get involved.

As much as it pained him to show restraint, Kole did not give orders to shoot. Instead he instructed a few of his troops to, "Help this man up."

They stepped forward and found Lemon's hands restrained by handcuffs. They led him out of the inner circle quietly, though Lemon continued to scream bloody murder.

"Shoot! Why y'all ain't shooting? Look what they did to me! ***Kill 'em all****!"*

Kole casually marched around the smaller circle, surveying the work his men had done. By then some of the whites realized the armed men were all black, and they were certainly not members of a police force. They cursed them; a few using the N-word with a hard *r*, as if their lives didn't hang in the balance, and these particular N-words weren't itching to lay them all down.

Kole ignored their stares and jeers as the fire licked the sky and his men maintained more composure than he would've at their age.

Finally he yelled, "***Who's in charge of this bullshit***?!"

He thought he'd have to bust a few heads to get an answer, but one brave soul spoke up right away.

"I am!"

Kole turned and saw a middle-age man who looked weather worn and war torn. He gestured with the barrel of his gun.

"Get up. ***Get your ass over here****!"*

Surprisingly, the white man showed no fear as he rose from his knees and stepped in Kole's direction. All eyes were on the two of them. Kole turned and walked back to the trees, where they left their vehicles. The white man grinned and wiped his hands on his pants as he followed him.

CHAPTER 69

"MAN, WHAT THE fuck is wrong with you?"

Kole walked far enough to give them a little privacy, but not too far. He could still see the white man clearly by the moonlight and firelight. If he tried to take off, Kole was confident he could drop him with a few rounds in the back.

The supposed leader of the racists continued to smile at him, which aggravated Kole further. If there wasn't so much at stake, he would've shot him right then, just on principle.

"What the fuck is wrong with *you*?" his antagonist asked. "Jumping all out the woods, like y'all green berets or something."

Kole kept his weapon trained on his chest. He sighed deeply before saying, "I know y'all wasn't about to do what I think you was."

The white man chuckled. "If you think we was about to lynch us a nigger, yeah, we was about to do that."

Kole couldn't believe he was this brave. "You gon' call him a nigger with an assault rifle pointed right at you?"

"What difference does it make?" the man asked. "You gon' kill us anyway, ain't you? If you expect me to beg for my life, you barking up the wrong tree. I'ma die like a man, just like I lived."

His country twang was so thick, Kole guessed he was from the Louisiana swamplands. As much as he hated him, he had to respect that he was willing to die for his convictions.

"If I wanted you dead, you wouldn't have seen us coming," Kole told him.

The white man frowned and cocked his head. "Is that right? Well, what'd you crash our party for? Y'all wanna roast some marshmallows?"

Kole's nostrils flared as he took another deep breath. "You making it real hard not to kill your cracker ass."

"Tell you what," the man said. "Why don't you say what you want, so we can get on with this? You got your boy back. What else is there to talk about?"

"How about this dumb-ass fire you got going. You know how many feds would've been up your ass, if you had pulled that off?"

"Don't matter," the man said seriously.

"How come it don't?"

"'Cause after what happened to our people, we have to send a message."

"Your people? You talking about the Woods in that duplex?"

The white man's smile finally ebbed. He nodded. "Yeah. Them was my people."

"You don't think they had that coming, after what they did to *my* people?" Kole asked.

"I don't know who the hell your people are."

"They killed my brother Moon. You knew about that?"

"Your brother?"

"Yeah. My brother."

"So y'all with that – what do you call it? Some kind of organization?"

Kole nodded slowly. "Did you know about the hit on Moon? You had something to do with it?"

286

"Not that it matters at this point, but I told Trey not to do it. He was a knucklehead, though. Always been that way. Never was one to look both ways before crossing the street."

Kole noticed a change in the man's voice when he spoke about Trey. "He was somebody to you?"

"My son," the man said. "Travis Oakley the third. We called him Trey. I always knew his rash decisions would get him killed one day. But I never thought it'd be one of you that got him. And the way it happened…" He shook his head. "They choked him to death. Didn't even have the decency to put one between his eyes. Can you imagine what it feels like to get choked to death?"

Kole's eyes widened. He couldn't believe his misfortunes. The last time The Organization got into a war this big, they were going against MMG because *their* leader's son got killed. Here he was again, talking to the father of a slain boy, trying to get him to back down from what was probably the worst pain he'd ever experienced.

He decided the worst medicine should be administered quickly. "I killed your boy."

Travis Oakley II stared at him, unblinking.

"I choked him," Kole said. "Watched him take his last breath. I don't regret it 'cause, like I told you, he killed my brother. I think that makes us even."

The man stared at him for a long time after that revelation. "You killed my son?"

Kole placed his finger on the trigger of his weapon, expecting him to make a dumb move. "You heard me."

Travis shook his head slowly. He frowned and looked Kole up and down. "Yeah," he commented. "Looks like you're big enough to pull that off."

Kole didn't respond to that.

"Tell me something," Travis said. "Did he fight you back?"

Kole cocked his head.

"I don't wanna hear that my son went out like a little bitch," the man clarified.

Kole's eyebrows bunched as he told him, "He fought me."

The man stared at him for a while longer. In the darkness, with Kole's back to the fire, he couldn't make out much. Kole was mostly a shadow, larger than life, with eyes that were teaming with demons.

"Can't see you too good," Travis said, "but it don't look like he got any licks on you."

Kole considered his son's weak attempt to save his life and didn't reply.

The white man's eyes narrowed before he moved again. This time he came charging forward. Kole saw it coming a mile away, but he only had a split second to come to terms with the fool's audacity and decide how he wanted to counter him.

Still hoping to avoid a bloodbath, he lowered the barrel of his rifle and fired at his legs. He let off one shot that sounded like thunder in the quiet environment.

BLAT!

He hoped to drop the redneck, but they were too close. Travis' hands were on him before Kole could determine if his shot hit its mark. The white man reached for the gun, and it went off again.

BLAT!

Kole's heart froze. He didn't think Travis could wrangle the rifle from his hands, but the older man was strong. Reeling from the death of his son, the redneck's blood flowed with ice cold courage and reckless abandon.

The rifle fell to the earth, and the leaders tussled in the darkness. The moment it hit the ground, Travis came up with a right hook that caught Kole flush on the chin. He grunted as his head snapped hard to the side. Unnatural stars clouded his vision. From a detached, third person perspective, Kole felt himself falling. The trees seemed to spin around them. Acrid smoke singed his nostrils.

"Want me to do him? *Say the word!*"

The voice pushed through the cotton in Kole's mind, and reality came screaming back at a dizzying pace. Kole realized it was Byrd speaking. He couldn't tell where his comrade was, but he was grateful that he'd come to his aid.

"*No!*" he snarled as he warded off more haymakers.

Travis swung from the fences now, no doubt with the same bare-fist tactics he'd honed in prison. Kole was acutely aware that the man had him fully mounted. He shook off the last of his disorientation could hear him speaking. Desperate and deranged, Travis screamed as he pummeled him.

"*You killed my son, you fucking nigger! You killed my boy!*"

Kole growled, and rage filled his eyes. His heart thundered. Being on his back, with a grown man on top of him, was a worst-case scenario. The words spewing from Travis' mouth further infuriated him. Despite it all, Kole did not regret his decision to shoot for the legs. What was happening that night was much bigger than the two of them.

"*Get the fuck off me!*"

He fought back in earnest, but his position left him at a disadvantage. Travis' son had found himself in the same predicament, and he wasn't able to save his life. But Kole was no skinny white boy. He took a few more blows to the head when he mounted an offense, but it paid off. He landed a crushing blow to the white man's skull that stunned him. Before Travis could recover, Kole kneed him in the balls and chopped him in the throat.

The redneck's eyes crossed, and he fell forward, wincing from multiple sources of pain. Kole scrambled from beneath him and quickly reversed positions. As soon as Travis' chest hit the ground, Kole straddled his back. He boxed his ears and jaws with hard, swift blows that incapacitated the threat in a matter of seconds.

He berated him with his final three blows

"*Fuck (Bap!) is wrong (Bap!) with you (Bap!)?*"

Travis lie flat, every one of his limbs limp. With his last bit of strength, he turned his head to the side and exhaled roughly, stirring the dirt around his mouth. Kole stood on his knees, both fists balled. His chest heaved. Blood ran from a blow he didn't realize he'd taken to the nose.

"You want me to do him?"

"*No!*" Kole shouted.

He looked up and saw Byrd was accompanied by two more soldiers. The trio had their rifles trained on the downed racist. Beyond them, Kole heard the crowd near the fire growing agitated. The white voices threatened to throw caution to the wind to find out what was going on. The black men promised to bust a cap in anyone who was foolish enough to try.

Kole made it to his feet and backed away from the body on the ground. He searched the grass for his weapon but was unable to find it in the darkness. Byrd assisted with his flashlight.

"It's over there."

Kole bent and hefted his rifle. Blood stained his bared teeth. He returned to the beaten man, who surprised him by attempting to rise to his knees. Kole knew he hadn't beaten him *mercilessly*, but still... He'd laid out plenty of people with fewer blows. As much as he hated this man and everything he stood for, he had to admit this was one bad motherfucker.

He kicked him in the ass and sent his face flying back to the dirt.

"You just don't get it," he breathed as he advanced on him.

"*Fuck you,*" the white man panted. "*Fuck all y'all-*"

Kole silenced him by snatching his shirt collar, effectively cutting off his windpipe. Travis weighed as much as he did, but Kole dragged him back to the fire with one hand. All eyes were on them when they emerged from the tree line. Kole thrust his enemy forward, and Travis rolled to his side, coughing raggedly. His face was bloody and lumped; with multiple contusions. In the firelight, Kole saw that his shot had hit its target. Travis' right leg bled from a wound to the thigh.

It wasn't his intent to make a statement, but the scene couldn't have been more powerful. Kole stood, armed, enormous and victorious, with the epitome of white power crumpled at his feet.

The visual was enough to make two of their captives rush to their leader's aid. They didn't make it more than a few feet before soldiers from The Organization pounced on them like a pack of hyenas, kicking and gun-butting them once they were down. Kole did not stop them. His men deserved an opportunity to vent their fury. They backed away when the racists were sufficiently bloodied and unconscious.

The rest of the rednecks continued to hurl insults at them, pushing the tension to the breaking point. Beyond the commotion, Kole was surprised to hear someone chuckling. He followed the sound to none other than Travis Oakley II. The man spat blood as he pushed up on his arms. As Kole watched, he made it to a sitting position; his ass flat on the ground.

He didn't appear pained by his gunshot wound, but he looked Kole in the eyes and said, "I'da knocked you out, if I wasn't shot. Don't you niggers ever fight fair?"

Kole's contempt grew at the same pace as his veneration. The conflicting emotions made him want to charge forward and deliver a kick to the man's already misshapen face.

"Is this what you call fair – forty of you out here jumping one of my guys?"

Travis didn't have a response for that. Instead he took a few deep breaths and said, "Whatever you plan on doing, you might as well get it over with. I don't know about everybody else, but I already told you I ain't begging a nigger for my life. If it's my time, I'm ready to take what's coming to me."

Kole locked eyes with some of the other white faces. He couldn't tell if they were on the same accord. As for the soldiers in The Organization, they were eager to lay every one of the crackers down. They prayed Kole would give the word.

As much as it pained him to show restraint, Kole spat and told Travis, "I think it's time for us to go our separate ways. I don't wanna kill you and all your men. And you damn sure ain't lynching nobody. In return for letting y'all live, you drop all animosity you have for my group, and we'll call it even."

Travis sneered at him. "How the hell are we even? You killed five of our people – my son included! Trey only killed one of yours."

"Moon was worth fifty of you sorry sonsofbitches!" Kole snapped. "And you said you didn't green light that hit. If your son was acting out of pocket, ain't no sense in defending that move."

"You worried about what's gon' happen if y'all kill us," Travis deduced. He wiped blood from his mouth and snickered.

The whites were all quiet now, listening intently as their leader made a life-or-death decision for them.

"I ain't worried about more of y'all honkeys coming to town," Kole said. "I'm worried about the *feds*. Unlike you idiots, my team don't wanna bring this much heat, unless it's necessary."

Travis considered that. Behind him, the fire crackled, burning brightly. "I don't know... My boys itching to lynch somebody. Judd lost a cousin in that house y'all shot up."

"My men are itching to murder everybody who had something to do with Moon getting killed!" Kole countered. "But if I tell 'em to stand down, they'll do it. You said you was the shot-caller. Don't you have the same control over your people?"

"I do," Travis said. "But when it's a time to kill, it's a time to kill..."

One of the other rednecks finally spoke up. "*Shut the fuck up, before you get us all shot!*"

Travis grinned, without turning towards the voice.

"Y'all ain't killing none of my people," Kole repeated. "If you lay a hand on one of my men, I don't care if it's a week from now or ten years from now, I will hunt your ass down. Believe that. And you best leave my woman alone too."

"Your woman? That was you in the Infinity last night?"

Kole nodded.

"Well, hell, you're just a regular badass, ain't you? Too bad you weren't born white. We could've used you in our ranks."

Kole could care less about the compliment. "Either give me your word right now that you ain't got no more beef with The Organization, or it's finna be a massacre. I'm done talking. We been out here long enough."

The white man reached, but it was only to wipe blood from his eyes. The move almost cost him and his crew their lives. He sighed and said, "Alright. You got my word. But just so you know, a civil war's coming. When we meet again, it won't be because of any of this other shit. It'll be because you're black, and I'm white, and one of us has to go."

"A civil war? Didn't y'all already try that?"

"It's different now, with Trump, Vance... The pure race is rising up all over the country. Even your police commissioner is on our side. Why you think he's coming down so hard on you niggers and beaners?"

Kole tried not to react to that. "Y'all just let a bunch of niggas get the drop on you, so good luck with your war."

"Mark my words," Travis warned.

"Whatever, man." Kole was eager to be done with this. "Come on. We out," he barked to his team. "Don't turn your back on 'em, but don't shoot nobody. It's over."

His men obediently began to retreat.

"*Nooo! Kill 'em!*" Lemon screamed. "***Kill 'em all!***"

"*I said it's over!*" Kole barked, and Lemon piped down.

As they backed into the darkness, he heard one of the rednecks say, "Come on. We can take 'em."

"Stand down!" Travis yelled at him. "You try anything, I'll kill you my damn self!"

Everyone in The Organization returned to their vehicles with no problem. It was a long, slow drive back to Overbrook Meadows, but they made it.

As he drove, Kole contemplated everything that had transpired since Moon died. Counting the two hitmen, seven people had paid the ultimate price for Moon's death. The Organization hadn't lost another soul, but nothing made up for the loss of their beloved leader.

Twenty years from now, Kole would still have tears in his eyes when he thought about his best friend.

EPILOGUE

CHAPTER 70

Her soul is musical
It sings to me
Her heart strings
Are a symphony
Her harp strings
Sound so sweet to me
Her hot skin
Tastes like ecstasy
Like chamomile
Honey
Vanilla tea

DANA AND TARIQ did not return to their home immediately.

Kole returned to his, but it was only to offer himself as a decoy. If the Woods and other white gangs were still gunning for him, he wouldn't make it hard to find him. As a precaution, he had several men with him at all times for the first month. Two posted up in his house, while the third provided surveillance from the street. The men split shifts, rotating frequently.

Their assistance was never needed, but the bond Kole had with these men deepened during the weeks following the incident in Waxahachie. They implored him to stay on as head of The Organization. They all believed Byrd was capable, but there was no denying Kole's expertise was second to none. No matter what room he entered, he was immediately the alpha male. Kole declined their offers to remain in the group.

"I only came back to find out who killed my brother," he told them. "That's taken care of. Now I gotta move on. I'm not turning my back on y'all. You know I'm always here when you need me. But I got my own life to live. I got a woman now, and we settling down. It's time for me to live the straight and narrow."

Not surprisingly, it was Byrd who was the most insistent that he stay. They met at The Moonlight one afternoon to oversee a few renovations. The club had been closed since Moon died. Kole knew his friend wouldn't want it to remain that way. The Moonlight had always been one of the best attractions on the city's south side. After speaking with Carla, Kole made the club's reopening his top priority.

"You know we need you," Byrd said as they strolled through the brightly lit nightspot.

The sound of skill saws and hammering was a welcome change to the solemn stillness that had permeated the building since its owner's murder.

"The boys are saying ain't nothing gon' change your mind," Byrd said. He and Kole walked across the freshly waxed dance floor.

"You not the one putting them up to that, are you?" Kole asked.

"What, asking you to stay?"

Kole looked over at him and nodded.

"Nah, man," Byrd said. "I'm sure they have their reasons."

"I know you're not worried about running the group," Kole told him. "'Cause you showed me something when we was taking care of that business for Moon. Everybody knows you got what it takes."

Byrd stopped walking and sighed. Kole turned to face him.

"I know what I'm doing," Byrd confirmed. "My problem is having the weight of all those lives in my hands. When you came back to help, we didn't lose nobody. You be having everything planned so perfectly. Even when we saw what they was finna do to Lemon, you kept a cool head. Nobody died that night. I can't lie, if it was my decision, we might have busted on them crackers."

"If a situation like that comes up again, that'll be your decision to make," Kole told him. "The thing about being a good leader is calculating every life you put in the balance."

"That's what I'm saying," Byrd said. "It's so many of us. We 250-strong now. Every time I give an order, one of them could die. That's a lot of pressure."

"That's why you'll make the right decisions," Kole assured him, "because you care about every last one of them. It may seem like you're playing chess sometimes, but you know every pawn you sacrifice has a mama, a sister, maybe a baby-mama, some kids. You gon' think about all those people before you make a move, and you'll ask yourself if the reward is worth the risks. If so, you'll do whatever you can to make sure all of your pawns come home. I know you will."

"You'll have my back if I reach out to you?" Byrd asked. "If I need help coming up with a game plan?"

"Of course I will. Me and Moon started The Organization damn near thirty years ago. I'll be an unofficial captain *for life*. Anytime you need me, you better pick up the phone. Plus I'll be at this club a lot, making sure everything runs smooth."

They approached the new construction area and marveled at the workers' progress.

"Bet Moon never thought there'd be a VIP lounge like this," Byrd said.

"You'd lose that bet," Kole told him. "Moon was always thinking big. He wanted to build a retractable roof, so he could *really* get some moonlight in here."

"Damn," Byrd said, his eyes widening. "You think we should do it?"

"He did some research," Kole said. "Turned out, the price tag cost more than the whole building. That's why Moon scrapped the idea. But maybe one day we'll splurge on it."

The men were quiet for a second before Kole asked, "Who'd you pick for the new manager?"

Byrd gave him a look and said, "I know you gon' think I'm tripping, but so far Lemon is at the top of my list."

"No shit?"

"He good with numbers," Byrd explained. "And he real good with people. He can be the life of the party, but when he gets serious about something, people respect him. You know he got that rep. I know Moon didn't want no violence in here. No shooting. I think when Lemon lays down the law, people will respect it. Don't nobody wanna get on his bad side."

Kole nodded, smiling. "And you over here worried about being a good leader. I told you you got this. You ain't done nothing but make smart moves since I met you."

Byrd smiled, his chest swelling.

CHAPTER 71

THE SWELTERING HEAT of June was nothing compared to the blistering July temperatures. August offered much of the same, but summer was on the decline by then. The change of seasons brought new beginnings.

On Saturday, August 25th, Kole and Dana loaded her SUV with all of the clothing and supplies Tariq thought he'd need to make it through his first semester of college. They set out at 4 am and made it to Florida at 5 pm. Kole did the bulk of the driving, while his passengers chatted and sometimes napped along the way.

When they arrived at his dorm, Tariq was eager to get his things inside and send his mom and her boyfriend on their way. Dana was equally eager to help him unpack and tour the campus before they left. Even though he never raised a child of his own, Kole was on the same accord as Dana. He'd been in Tariq's life for almost two years. He'd grown very fond of the boy. Tariq surprised him with heartfelt words before Kole and Dana hit the road again.

"Take care of my mama," the teen said after an extended bro-hug. "I may not always like what you do, but there's no doubt in my mind that you love my mama, and you always put her first.

I know you won't do anything to hurt her or let anything happen to her."

Kole told him, "You right about that. You ain't got nothing to worry about."

He and Dana decided to spend the night in a hotel before they took off the next morning. On the way there, Dana cried for the first time during the trip.

Kole placed a hand over hers. She looked at him and smiled wistfully.

"You think he's gonna be alright?" she asked.

"You know he'll be *better* than alright," Kole replied. "You did a great job raising him. He'll continue to make us proud, every month and every year."

The fact that Kole said *us* made Dana's tears flow even harder. Tariq was a senior in high school when they started dating, but that never stopped Kole from reaching out to him; offer himself as a mentor and father figure.

"I'm gonna miss him *soooo* much," Dana said.

Kole nodded. "I know. But this is your goal as a mother; to push your offspring out the nest and let 'em fly. Tariq ain't hit the ground once, so you know you did a good job."

Dana sighed.

"Just remember everything you learned," Kole said, "so you'll do as good a job with the next one."

Dana's smile broadened. "I will," she promised. "But I'll be crying when he goes off to college too."

"*He?*" Kole frowned. "I think you're mistaken. I'm looking forward to a baby *girl*."

Dana's heart shuddered, ever so sweetly. "Are you sure about that? Do you have any idea how hard it is to raise a teenage daughter?"

"I got no problem chasing knot-headed boys away."

"What about puberty, periods, prom night – all those days when she wakes up and decides she hates both of us."

Kole frowned. "Shit. What's it like with teenage boys?"

"About the same," Dana said with a chuckle. "Except no periods, and you don't worry so much about prom night. Just have to teach them to wrap it up, so they won't bring any babies home."

"Still think I'd rather have a girl," Kole decided. "I don't want no little punk calling me *daddy*."

"Spoken like a real *thug*," Dana said with a shake of her head.

"Hey, I'm retired," Kole responded. "I'm an *ex*-thug."

CHAPTER 72

A FEW MONTHS after they returned from Florida, Kole awakened Dana one balmy Sunday morning and asked if she'd like to accompany him to the cemetery. Without question, she said she would.

The mood at Maplewoods was somber. The property was deserted when they arrived. Kole helped Dana out of the car and held her hand as they walked to Moon's grave. She hadn't been there since the funeral. His headstone was large and beautiful, with "*OG MOON*" inscribed across the top. Beneath that was "*SEE YOU IN THE MOONLIGHT.*"

Kole did not speak as they stood at the gravesite, but Dana could tell he was having a whole conversation with his best friend. Before they returned to the car, Kole left flowers he'd brought with him. He dropped to one knee to adjust the bouquet, with no regard to the new slacks he was wearing.

He stood and produced another offering, this time from his jacket pocket. Dana was more intrigued than excited when she saw it was a ring box. Even when Kole turned to her and opened it, her heart didn't freeze until she saw there were two rings inside; an engagement ring and a wedding band.

"I know a cemetery ain't the best place for this," he said, looking into her eyes. "I watched enough movies to know women like to remember the date and time you get engaged; where it took place and what y'all was wearing.

"I'm doing it here because this is something my brother wanted most of all, for me and you. I'm not doing it for Moon. I'm doing it because I love you. I know we gon' spend the rest of our lives together. And we gon' raise our baby right."

Dana stood stunned, unable to move. There was so much wrong with this proposal. First of all, was it even a proposal? There was no question in his speech. Also, Kole had been down on one knee a moment before he offered her the ring. Why didn't he remain there and propose to her properly?

Of course all of that went against who Kole was and what she expected of him. Rather than balk at the setting and his delivery, her heart thundered. Her eyes filled with tears. Her hand trembled as she reached for the rings.

Kole steadied her hand and slid them on himself. He pulled her into his arms, and they kissed above Moon's grave.

She didn't formally accept him that day, but two weeks later they went to the courthouse and gave their official *I do's*.

Dana's heart had never been so full.

CHAPTER 73

DURING CHRISTMAS BREAK, Tariq returned to Overbrook Meadows to spend the holiday with his family. He wasn't upset when Dana immediately put him to work upon arrival. She hadn't lived in her home since she and Kole married. She recently found a realtor who placed the house on the market.

With help from a crew of movers, Kole had most of their belongings packed up and taken across town already. They'd left Tariq's room as-is, worried he might take offense to someone going through his things.

He surprised them by saying, "You could'a called and asked me. I would've been happier if I got to the new house and all my stuff was there already."

"I tried to tell yo mama that," Kole replied.

"Yes, you can blame me," Dana said. "If you don't wanna do it, we can get the movers back over here."

"Well... you might as well let me go through it right quick," Tariq said. "It might be *some* stuff I do wanna pack myself..."

Dana drove him to their old home, and Tariq took a dozen boxes to his room, while she cleaned the kitchen one last time. A couple of hours later, he emerged from the room carrying one of the boxes. He had so much tape on it, Dana frowned when she asked, "What's in it?"

"Nothing," he said sheepishly. "The movers can take the rest. I'll bring this one to the new house myself. Don't mess with it when I go back to college."

Dana was still curious later that night when she went to bed with her husband.

"What do you think is in it?" she asked him.

"I'm sure you don't wanna know," Kole said.

"No, I really do."

"If I had to guess," Kole said, "I'd say love letters and porn."

"Jeez," Dana exclaimed. "That box looked kinda heavy."

"They got these new dolls," Kole said, "it's just the ass and the front. No legs or upper body..."

"Okay. I don't wanna know."

He laughed. "Told you."

CHAPTER 74

ON FRIDAY, JANUARY 4th, Kole brought Dana a newspaper before retreating to the kitchen to make breakfast. She was surprised when she saw it was the Chicago Tribune, rather than the Overbrook Meadows Telegram. Her befuddlement deepened when she realized the paper wasn't folded indiscriminately. It was folded to display an article. The headline read: **MAN BRUTALLY BEATEN – POLICE SEARCHING FOR SUSPECT**.

According to the story, a 67-year-old Chicago native was beaten within an inch of his life by an unknown assailant. The victim was admitted to the hospital with multiple fractures and contusions. Several kicks to the stomach had bruised his liver and spleen. The victim could offer no motive for the attack, only to say his attacker called him by name and began punching him when he confirmed his identity. The beating occurred in the driveway of his home.

The victim described the culprit as a large, very muscular black man with dark skin and the coldest eyes he'd ever seen. The article indicated the victim may never fully recover from a brain bleed. The police had no motives, witnesses or suspects. They implored the public to come forward with any information they could offer.

Dana was not surprised to see the beaten man's name was Harold Scott. She quickly confirmed the date of the attack coincided with a recent trip Kole and Byrd had taken to the Windy City. Kole hadn't returned to a leadership or even an associate position in The Organization, but Byrd asked him to tag along while he established a new connect up north, and Kole obliged.

Dana only mentioned Harold Scott's name once the entire time she and Kole had been together. Looking back on that day, it didn't surprise her that he remembered. Even though Dana's abuse at the hands of Mr. Scott was decades old, and he may have moved on with his life and never abused another foster child, Kole wanted him to pay for what he'd done to his wife.

Dana had overcome her shock by the time Kole returned with her breakfast. He carried it on a tray; made to be eaten in bed. Despite what she'd just read, Dana couldn't help but smile as her man brought the food to her. She placed the newspaper aside and shook her head disapprovingly.

"Least I let him live," Kole said coldly. "At that age, it wouldn't have taken much to snap his neck."

Dana cringed. "Speaking of age, don't you think he's too old for what you did to him? You're too old too."

"If it ain't no statute of limitations on murder, it shouldn't be one for what he did to you," Kole replied. "Are you saying I'm too old to whoop up on somebody, but I'm not too old to be a father?"

As he spoke, Kole realized his breakfast tray no longer fit over Dana's lap, even with her sitting up. Her belly was too big. Their daughter Carmen was due in a couple of months. Dana was still surprised Kole didn't prefer a bouncing baby boy.

"You're gonna have to eat over here," he said, taking the tray to her desk.

He left it there and returned to help Dana out of bed. Her mobility was impaired these days. Thankfully Kole didn't mind assisting her with anything. Her new walk was now more of a waddle, which he found cute.

Dana took a seat at the desk, and Kole removed the shiny lid on her tray. He'd made French toast with oatmeal, coffee and a fruit bowl. Dana's mouth watered as she lifted her fork.

She was no longer bothered by the many contradictions Kole was as man and as a husband. A couple of weeks ago he beat a man so heinously, any law-abiding citizen would surely turn him in. This morning he made breakfast and cared for his wife so tenderly, any single woman would kill to have him as her spouse.

"Thanks baby," she told him.

She looked up, offering a kiss. Kole planted a soft one on her lips. He brushed her hair back with his fingers and sucked her bottom lip.

"Gotta run some errands," he told her. "Anything you need before I take off?"

"Mmmm, I dunno. Some dick?" she said honestly and hungrily.

Kole laughed that off until she reached with both hands and unbuckled his pants. He watched her, not sure if she was serious. Sure enough, she pulled his boxers down and leaned forward, taking him into her mouth. Kole wasn't erect, so she could take him all the way in, which was a rarity. Kole's stomach tightened, and he sucked air between his teeth.

"Damn," he breathed. "Who knew pregnancy would make you so horny?"

By then his erection had swelled. Dana had to back away before saying, "I'm sorry, but this breakfast is gonna be cold by the time I get through."

Kole told her, "That's cool. I'll throw that shit away and start from scratch."

"You don't have to do that," she chuckled, speaking into his dick like it was a mic.

"It's no problem. I don't mind."

He placed a hand on the side of her head, and his fingers disappeared in her soft mane. He slowly guided her mouth back to his pipe and shuddered when he hit the back of her throat.

"Don't mind at all..." he grumbled.
Even with her mouth full, Dana had to giggle at that.

KEITH THOMAS WALKER

ABOUT THE AUTHOR

Keith Thomas Walker, known as the Master of Romantic Suspense and Urban Fiction, is the author of more than two dozen novels, including *Fixin' Tyrone*, *Life After*, *The Realest Ever*, the *Backslide* series, the *Brick House* series, the *Finley High* series, the *Asha and Boom* series, and the *Blurred Lines* series. Keith's books transcend all genres. He has published romance, urban fiction, mystery/thriller, teen/young adult, Christian, poetry and erotica. Originally from Fort Worth, he is a graduate of Texas Wesleyan University. Keith has won numerous awards in the categories of "Best Male Author," "Best Romance," "Best Urban Fiction," "Best Young Adult Romance," "Best Duo," "Book of the Year," and "Author of the Year," from several book clubs and organizations. Visit him at www.keiththomaswalker.com.